Praise for the first two books of award-winning author Theresa Michaels's exciting trilogy, The Kincaids

Once an Outlaw

"...a delightful, fast-paced and rip-roaring adventure novel... 5★s."

—*Affaire de Coeur*

"...Ms. Michaels illustrates once again why she is one of the brightest stars in the genre today."

—*Romantic Times*

"Theresa Michaels does it again!... Captivating!"
—*The Literary Times*

"*Once an Outlaw* is romance at its finest.
5 Booklover ❤s"

—*Booklovers*

Once a Maverick

"Riveting... Readers are in for a very special treat."
—*Romantic Times*

"Breathtaking! ...one of the best romances ever!"
—*The Literary Times*

"The action never lets up...a terrific western romance."
—*Affaire de Coeur*

Dear Reader,

The third book in award-winning author Theresa Michaels's Kincaid Trilogy, *Once a Lawman,* features the oldest Kincaid brother, Conner, a small-town sheriff who must choose between family and duty as he works to finally bring to justice the criminals who've been plaguing his family's ranch. Described by *Romantic Times* as "breathtaking," *Affaire de Coeur* as "delightful," and *The Literary Times* as "sizzling," this one is sure to please.

Miranda Jarrett's characters have gone up against all manner of villains and disasters in the past, but Captain Nick Sparhawk, the hero of *Sparhawk's Angel,* is in real trouble. His tormentor is a meddlesome angel bent on matchmaking. Don't miss this tale that *Romantic Times* calls "delightful, unforgettably funny and supremely touching."

A sensible novelist brings love and laughter to the wounded soul of a neighboring earl in Deborah Simmons's new title, *The Devil Earl.* And an indentured servant is torn between her affection for her good-hearted master and her growing love for the rugged frontiersman who is guiding them to a new life in the territories in Ana Seymour's new Western, *Frontier Bride.*

We hope you will enjoy all four titles, and come back for more. Please keep a lookout for Harlequin Historicals, available wherever books are sold.

Sincerely,

Tracy Farrell
Senior Editor

Please address questions and book requests to:
Harlequin Reader Service
U.S.: 3010 Walden Ave., P.O. Box 1325, Buffalo, NY 14269
Canadian: P.O. Box 609, Fort Erie, Ont. L2A 5X3

THERESA MICHAELS

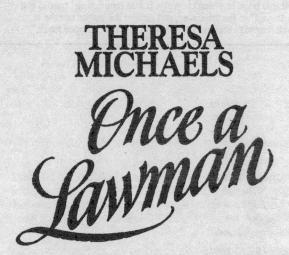

Once a
Lawman

Harlequin Books

TORONTO • NEW YORK • LONDON
AMSTERDAM • PARIS • SYDNEY • HAMBURG
STOCKHOLM • ATHENS • TOKYO • MILAN
MADRID • WARSAW • BUDAPEST • AUCKLAND

ISBN 0-373-28916-2

ONCE A LAWMAN

THERESA MICHAELS

is a former New Yorker who resides in south Florida with her husband and daughter—the last of eight children—and three "rescued" cats. Her avid interest in history and her belief in the power of love are combined in her writing. She has received the *Romantic Times* Reviewer's Choice Award for Best Civil War Romance, the National Readers' Choice Award for Best Series Historical and the B. Dalton Bookseller Award for Bestselling Series Historical. When not writing, she enjoys traveling, adding to her collection of Victorian perfume bottles and searching for the elf to master her computer.

To Adene, Audrey, Belinda and JoAnn.
I treasure your friendship.

Chapter One

∗

Annoyed. Angered. Alarmed. Conner Kincaid sat behind the battered desk that had belonged to Verl Jenison, the previous sheriff of Sweetwater, and reviewed the shifting state of his emotions. Never had his temper been so sorely tested and he eyed the cause of it. Tall and willow slender, Miss Belinda Jarvis paced the small confines of his office.

He had tagged her as Eastern born and bred without hearing her speak a word. From the feathered concoction that graced her upswept blond hair to the tips of her high-buttoned shoes to the delicate lace-trimmed collar peering above her tobacco brown short caped jacket and the finely woven plaid draping her bustle, she was every attractive inch a wealthy, fashionable lady.

If it weren't for the fact that she posed a threat to his family, Conner would have explored the heated spark that flared to life the moment she barged into his office demanding his immediate attention.

Even Seely Morehouse, sleeping off his latest binge in the single jail cell, had rubbed red-rimmed eyes and muttered about angels and devils coming to get him when he saw her.

But there wasn't anything angelic about this woman. As if his thought had been spoken, she suddenly stopped pacing and looked at him.

Conner met her direct gaze with his own cool stare, giving away nothing of his inner turmoil.

Taken individually, her features were not exceptional. The brows and lashes framing her large brown eyes were mink dark, in decided contrast to her blond hair. Her nose was straight and her chin a shade on the pointy side. His gaze lingered on the generous shape of her mouth. The deep rose color of her lips lent her skin a creamy tint like a blazing star flower. It was the kind of mouth a man might speculate about.

Conner was man enough to look his fill and reach his own conclusions.

He was intrigued by the gleam of intelligence he saw in her eyes as she continued to stare at him. Other men might call them bluestockings, but he had always found independent-thinking women attractive. And this one was no exception.

Belinda Jarvis rarely became unsettled by a man's staring. But there was something about this man that made her struggle to retain her accustomed poise.

"Well, Sheriff?" she asked to break the uncomfortable silence. "You have had time to read my brother's last letter and make a decision." She pointed at the paper lying on the desk in front of him. "You did read it? I assume you can read."

"Yes, ma'am. I get by."

She ignored the decided edge of sarcasm. "That saves me time searching for someone you trust to read it to you."

There was something dark and dangerous about the sheriff's face. Belinda was annoyed that she noticed that his jaw appeared squared from granite. His smile was not quite a decent one, and combined with the blatant appraisal in his cool gray eyes, it was too much. She lowered her gaze by cowardly inches— throat, shoulder, chest...then chided herself for such foolish behavior. She had to remember that all she needed was for this man to do his job.

"I did not mean to insult you, Sheriff."

Like hell you didn't, lady. Conner tilted back in his chair so that it balanced on its rear legs. "None taken, ma'am."

Belinda wanted to wipe the cocky grin from his lips, but she merely inclined her head in acknowledgment.

"Now, shall we get back to business? The letter clearly states that should anything happen to my brother and his wife, I am named guardian of their son. All I require of you, Sheriff, is your cooperation in claiming my nephew."

Conner eased his chair forward. His hands gripped the edge of his desk. "There is no doubt in your mind that your brother and his wife are dead?"

"None." Once more Belinda struggled to maintain an air of calm control. She knew she sounded cold and callous. "My brother and I were not close. He refused the place waiting for him in our family's business and in society."

She paused, unwilling to explain that the family had been against his choice of wife until he confessed that she carried his child. But once married, Robert had refused to forgive the family for the cruel things they had said about the woman he loved.

"What makes you think that the child is still alive? This is rough country, ma'am. If you're so sure his parents are dead—"

"Sheriff, please," she interrupted. "I've already told you. I'm sure. You will simply have to accept my word. I am not in the habit of having it questioned."

"That so?" His tone was polite, but the slightest blur of a frown drew the slash of his eyebrows together.

"Yes, indeed." Like a slippery length of fine silk, Belinda felt her grasp on both her poise and patience begin to slip.

The ruggedly handsome sheriff was younger than she had been led to believe, and, unlike most men she came into contact with, had not fallen all over himself trying to accommodate her.

She was not vain about her appearance, but she had realized at a young age that she had been blessed with an attractive face and figure. If men wished to be blinded by a woman's looks, she had learned not to argue with them. What she had learned was to turn their fawning to her advantage and use her intelligence, free from any male interference.

Her family wealth usually insured cooperation whenever she demanded it. But this lawman, watching and appraising her every word and move, appeared immune.

"You still harbor doubts," she accused. "Will it satisfy you that I am telling the truth, if I repeat my story?"

"Sure would help me keep things clear." Conner had her where he wanted her: angry and defensive. "Go on."

Her hands clenched and she looked away from him. "The Pinkerton National Detective Agency has investigated this matter at my request. Allan Pinkerton was a personal friend of my father. My family aided him when he first established his agency in Chicago. Even you must agree they are the best that money can buy."

"Never had any call to *buy* myself some fancy detective, ma'am. I'll just take your word for that."

"By all means, do so," she snapped, facing him. The irritating clodhopper! She was not going to lose her temper. She was not going to allow him to provoke her. Taking a deep breath, then releasing it, Belinda continued.

"Their report, made after months of investigation by several of their best detectives, concludes that my brother and his family never reached their destination in California. They did confirm that my brother traveled with another family. Neither family left the Arizona Territory."

"And did your fancy detective agency bother to inform you that the territory is a mighty big place, Miss Jarvis? They could be anywhere."

"No. My coming here to Sweetwater was not a random choice, Sheriff. The last time my brother stopped to buy supplies was in Apache Junction."

Conner's gut tightened at the mention of the town that linked his brother to her story. He wanted to usher her out of his office, then personally escort her out of town. "That's a way north of here. Men go off all the time. Some catch gold fever and are never heard from again. 'Pache could've gotten them. Flash floods, rock slides, there are a hundred ways for men to die out here."

"I am aware of all that." *Calm. Just be calm with this dense, backwoods excuse for the law.* "When I was informed of where my brother was last seen, I was told about a widow who had recently left the area in the company of an outlaw and two young boys that were not hers. There is no doubt in my mind that these people have my nephew. But I had to come West to discover the truth for myself.

"The widow's ranch was deserted, but she had returned twice and both times was seen leaving with loaded wagons. The last news I had claims that this widow lives on the Kincaid ranch. Nothing will deter me from following that lead."

"If you're so all-fired sure that you're right, why don't you just ride out there and claim your lost nephew?"

"Are you deliberately trying to provoke me, Sheriff?"

"I'm trying to get at the truth."

"You have a strange way of doing so. I cannot risk having the boy hidden away from me. You do not understand what is at stake."

"Guess not. But I'm not sure your concern is for the boy's welfare at all."

"You know nothing about me or my feelings. Do not presume to pass judgment on me. I would not have traipsed about this hostile country if I did not care about the boy. For all I know they could be teaching him to steal. My brother never intended that his child be raised by an outlaw. Even a man like you must admit the very idea is enough to give one nightmares."

Conner glanced to the wall where yellowed Wanted posters covered the rough planks. Faded images of the James brothers, the Youngers, Charley Pitts and Ty Hardin stared back at him. The names and the varying amounts of monies offered for the men, dead or alive, only served to remind him that Belinda Jarvis believed that his brother Logan really was the outlaw he had been forced to play to bring a band of robbers to justice.

"Sheriff, your continued inattention is annoying. I wonder if you understand the very serious nature of my request for your help. Am I wasting my time attempting to elicit it?"

His gaze returned to her. She refused to allow that cool, hard stare to intimidate her. Her pride would not allow a small-town lawman to succeed where wealthy, powerful men had tried and failed.

She stepped closer to the desk. "I demand to know if you are going to help me. You cannot doubt the evidence I have presented. You are sworn to uphold the law. If these people have my nephew in their clutches, I want them arrested and my brother's child returned to me. For all I know, they may have had something to do with my brother's death."

It was with a great deal of annoyance that Belinda realized she leaned over the desk. Straightening, she felt the pool of sweat gathered between her breasts. Beneath her hat, her hair felt damp against her head. With gloved hands, she patted her temples. She did not want him to see how upset she was. Men took advantage of women when they were vulnerable.

Fanning herself with one hand, she resumed her pacing. The hot, sultry air stirred as she walked back and forth in the small office.

Through the open door, she glimpsed the dusty street. A longing for the lakeside breezes of her home swept over her. She paused, thinking she had been wrong to come here on her own. Perhaps she should have allowed the detectives to handle this. But the boy had suffered enough alone. She could not allow strangers to fetch him home where he belonged.

Conner watched her. He was not a man who deliberately provoked anyone's temper. At least he hadn't been until this woman snapped accusations and demands at him like the rapid fire of a repeating rifle.

Her insistence that he arrest his brother slammed into him with a burning sensation that notched his temper higher.

The tap-tap of her high heels hitting the wood floor revealed her agitated state. He caught every one of the glaring looks she shot at him.

"I'm giving the matter a great deal of thought."

"Thought? What is there to think about?" Belinda stood in the middle of the room. Her eyes filled with disbelief. "Either you believe me or you don't!"

"No need to yell at me. I hear you just fine. And don't get your bustle in a coil, Miss Jarvis. Take a seat, even if the accommodations aren't what you're accustomed to. All that prancing about is distracting."

"Prancing?"

"Pacing. Prancing. All the same."

Conner followed her gaze to the rickety slat-back chair in front of his desk. He hadn't gotten around to fixing up his office and had refused the Kincaid ladies' offers of help to do it. He didn't even have his new name sign hung outside the doorway. A fact that annoyed his mother since she had had one made for him. Most of the past two months had been spent visiting the outlying ranches to thank the families for their support in the election and to reassure them that he would see an end to the rustling.

"Stop daydreaming, Sheriff. I would never be dismissed like this in Chicago. My family name and wealth would insure—"

"Perhaps your eyesight's poor. This isn't Chicago," Conner reminded her. He could no more stop his grin than he could stop breathing. Belinda had color in her cheeks. Deep rose-red flags that signaled her anger.

"I am well aware of that fact, Sheriff."

"Good. That was my sole intent. As you keep reminding me that I'm the only law around here, we'll do things my way."

"Slow as molasses on a winter morning."

"Most women don't complain about it. There's a heap of pleasure to be found that way." Conner was surprised to see the deepening color in her cheeks. She wasn't a girl fresh from the schoolroom, or in her case, some fancy boarding school. His gaze drifted down to the rapid rise and fall of her breasts. "No, ma'am, slow ain't reason to complain."

He was goading her and Belinda stopped herself from answering with a retort that would have the man sputtering. The lace trimming her high-necked shirtwaist constricted her throat. She raised her gloved hand to hide her need to swallow several times. She refused to think about him and his slow idea of pleasure. Bragging, that's all it was. He was staring down at the letter, clearly ignoring her, and that smarted.

Conner heard her furious mutterings as she paced to the doorway and stood there with her back toward him. He was torn. The past two months had brought him contentment. His younger brothers were running the ranch and overseeing the mining operations. He was free to follow his dream. A dream to see the territory safe for families to settle.

As a Kincaid, Conner wanted to send this woman packing.

As the sheriff, he had no choice but to consider her request that he help find her nephew.

It tempted him to see the Eastern society darling sent on a wild-hog chase through the territory.

The fact that such a thought was present forced him to admit how torn his loyalties were. And how close he was to losing his infamous temper. It didn't help that he suspected the lady packed the devil's own temper, too.

Without looking at him, Belinda prodded him again for his decision.

"I'm not ready to make one. You'll just have to wait."

Her shoulders drooped as if the starch dissolved from her, and Conner almost felt sorry for his harsh tone. In moments, she presented a rigid back to him again. He had to admire her strength.

But if what she claimed was true, she would destroy his brother Logan's happiness. Conner didn't want to think what it would do to Jessie. If the corset-cinched Miss Jarvis had her way, one of the boys that Logan and his wife Jessie intended to adopt would never bear the Kincaid name.

The trouble was, the letter she had given to him only made mention of a son, but didn't name the boy.

He struggled to recall if anyone had mentioned the name Jarvis. He didn't remember hearing it. Kenny, at thirteen, was mature beyond his years. If the boy had schemed to keep something hidden, then hidden it remained. And little Marty... he followed Kenny's lead like an adoring puppy. It made no sense that he would have lied about who he was. She had to be wrong. Kenny claimed they were cousins. Marty never denied it.

Belinda Jarvis, with her fancy Chicago detective's investigation, was looking for one boy, not two.

The loose ends nagged at him. They had all taken Kenny's word that there were no family members for them to go back to. What if he had lied?

He couldn't ignore the fact that his brother's wife, Jessie, came from a ranch close to Apache Junction. Logan, pretending to be an outlaw, had his life saved by two orphan boys after he'd been wounded in a robbery and left to die, and they'd taken him to Jessie.

The one thing Conner was certain of was that he needed time to do his own investigation.

He'd have to be very careful in questioning the boys. He didn't want to alert his mother to what was going on. Macaria had welcomed those two boys as if they were her own. He and his brothers had breathed one long sigh of relief that Macaria's attentions to her former suitor and new neighbor lessened considerably.

It had been a shock to learn that Charles Riverton, the man he and his brothers suspected of being behind the robberies and the rustling, had once courted their mother. They had become a little desperate when Macaria defended the man against their suspicions. The arrival of the boys to distract her had been a blessing.

He couldn't stop thinking about his family's reaction to Belinda Jarvis and her letter. In a matter of a few months the two boys had slipped into the weave of the family as if they had been born Kincaids.

And what would this do to the boys? They were as excited as everyone else that the Kincaid nursery would soon have a new baby in the cradle. His youngest brother Ty's wife, Dixie, was due to give birth in a few weeks.

He flashed a stare full of the anger churning inside him at Belinda's back. Like a dust devil, she had swirled in from nowhere to wreak havoc. Unfortunately, Conner did not believe she would disappear as suddenly as she had arrived.

"Sheriff," Belinda said softly, slowly turning around to face him. "I, too, have done a great deal of thinking. Is there a problem that we need to discuss?"

"Problem?" Conner repeated, shaking off his black thoughts.

"Yes, a problem. I should have realized that there was one, with your reluctance."

"You'll pardon me, ma'am, but I'm not following you."

"This man, this Kincaid, he's an outlaw. Are you afraid to confront him?"

Conner stilled. He shook his head as if he hadn't been sure of what she said. "Are you accusing me of being a coward?"

The oh-so-soft tone of his voice should have warned her, but Belinda, intent on having this over with, dismissed it.

She came nearer to the desk, glancing around the poorly furnished room. A blackened potbellied stove mounted on a slab of stone filled one corner. The series of pipes that rose to the hole cut through the roof appeared to be a rusted, flimsy affair. Next to the stove stood a table. One broken leg was tied with twine, another was balanced with the aid of an overturned enamel cup. The crowded top held coffeepot, plates, fry pan, cups and canned goods. She knew that the door behind him led to a jail cell, and the building did not appear large enough for there to be more than one.

On the wall opposite the Wanted posters, a battered bureau missing one drawer and several drawer pulls stood below a filled gun rack. The scarred desk and two chairs completed her survey. Poor, indeed.

Belinda found bribery a distasteful chore. But she had learned that bribes were necessary when one wanted things done immediately and to one's satisfaction. She frowned as she closed the short distance to stand in front of the desk.

"I asked you a question, Miss Jarvis. Are you calling me a coward?"

"You misunderstood me. I never meant to insult you, Sheriff." Conscious of the delicate line she walked, her tone conveyed intimacy. "I would imagine a man like you constantly risks his life for very little pay. I seem to recall that marshals earn as little as five hundred dollars a year. There was an article in the—"

"Yeah, you read that right. There's little pay. But sometimes a man takes on a job for other reasons. I don't see that what I'm paid to do my job has any bearing on your business. And I'm not about to forget that you called me a coward, no matter how fancy a spin you put on the words."

"A poor choice of phrase on my part. I see before me a man who requires some added reward for doing his job."

Placing her reticule on the desk, Belinda opened the drawstring and removed a thick wad of folded bank notes. She narrowed her eyes fractionally when she saw him hunch forward to stare at the money. A cold smile touched her lips.

"You appear to be a smart man. How much will it cost me to have you accompany me to the Kincaid ranch to retrieve my nephew?"

Chapter Two

Conner's gaze rose slowly from the money until it locked with hers.

Belinda's frown deepened. There was the promise of fury within the silvery depths, but she held his steady gaze with her own, missing the way his fingers tensed before he controlled himself.

"Since I'm just a small-town lawman unused to your city way, I want to be real sure that I understand you this time."

Hearing that very soft voice once more, Belinda again found herself ignoring it and the warning that flared within her.

"Of course. Take all the time you need." The man had obviously been given a badge for his brawn, not his intelligence. She had made her request as plain as could be.

"You are offering me a bribe."

This time Belinda heeded the warning that whispered through her. "Think of it as a gift of gratitude for your help."

"A gift of gratitude? That's a nice turn of phrase. Tell me, Miss Jarvis," Conner said, shoving his chair back to stand, "are you always this insulting to the men you deal with? Must you pay them for *every* service performed?''

Inwardly cringing at what he implied, Belinda took a hurried step back. She refused to dignify his questions with answers.

She had not realized from his seated position how tall he was. He easily topped her own significant height by a good six inches. Muscular, male inches. As he slowly leaned forward over his desk, her gaze was drawn to the taut pull of cloth across his chest and shoulders. She revised her first quick summation of the man. He was not a backwoods hick. His shirt was made of a fine linen weave fitted to his impressive body by an expert hand, for the cloth moved with his every deep breath.

''Miss Jarvis, I asked you questions. I'm not a man accustomed to waiting for answers.''

Belinda didn't need him to tell her that he was used to having his questions answered. That commanding tone of his voice had not developed overnight.

''It appears that I have made a grave mistake about you, Sheriff.''

''Do tell. A grave is exactly where you could wind up, flashing that much cash around.''

''Be satisfied,'' she snapped in reply. ''The admission was not an easy one to make.''

She tucked the money back into her reticule, venting her anger by yanking the drawstring tight.

''I suppose you will still require more time to reach a decision? Perhaps you would like to send a telegram to the Pinkerton Agency to confirm what I have told you?''

''How very kind of you to understand my position.''

"You are practically accusing me of being a liar! I do not tolerate anyone questioning my word. And there is no need to mock me."

"On the contrary, Miss Jarvis, I feel the greatest need to do so."

"Blunt, are we?"

"Honest, lady."

A battle gleam shone in her eyes. "There are other ways to accomplish what I have come for."

"And I'll bet you know them all. Honest or dirty as can be. Be warned, honey. This is my territory and you're way out of your hothouse city league here."

"Are you threatening me, Sheriff?"

"Just warning you. Things happen. A woman alone—"

"I am not a weak, hothouse flower, Sheriff."

For the first time since she had entered his office, Conner allowed full rein to the male speculation that had hovered in his mind, growing steadily as the minutes passed. His gaze roved over her from head to toe and slowly, very slowly, charted a return course until he once more looked at her eyes.

"Now, there's a point we both agree upon, Miss Jarvis. You're no hothouse bloom. You're more like fireweed, the first to throw deep roots into barren soil and the last to die."

A weed! He compared her to a weed! Belinda itched to slap the grin from his lips. She had to trust her instinct that warned anger would gain nothing with him.

"Why, Sheriff," she cooed in a sugar-sweet voice, "I do believe you are attempting to flirt with me."

"Honey, if I was flirting with you, you wouldn't have any doubt about it."

From the sudden tightening of her jaw, Conner imagined he heard the snap of her teeth coming together.

"I have underestimated you."

"You—" he leaned farther over the desk to confirm "—sure as hell have."

Belinda knew a challenge when she faced one. Without stopping to think, she braced her hands on the edge of the desk and leaned forward until her nose almost touched the tip of his.

"Mr. Lawman, before I am finished with you, I'll have your badge."

"It's all yours, honey. Just come and take it."

For an endless moment Conner forgot everything this woman threatened. He absorbed the full force of her gaze and the tempting scent of her floral perfume. Sexual tension hummed between them, as basic and as primitive as could be.

"I was not making an idle threat," Belinda whispered. She seemed unable to pull back from the compelling, blatantly sensual snare enfolding her. It was his eyes. Had she truly thought their gray color cool?

"There's nothing idle about this," Conner stated in a husky voice. "You still want the badge?"

The invitation in his eyes and voice had nothing to do with the brass star on his chest. Like the sultry heat that filled the morning air, his invitation to just come and take it hung between them.

"No," Belinda murmured, unsure of what she was refusing.

"Oh, yes," Conner whispered, throwing caution to the four winds.

He slanted his head slightly to the right.

Belinda tilted hers to the left.

He had only thought the shape of her mouth generous, now he confirmed how very generous her lips were. Warm, silky, smooth flesh met his mouth in a kiss that enticed and beguiled him into wanting more. He caught the hitch in her breathing and felt the fine trembling of her lips that bespoke an innocence he dismissed.

Belinda startled herself by thinking that their lips fit together perfectly. Dangerously so. She had kissed a number of men since she had made her debut into society seven years ago. But she could not recall a man who kissed with such skill, as if he knew what he wanted and exactly how to get it. *Slow as molasses on a winter morning.* That was how he tasted her mouth. She was being seduced by the gentle ply of his lips and tongue.

Her murmured request for more broke across Conner's mouth and roused him. What in the blazes was he doing seducing the woman who could wreck his family's happiness? With an abrupt jerk, he pulled back.

Raking his hands through his hair, he closed his eyes. *Of all the dumb mistakes . . . and I'll be damned before I apologize to her.* But her whispered *more* replayed in his mind until the word branded itself there.

Belinda barely managed to stop herself from falling facedown on the desk when the kiss ended so abruptly. She slowly straightened, then turned away. Her reaction flustered her. At the very least she should have protested the liberty he had taken. *Taken? Or did you allow it? Honesty called for the admission that she had invited his kiss.*

She caught herself raising the tips of her gloved fingers to her lips. *Stop behaving like a schoolgirl who has just had a first kiss.* The admonishment did little good. That was exactly how she felt. Why had he stopped? She was not an expert, but he seemed to have been caught in the moment just as she had been. And why did he remain silent?

Belinda had to seize the opportunity to be in charge. "This should not have happened."

His grunt could have meant anything, agreement or disagreement.

"I do not know what came over me. Not that I am apologizing. There is no need for either of us to make an apology. After all, we are both adults. This was merely a moment's vagary. I am not prone to such irresponsible behavior."

I'll just bet you're not. For you, lady, sex had better be tied in fancy lace-trimmed sheets with a big satin bow around a few sparkling gems before you'd let your hair down for a man.

Far from being calmed by his summation of her character, Conner found himself still irritated by her cool, crisp explanation. Why should it matter? So what if the kiss meant nothing to her? It didn't mean a damn thing to him. He wasn't some green kid still wet behind the ears. But the irritation lingered and turned on himself for allowing her to distract him from the business at hand.

"Just forget about it," he stated impatiently. "Tell me where I can get in touch with you. Once I've checked things out, I'll let you know my decision."

So very cool. Mentally taking herself in hand, Belinda shrugged off the lingering sensual snare that he had spun so effortlessly. What possible difference could it make that this uneducated, uncouth, small-town lawman dismissed her so easily? It must be the heat that affected her. She turned around but could not meet his gaze.

"You're staying..." Conner prompted.

"My Uncle Phillip made arrangements for me to stay with a friend and business associate of his. I am sure you are aware of Mr. Riverton's contributions to—"

"Riverton?" Conner almost snarled the name. "Of the Circle R ranch?"

"I believe that is the name." Taken aback by the venomous tone of his voice, Belinda grew wary. "Does this create a problem for you?"

Conner nodded, confirming private thoughts. He swept his gaze over her once more. This time there was no male appreciation, no heat at all in his eyes.

Conner mentally placed a No Trespass sign flat across the agitated rise and fall of her chest: danger, poison water. He should have known in the first few minutes of her arrival when she announced who she was, trying to impress him with the number of stockyards her family owned in Chicago, and the amount of real estate, that she had a connection to Riverton. Not that it mattered. He was still going to check out her story and Riverton was still going to pay for his crimes against his family.

"I sent that boy hanging around the depot—"

"Shelden's boy Steven. He's always hanging around old Wally, listening to his stories."

"Well, he appeared old enough to ride out to Mr. Riverton's ranch with word that I had arrived. The ticket agent is holding my luggage until a wagon or buckboard comes." Puzzled by his stare, Belinda raised her chin a little, her voice sharp. "My uncle assured me that Mr. Riverton would aid me in any way he could to help me accomplish my goal."

"Lady, if that's another of your threats, forget it. Riverton isn't worth the spit it takes to say his name. If he, or any man working for his brand, sets one foot on Kincaid land, there's a bullet marked and waiting."

"My, my, Sheriff, you do seem to have a problem." She could not resist the opportunity to test his mettle. She was still piqued that he had dismissed her as a woman so easily. "What a strange thing for a man of the law to approve. And it is approval that I hear in your voice.

"Perhaps," she said, toying with the pearl buttons on her glove, "you are the wrong man to help me. You seem to have a deep regard for this Kincaid family, despite the fact that they harbor an outlaw."

"Damn right I do, lady. That *outlaw* you keep harping about is my brother."

Belinda's head jerked up. She stared at him with a dawning horror. "Your brother?" she repeated. "You are a Kincaid? You led me down a garden path all this while. You conniving, miserable excuse for a man. You..." Her gaze darted around in search of something to throw at him. Finding nothing, she lost her temper.

"You lying cur. You... you... bastard!"

"Not me, honey. My folks tied the knot long before I came along."

"Don't you dare call me *honey.*" She briefly closed her eyes as the heat of temper permeated her body. When she glanced at him again, his mocking grin made her grit her teeth.

Having her attention once more, Conner couldn't stop himself from prodding her temper. "I won't call you *honey*."

"Thank you," she replied in a starched voice.

"*Brine* would suit you better."

"Brine? My name, sir, is Belinda. Not that I have given you permission to address me by my first name. I am, and will remain, Miss Jarvis to you. And you are still a bastard."

Executing an about-face with almost military precision, Belinda marched out of the office.

"Damn, and double damn," Conner muttered, coming around his desk and kicking the rickety chair. He had only wanted to break through the society lady's highfalutin manner, not reveal that he was a Kincaid, until he had time to check out her story.

"Some days it don't pay to pull your boots on." Still muttering, Conner snatched his hat and gun belt from the peg near the door and went after her.

Conner immediately canted his hat brim to shield his eyes from the sudden glare of the sun. Spring had come early to the territory this year. It was the middle of the week and few people milled about town.

Two horses stood hitched to the rail in front of Shelden's Mercantile across the street from him. The animals' heads were down, their tails slowly swishing back and forth to stop the flies from settling on their hides.

He waved to Mose Riley who waited for his checker partner to arrive. It was a town joke that Millicent Haines, the preacher's wife, made her father spruce up before he could sit in front of the mercantile to share war stories with his old crony while they belabored every move.

Conner glanced at the swing and sway of Belinda's bustle as she marched on, looking straight ahead. Damn but she was a fine-looking woman!

It was quiet enough for her to hear the clank of his spurs hitting the wooden sidewalk when he followed her. Beyond the mercantile, the sound of a hammer rang out from Tom Sweet's forge. Owner of the livery and blacksmith shop, Tom and Walter Waterman had founded the town. Walter owned the bank, ran the telegram office and partnered his son in the freight line.

Conner spared a quick look into the new plate glass window of the Sweetwater Weekly Gazette. Mark Dryer had taken over the paper six months ago and had come out in support of Conner's bid for election. He could see Mark hunched over his typesetter but didn't attempt to gain his attention.

The light breeze carried the odor of tanning leather. Conner waved to Carl Gladden as the man repositioned the hide he was nailing to the drying board. He noticed that Carol broke off in mid-wave to stare at Belinda who was crossing the rutted street and heading for the stage depot.

Broom in hand, Rob Long stepped out of the door to his café. "Mornin', Conner. That's a fancy packaged bit of goods."

"If you're thinking about unwrapping it, Rob, wear gloves. You'll need thick ones to protect your hands from the thorns."

"Like that, is it?"

Conner stifled his impatience and stopped. "Woman has a tongue sharper than one of Carl's skinning knives."

"Thank goodness Deana ain't like that. Couldn't live with her. My sister made fried chicken and dumplings for lunch. Know you're partial. I'll tell Deana to save you some."

"Thanks, Rob, but I need to ride out to the ranch. Seely Morehouse could use a good meal. Don't know if his missus is coming to fetch him today. And Rob, this time put it on my bill."

"You seem a mite edgy, Conner. That woman bring trouble your way?" Rob glanced across the street at the woman who stood beneath the stage depot's sheltering overhang. He looked at Conner. "Only asking, 'cause she asked old Wally a heap of questions about the Kincaids before she went looking for you."

"Did she now?" Conner mused. Once more his gaze focused on Belinda.

"Musta been a surprise when she found out who you were. Old Wally tried to tell her twice, but she'd fire another question at him till he gave up."

Conner noticed the rising cloud of dust at the opposite end of town. He picked out the new buggy that had caused a stir when the freight line delivered it two weeks ago.

"Riverton," Conner muttered under his breath. "So the great man himself has come to town to fetch her."

Four Circle R riders followed behind, and as the small carriage swept by, Conner's harrowed gaze fixed on the profile of Charles Riverton beneath the buggy's collapsible leather hood. He hated admitting to himself that the man handled the perfectly matched team of bay horses with an expert hand.

"Fancy rig for a fancy lady," Rob said.

Conner ignored him. His attention remained on the man he hated. Bringing the prancing team to a stop with a flourish, Charles stepped down. He smoothed his frock coat before he swept his white panama hat from his head to greet Belinda. The faintest shiver of contempt pulled at the corner of Conner's mouth. Belinda's smile, as she allowed Riverton to raise her gloved hand to his lips, set his back teeth on edge.

Seeing Conner was lost in thought, Rob once more murmured, "Like that, is it?" He began to sweep the walk in front of the café.

The last thing that Conner wanted was a confrontation with either Belinda or Riverton. He saw that Wally was already loading her luggage into the buggy's boot. Not one of Riverton's men dismounted and offered to help. But then, Riverton hadn't hired them for their manners, just their guns.

He was wasting time standing and staring. As he moved to turn back, Conner caught Belinda's gesture toward his office. So she was telling Riverton what had occurred between them. Immediately Conner amended his thought. She would no more tell Riverton about the kiss she had invited than he would.

"Rob, keep an eye on things for me. I should be back before dark."

"Sure thing. Regards home, Conner."

Cutting down the alley next to Long's Café, Conner headed toward the lean-to the town fathers had built in the back of the jail. Within minutes he had tossed a saddle on his gelding, Sour Mash. He mounted and rode for home, thinking about how he was going to break the news about Belinda Jarvis.

Chapter Three

Belinda had refused to acknowledge the sheriff's stare, but the moment his burning gaze lifted, she had sighed with relief that he no longer watched her.

"My dear, has something upset you?" Charles Riverton asked, replacing his white panama on his head. "You appear distracted. Did Kincaid do anything to—"

"The sheriff? Why would you think that? If anyone did any upsetting, the blame is mine for the news I gave him. Please," she said, momentarily resting her hand on his arm, "do not concern yourself."

Seeing that all her luggage was secure, she thanked Wally. Since Charles had not tipped him, she removed a dollar gold piece from her reticule and gave it to the old man.

"That wasn't necessary. Wally is paid to—"

"Charles, I do understand that things are done differently out here. But please, allow me to make my own decisions about any service rendered to me."

There was a brief flash of anger in his dark eyes.

"Of course. I had forgotten how independent you are. I won't repeat the mistake, my dear. Come," he offered, holding out his hand to help her onto the narrow buggy seat. Once she was settled, Charles stood a moment looking at her. "I swear you're more lovely than memory served. And if Kincaid forgot he dealt with a lady, I promise you he'll pay for it."

Hearing the underlying threat of violence in his voice, Belinda felt a pang of alarm. She looked at his muscular body, dressed as finely as any gentleman of fashion to be found in a Chicago drawing room. Remembering Kincaid's reaction to the mention of Charles as her host, Belinda surmised that Charles felt the same way about him.

"I assure you, Charles, there is no need to be disturbed. The sheriff was not so much unpleasant as he was blunt." She had to stop. Charles wore a strange look. A disappointed one, she thought. But she was troubled at finding herself once more rushing to defend Kincaid. How could she? The man had tricked her. Truly this heat affected her mind.

"I'm sure your Uncle Phillip told you that I'll do everything in my power to aid you." He seated himself next to her and untied the reins from the short brass rail that trimmed the foot box. "At the risk of sounding boastful, my power is considerable in the territory. But I admit that I'm puzzled, my dear. Phillip never mentioned exactly what it is that brings you here."

"At my request," she answered. Belinda thought of his boast, and of her threats to Kincaid. She could end the matter now. All she had to do was tell Charles what she wanted.

The unease that had begun the moment Charles lifted her hand to his lips and she had looked into his dark eyes grew at an alarming rate. Charles would exact a price for his help. Belinda did not believe she was being vain to think she would be a part of it.

She rocked back on the seat as he urged the horses into a brisk trot. The four accompanying horsemen aligned themselves two on each side of the buggy. Their hardened appearance added to her unease, although she tried to excuse it. According to the newspaper stories she had read there were many threats to life in the West. A man of Charles's wealth and power would be a target.

Many gentlemen of her acquaintance had bodyguards. Why then did the uneasy feeling remain?

The sheriff's office passed in a blur. She saw that the door was still open. Separated by a few building lots, two saloons lined the street opposite each other. She turned and leaned out of the hood's protective shade to see the name signs painted above each saloon. The Dugout and Potee's were two more names she would add to the list she was making for Christian De Young, her man of business. Fond of reading dime novels, he had wanted to accompany her on this journey, but with the threat that her cousin Albert presented to the family business, Belinda had had to refuse his request.

"My dear, I can't help but ponder your reason for making this trip alone. Won't you ease my mind and tell me?"

Belinda glanced at the strong line of his profile. She could and did use feminine wiles when it suited her purpose. She could also infuse her voice with enough starch to wilt the most persistent men.

"You will forgive me, Mr. Riverton, but—"

"Charles, my dear, please. I assumed we moved beyond that formality when you used my first name at the depot. Calling me Mr. Riverton makes me sound as if I am your uncle's age when in truth there is a considerable difference in our ages.''

The slip of using his first name only reminded Belinda how upset her meeting with the sheriff had left her.

But now she had a new worry. The old roué had not been subtle with his hint. Think of him as anything but her uncle's contemporary? Never. Phillip had celebrated his fifty-eighth birthday a month early because of her leaving. Charles was ten years younger. She knew many women who had married older men, but twenty-some odd years older than herself was too old. If she had been thinking of getting married.

Kincaid was not an old man.

Belinda was startled by the thought. Where had that come from?

''My dear, you didn't answer me. May I call you Belinda?''

''I am not sure that my uncle would approve.''

''But Phillip is not here.''

''No, he is not. Charles then, if it would make you more comfortable. As I had begun to say, I am fatigued by my journey. The explanation is long and tedious. I am sure you will be gracious and allow me the opportunity to rest before I answer your question.''

Having been put in his place, Charles had no choice but to agree. ''All right, but I sensed from Phillip's telegram that the matter was one of some urgency.''

''It is.'' Her curt answer was rude. What was wrong with her? She might need this man's help. Alienating him would not insure his cooperation. She could not leave the matter entirely in the sheriff's hands, not when he was so close to it. Or could she? Kincaid had been insulted when she attempted to bribe him. Only an honest man would have reacted to that amount of money in such a way.

Or was it all a trick? Rubbing her forehead, Belinda did not have an answer. Rarely had she wavered in her judgment of someone. But Kincaid... and the heat... *and that kiss.*

Belinda wished to lapse into silence and simply study the swiftly changing landscape. But she would never find out more about the Kincaids if she did not engage Charles in conversation. Time to make amends for her curtness.

"Charles, I apologize. These past few months have been trying ones." Like most men, especially those who had wealth but craved power, Charles was not immune to her softened tone and implied flattery. Studying his profile, she caught the subtle move he made to straighten. She could easily imagine him preening under her avid gaze.

She sorted about for a quick change in conversation. The barren land offered no clue, then an idea came to her.

Belinda managed to turn a bit more on the seat. "May I ask you a personal question?"

Charles glanced over and saw the admiration gleaming in her large brown eyes. Belinda had a mind of her own, as he had found out, but she was young and malleable and very rich.

The thought of all that unclaimed wealth added warmth to his voice. "Ask away, Belinda."

"After we met last year, I admit I became curious about you." She was thankful that the deep ruts forced his gaze from her to concentrate on guiding the horses around them.

"Why has a man of taste and refinement chosen to live here? As far as I can see," she said with a graceful sweep of her hand, "there is no civilization. I have never understood what drives people to leave the cities where everything one could desire is at hand. It is no secret there are all manner of hardships to be endured in this untamed land."

"That's true enough, Belinda. We still have bands of renegade Apache plaguing our efforts to settle most of the territory. But the army has stepped up its effort to contain them on the reservations. The possibilities are endless for a man of vision to make his mark. I admit that I crave power to shape the government of this territory."

"Do I detect strong ambitions, Charles?"

"Why not? There is gold and silver here to fuel more than my dreams, Belinda. The kind of money the likes of Gould and the Commodore have at their disposal."

"The robber barons," she murmured, hiding her distaste.

Charles flashed her a rewarding smile. "Exactly so."

"Uncle Phillip was right about you." Belinda settled back against the padded seat, thinking of what her uncle had said. Charles had one god—power. Phillip had also informed her that Charles was unscrupulous about how he obtained it.

"Since I admire your uncle, I will take that as a compliment."

She did not make an attempt to disabuse him of this notion. She was comfortable playing this type of game with men like Charles Riverton. So unlike her disconcerting meeting with Sheriff Kincaid.

Belinda found herself reluctant to discard the image of Conner's face as it sprang to mind. This only added to her confusion. A strange shiver of sensual awareness spread over her, one she could not seem to stop.

"Tomorrow, if you feel up to it, I'll take you for a ride over my land. There is a primitive beauty to it."

"I shall look forward to that. Do you have neighbors close by?"

"The Kincaids are the closest. About an hour's ride. Why do you ask?"

"I was merely curious." That close? She could ride over and... and what? Snatch her nephew? Risk confronting an outlaw? She had to proceed with caution until she knew what opposed her. Kincaid, for one.

She did not understand this preoccupation with the man. Examining her feelings, Belinda knew she could not be attracted to him. Hard on the heels of this came a nagging voice demanding to know what had possessed her to kiss him. A stranger... an aggravating, arrogant... she could spend days making a list of things he was.

She toyed with the top button on her collar. The kiss had been merely giving in to a momentary impulse. And the heat, she reminded herself for the third or eighth time. Mentally defending her action, she knew there had been a great deal of heat generated by the sheriff's overwhelming masculinity. And those blatant innuendos about other women finding pleasure in his slow methods.

There, she could feel anger coming back over his fooling her with his initial civil manner. He had deliberately misled her into talking about his brother. His brother!

And she wasn't about to forget his accusation that she did not care about her nephew's welfare. Working herself into a fine state, she continued to review the situation in her mind. She had not informed the sheriff of the distance that her brother had forced upon their relationship. All her attempts to mend the breach had been rebuffed. She had never told anyone how much it hurt her to be denied seeing her nephew.

Matters had not been helped by their grandmother leaving the bulk of her shares in the family's holdings to Belinda. Robert broke away completely when he discovered their father's will read the same.

Robert had blamed Belinda for being left out of their wills, but she knew it was not true. The real cause had been Robert's refusal to take any interest in business.

Yes, the sheriff's accusation had stung, but Belinda was proud that she had hidden her hurt from him.

In the next breath, she admitted that Kincaid had given her something to think about.

The old man, Wally, told her the Kincaid family was an old and proud one. Very close-knit. Tighter than ticks on an old hound's skin, had been his exact words.

What if the Kincaids refused to honor her brother's request that she have his son? What if the boy refused to leave them?

The land passed in a blur. She admonished herself for having these doubts. Kincaid had well and truly flustered her. Those people had no claim on the boy. And no child could be allowed to decide his future.

It was this infernal heat that made her fortitude wilt and allowed these ridiculous thoughts to surface.

She would get what she came for and no Kincaid, be he sheriff or not, was going to stop her.

Chapter Four

"The whole thing is ridiculous!" Logan fixed his attention on the linen wrap he was replacing on his mother's favorite mare. "Can't imagine where you came up with such a tall tale, Conner." Crouched in the thick straw bedding, Logan shot his older brother a look.

"Haven't you got better things to do than sit in that office of yours and spin yarns? If you need work, there's plenty to do here."

"I'm not spinning yarns for your amusement, Logan. I saw the letter, I met the lady. But let it go for the moment. Sounds like you've got your plate heaped with work."

The wealth of understanding in his brother's gaze took the edge off Logan's anger. "Yeah. My plate's so full I haven't slept in my own bed for more than two nights running. Jeez, Conner, how the hell did you manage it all?"

"Just did." Conner shrugged. "Work needed doing, wasn't much choice."

Left unsaid between them was the fact that Conner had no one helping him. Their daddy's boots had fit Conner like they had been made for him, in all ways.

Or so Logan and their younger brother Ty had believed. It wasn't until Conner relinquished most of the day-to-day overseeing to them that they'd understood that Conner never wanted to be the boss. Santo's words came back in a rush to Logan: Conner had been a man before he'd ever had a chance to be a boy.

"It's not the work, Conner." Satisfied that the swelling had gone down on the mare's leg Logan nudged aside her curious nose and replaced the extra linen strips, tin of Three Horn Cure All, and bottle of Neatsfoot oil in his box.

"Then what's causing the problem?"

"Guess me and Ty are having a hard time divvying up who makes the decisions for what. Half the time he's gone up to hurry the carpenters to finish his house so he and Dixie can move in. Truth to tell, I guess I envy him. Jessie hasn't said a word about living in the big house, but she's a woman used to her own ways. Sofia rules the kitchen. You know that," he added with a grin that his brother shared.

"I just don't know when there'll be time to build our own place. And I can't take those boys away from Ma now."

"Nope, you can't. So most of the decisions fall on your shoulders because you're here and Ty isn't."

"Pack that truth in a bottle of snake oil and give the man a prize."

Conner rested his arms across the top slat of the box stall. "Here's another truth. Belinda Jarvis—"

"You can't believe her."

"Already told you that I do. There are too many facts that add up."

"No. It doesn't add up for me."

Conner heaved a weary sigh, "Logan, you can deny it all you want. But the lady has corset steel running up her backbone, and she's not going away. You can't ignore—"

"I'm not ignoring it." Coming to his feet, Logan shot his brother a narrow-eyed glare. "I'm listening to you and getting this real strange feeling that you approve of this woman. I thought you said she was as mouthy as a chicken house when the fox is around?"

"Did I say that?"

"Denying it?"

"Nope."

"What's with you, Conner? You admire this woman?"

"Heaven forbid. She's starched harder than—"

"Conner. Stop telling me how much you don't like her. Tell me instead that she can't take the boy away from us." Running one hand through his dark hair, Logan glanced around. "Jeez, what the hell am I going to tell Jessie?"

"Try nothing for now. I told you, I rode out here to warn you and only you. Don't say anything to Ma or Jessie. Tell Ty, if you want to. I'll do all I can to check out her story."

Conner opened the stall door for his brother, then latched it. Logan appeared dazed, as if it were finally sinking in that Conner was serious.

Logan didn't move when his brother placed his big hand on his shoulder.

"Listen to me, Logan, you can help me disprove her claim. If you're so sure she's barking up the wrong tree, get me proof. The boys have their family Bibles, don't they?"

Logan stared at the closed door of the storage room. "All their stuff is back there. Everything their wagons carried. I never asked them to go through it after the first time they refused. I took Kenny's word from the start that they were cousins with no kin to take them in. I can't believe that boy lied to me."

"We don't know for sure that he did. 'Sides, Kenny's got a way 'bout him that'll have the preacher thinking he's the sinner to be saved."

Conner shared his brother's laughter. It quickly faded. "We need to talk to Kenny first."

"Well, we can't. Santo took the boys and Jessie up to the canyons to hunt for berries. You'll have to stay till they come back."

"All right. But think hard about this, Logan. If Miss Jarvis is right, she's got the law on her side."

"The law?" Logan dropped the wooden carry box, kicked it aside and lunged for his brother.

"Say that again," Logan demanded, grabbing hold of Conner's arm.

"You heard me plain enough. If she's right, Logan, I'll have no choice but to turn over the boy to her."

"The hell you will." Logan drew back his arm and let a punch fly at Conner's jaw.

Conner ducked his head to one side. The blow struck his shoulder. Logan lunged at him. Conner barely managed to shove him back, for they were of similar height and build. When Conner saw that Logan was coming at him again, he laid into his brother until he had him slammed up against the support beam. Dust filtered down from the rafters, choking them both as they struggled.

Breathing heavily, Conner was the first to back away. "Damn it, Logan, stop. I don't want to fight you."

Chest heaving, Logan glared at him. He had supported Conner's decision to go after the sheriff's job. But this...this was betrayal of the worst sort. He shook his head. "I can't believe you're standing there, standing against me, against us."

"I'm not against—"

"You sure the hell are! You're standing on Kincaid land, Conner. Standing there and telling me you'll break my Jessie's heart, not to mention what taking one of those boys will do to Ma. And my boys, Conner? What about them? Did you once think about what separating them will do? After all Kenny and Marty have been through, losing their folks, living hand to mouth, scared and alone. You think I'll let a stranger tear them apart after they almost died trying to save my life from outlaws."

Logan's voice became hushed. "If you dare try taking—"

"Don't threaten me, Logan."

"Don't get up on your high horse with me, Conner. You're not the ramrod of this outfit anymore. You're nothing but a brass badge who can't remember his family always came first with him."

"And you're angry with the wrong person. Stop saying—"

"I'll have my say—"

"Logan! Don't say another word. You'll regret it, like I'm already doing. And lower your voice before the whole ranch knows why I came out here."

"Afraid you'll tarnish the Conner-can-do-no-wrong image? Go to hell." Logan swiped his hand across his mouth. His tongue probed his tooth. His jaw was already starting to swell from where it had connected against the wood.

Conner rubbed his hands up and down his thighs in an effort to control his temper. His effort wasn't helped by having Logan glare at him as if he were something that had crawled out from beneath a rock. Damn Belinda Jarvis!

"Logan, listen. I—"

"No. You listen." He fixed his gaze on his brother's face. "I'll talk to my boys and find out if there's any truth to this claim. I'll get out the Bibles, too. But I don't want you anywhere near them."

"You've got no right—"

"I have every right, Conner. I'm the closest thing to a pa those boys have. I can't believe you'd forget who that woman is staying with. Before you rode out here, did you once think that Riverton put her up to this?"

"Why? What would he gain—"

"Plenty, Conner. This could be his ploy to split us apart."

Raking his hand through his hair, Conner let his hand fall to his side. As long as Logan was willing to reason this out, he had to make another effort. But it was tearing him inside to take the opposite side at every turn.

In a calmer tone, he answered his brother. "On the ride out here, I thought about the possibility of Riverton setting this up. I may not like what Belinda Jarvis had to say, but I'd stake a heap on her believing every word. You weren't there, in my office, when I told her that you were my brother. Like I told you before, she had this report from the Pinkertons that an outlaw and a widow left Apache Junction with two boys that didn't belong to them."

Conner saw the mutinous expression forming on Logan's face and held up one hand. "Just let me finish. Much as I'd like to tie this neatly up and lay it at Riverton's door, I can't. For two reasons," he hurried to add before Logan could say a word.

"He couldn't be sure that it would split us up. And even if he somehow figured a way to use this to his advantage, there's still Belinda.

"There's no way that woman faked her reaction when I said you were my brother. She didn't know that I'm a Kincaid. Riverton would have told her that."

Logan stepped back from Conner. "And that's it?" he demanded. "That's all you've got to say? You're willing to tear this family apart on the word of some woman who didn't act like she knew you were a Kincaid?"

"Take the damn wood out of your ears, little brother! I said I'd send telegrams. I'll verify her story before I let her near this family. My family, Logan. Just try and understand that I've got a job—"

"Shove your job, *big* brother. Shove it to hell and gone!" He turned his back on Conner and headed for the door.

"Logan." Conner started after him, then shook his head, knowing it was useless to try and talk anymore.

He didn't understand what had happened. Logan was usually the calm one, always willing to listen to all sides. This time, instead of offering to help him figure it out so no one was hurt, his brother allowed anger to override good sense.

Churning anger had him swinging without thought. His fist connected with the solid wooden beam. Another shower of dust rained down on him. The anger was still there, and so was the beam, but now he sported skinned knuckles.

He would love to prove that Belinda Jarvis was in cahoots with Riverton to drive a wedge between the Kincaids.

He'd love it, but deep inside himself, he knew it was not true.

A last nagging doubt forced its way into his thoughts. If she hadn't been so easy to kiss, would he still believe her?

Conner eyed the spilled contents of the carryall. Old habits were hard to break. He hated things out of place, just like he hated loose ends. As he bent and picked up the items to replace them in the wooden box, Conner replayed his meeting with Belinda.

He had denied knowing much about the Pinkertons, but any lawman worth his forty-eight dollars a month knew the agency's reputation. But just as that part of her tale rang true, Conner sensed that Belinda had left a great deal unsaid.

And if he believed her, then Kenny had lied to all of them with his claim that he and Marty were cousins.

He had come to Logan as a brother, now he had no choice but to approach him as the law.

Chapter Five

Hot and tired, Jessie wished she had stayed home and let Santo take the boys without her on the hunt for the first wild berries of the season.

She had spread a picnic lunch in the shade cast by the rock wall of a slot canyon, contented to remain there while Santo, Kenny and Marty followed a set of animal tracks deeper into the canyon.

She had become discouraged by the empty search of so many small arroyos and canyons, looking for the elusive berries, but the happiness of the boys meant so much to her that she couldn't voice a desire to return to the ranch.

There was another reason she wasn't anxious to return, one she couldn't speak to anyone about. Not even to her husband. Logan wouldn't understand how difficult the past few months had been for her.

It wasn't that Macaria or Sofia resented her in any way. The women had welcomed her and the two orphan boys into the family. Even Dixie, her new sister-in-law, had offered friendship, but now Dixie was deeply enclosed in a cocoon with her husband as they awaited the birth of their first child. Rosanna, Sofia's daughter, was the only one to see the restlessness that plagued Jessie and eagerly relinquished her chores to help Jessie fill the hours.

Maybe too eagerly. There was something about Rosanna that bothered her. A vague feeling that began when the young woman questioned her about the effort to clear Logan's name. Jessie had been so startled that she knew her attempt to hide her reaction was not successful. And it wasn't the questions themselves that bothered her—after all Rosanna had grown up with the Kincaids—but the fact that she seemed to know more than Jessie did.

Touching the gold of her wedding band, Jessie brushed aside the unease. Perhaps it stemmed from her own sense of having lost a tiny part of her hard-won independence.

She had fallen in love with Logan's family as easily as she had fallen in love with her outlaw. But she couldn't help feeling that all the Kincaids had a place and she had yet to find hers.

Dixie would have the first Kincaid baby, and Macaria was occupied with the coming of her first grandchild.

And Jessie had . . . not the boys, not any longer. If Sofia wasn't spoiling them with her special treats, Santo or one of the men was teaching them necessary skills.

She couldn't even look after her own herd of cattle. Logan refused her offer to count them as part of the Kincaid herd. Santo, to forestall an argument, had come up with the suggestion that Kenny and Marty be responsible for them. She had forgiven Logan for turning down her gift when he later held her in his arms and explained that he wanted her to have something of her own.

She couldn't deny him, just as she couldn't deny that Santo had made a wise decision. Kenny thrived on responsibility and little Marty was thriving, too. His nightmares had lessened, wrapped as he was within the love and safety provided by family.

Both of the boys had put on weight, but Jessie didn't think she would ever take the sound of their laughter for granted. She would never forget how close she had come to losing them and Logan.

Shuddering with the memory, Jessie was wrenched from her thoughts by the sound of Marty calling her.

"Jessie! Jessie, come see. We found the rustler's camp!"

"Rustlers," she repeated, dread filling her. "Marty, wait." But as she scrambled to her feet and started for him, she saw his blond head disappear around a rock slide.

"Santo is with them. He wouldn't let anything harm the boys," Jessie whispered to herself as she ran deeper into the slot canyon.

Belinda was disturbed by the armed guards at the gate leading up to Charles's house. The concern remained despite the sight of a sprawling home that made her catch her breath.

Although her uncle and Charles himself had reassured her, she had retained her doubts about the accommodations she would find at the end of her journey.

Armed guards aside, her doubts vanished.

"Welcome to my home, Belinda." Charles offered his hand to help her alight from the buggy. "I hope you will think of it as your own while you grace me with your charming company."

The hushed intimacy of his voice forced her to look at him. His dark, almost black eyes, met her gaze with a warmth that Belinda did not return.

Unlike many men of the day, Charles had no mustache, or beard. His sweeping sideburns were neatly trimmed, but this close to him she saw the coarseness of his skin. She had been wrapped in thoughts of the sheriff—not a good sign—and never noticed Charles's fleshy jowl or the thinness of his lips.

An old saying of her grandmother's came to mind: Thin lips indicate a petty character. When his thick brown eyebrows pulled together in a frown, Belinda realized how long she had been staring at him.

"Thank you for your generous offer, Charles. I hope I shall not impose on your hospitality for too long." Belinda made an attempt to brush the fine red dust from her skirt.

"We shall see, my dear. Perhaps you will become enchanted with this land."

There was a hint of insistence in his voice. Belinda could interpret his tone in no other way. Once more she was disconcerted by the feeling that she had made a mistake. As Charles turned to issue orders about her luggage to the two men who had accompanied them up to the house, Belinda looked at his home.

Coolness in the face of desert heat was the goal of home builders, that and protection from dust storms, earth-shaking rains and marauding Indians.

The house sat on a slope of land so that, even standing where she was, she could see down to the gate, across the fenced corrals and pastures where he kept his blooded stock. He had pointed out the long stone bunkhouse, built of rock hauled from the mountains so he couldn't be burned out as many ranchers had been. Barns, stock pens, smoke houses and other buildings were clustered below.

Turning to the house, she admired the graceful arches of cool-looking whitewashed adobe that invited one beneath the dark-timbered supports and reddish tile roof. Wicker chairs and clay-potted plantings added to the cool welcome.

Charles took her arm and urged her to step onto the tiled entranceway. The double wooden doors were flanked by large gleaming brass and glass lanterns. Brass was repeated in the door's massive hinges, handles and studded design.

"These doors, Charles, the workmanship is exquisite."

"I'm rather proud of those myself. My business frequently takes me into Mexico. A small village priest approached me about buying the doors of his church in order to get the money to dig a new well. Since the stop didn't take me out of my way, I agreed to at least look at them. Those peasants often have an inflated sense of the worth of what objects they sell. But as you see, I was most pleased by the bargain we struck."

Belinda murmured admiration, manners dictated she do so, but her estimation of Charles Riverton fell several degrees. She had been brought up and truly believed that those fortunate to have wealth should do charitable works, not take advantage of those in need. Charles obviously did not follow that same path.

He was her host and her uncle's friend, she reminded herself. It was not her place to criticize him. But his admission added to the disturbed feeling that wouldn't leave her.

"Ah, Mrs. Dobbs. I wondered what was keeping you."

Belinda's attention immediately focused on the dour-faced woman who whispered to Charles. From the gray threading the severely pulled back hairstyle to the prune shade of her high-necked gown, unrelieved by any adornment, Belinda likened her to the matrons who worked in the local orphanage back home.

There was no smile of welcome as the woman stood aside and Charles made introductions before ushering her inside his home. Nor did Mrs. Dobbs speak when Charles instructed her to show Belinda to her room so that she could refresh herself.

"I especially hope that you find your room to your liking."

"I am sure that I will, Charles." She ignored the slight squeeze he gave her arm before releasing her. Belinda caught sight of someone peering at her from the doorway of one of the rooms down the hall. She angled her head to the side, but whoever was there was gone. She could not tell if it was a man or a woman, for a hat brim shadowed their face.

"Go along, my dear. Mrs. Dobbs will unpack for you. Then I hope you will join me for a light repast in the courtyard."

Belinda, longing for a hot bath, not his company, recovered herself enough to remember that he had deliberately distracted her when she questioned him about the Kincaids.

Her smile added to her assurance that she would love to join him. Charles was the only source of information she had about this Kincaid family. She needed as much local information as possible before she confronted them with a demand to return her nephew.

Following the silent Mrs. Dobbs down the wide, high-ceilinged hallway, Belinda peered into the open doorways of the rooms on either side.

She didn't see anyone and wondered if she had imagined that someone had looked out at her. She knew it was not her imagination that spawned the impression that Charles intended any visitor to his home to understand that he was a man who lived alone, a wealthy man, and one who had power. It was declared in the heavy wood lines of furniture, the leather and supple hide coverings, the thick Turkish carpets centered on every floor.

Mrs. Dobbs opened the door at the end of the hall and abruptly they were beneath a series of archways that encircled a large courtyard.

"This way, miss," Mrs. Dobbs instructed, indicating her left. "Mr. Riverton's suite of rooms are in that wing. Your room is here in the guest wing."

Belinda almost reprimanded the woman for her impertinent tone, but kept quiet. If Charles or his dour housekeeper thought she was interested in knowing where his suite was, they had both spent too much time in the sun.

She had not kept her freedom from the restrictions of marriage this long without being very careful. She had no intent of being railroaded into a compromising position and forced to wed.

"Tell me, Mrs. Dobbs, are there any other guests? I could not help but notice the rooms across the way."

"Those are the servants' quarters, kitchens, pantry and laundry rooms. Places you'll have no need of visiting while you're here."

"Then there are other servants here," Belinda said as she followed the woman. "I wondered who was

peering out from one of the rooms when I arrived?"
She deliberately posed it as a question.

"You are mistaken, miss. There was no one in the
house."

Belinda opened her mouth to argue, then shut it.
She had not been mistaken. Why would the woman lie
to her?

Belinda cast a longing look, wishing to linger in the
quiet of the courtyard. A spray of sparkling water rose
from the stone fountain centerpiece around which
potted flowers bloomed. Their scent was faint, their
colors vibrant against the other shrubs and greenery
contained in the large clay pots.

A few benches were scattered about, several forming the basis of informal seating groups along with
chairs and a table. The entwined vine and floral de-
signs of the pieces reminded her of the intricate gates
and balcony rails of the homes in New Orleans.

Hearing her name, Belinda saw that Mrs. Dobbs
stood in an open doorway. Her impatient look made
Belinda hurry. She was as eager to be rid of this disapproving woman as the woman was eager to be gone.

Having the example of Charles's taste in heavy, dark
furnishings in mind, Belinda was unprepared for the
guest room.

The drapery covering two windows that over-
looked the courtyard were pale shades of lilac, blue
and pink flowers on a cream background. The drapes
were tied back to reveal the sheer Brussels net lace
curtains.

The delicate colors were repeated in the silk dam-
ask upholstery of ornately carved walnut furniture
that had been created for a woman.

Spiderweb-fine lace formed the canopy for the four-poster bed. Small, plump cushions invited one to recline on the backless tufted couch. In front of the windows, two gilt chairs were separated by a table where three cupids held a silver-worked clock between them.

Belinda turned slowly, her gaze noting the near-perfect combination of color and furniture so dear to the feminine heart. She couldn't stop the chill that shivered up her spine. It was too perfect. And the colors...

Feeling Mrs. Dobbs's gaze upon her, Belinda forced a smile as the woman wasted no time beginning the process of unpacking.

The dressing tabletop rapidly filled as the woman removed hairbrushes, combs and various toiletries in their matching silver containers from the smaller portmanteau.

As she strolled around the room, Belinda felt her heels sink into the thick floral-patterned carpet. The scent of cedar drifted from the now open wardrobe doors.

Drawn to admire the porcelain oil lamps with etched glass globes and crystal prisms paired on the cheval dresser, Belinda could not stop another chilling shiver.

Removing her gloves, she placed them next to the footed tray painted with pale pink roses and trimmed with gold. A matching hair receiver, ring tray and covered box sat on the tray.

Belinda glanced at her reflection in the standing pier glass in the corner. Her brows were drawn in a frown reflecting her puzzled thoughts.

She saw that Mrs. Dobbs paused to stare at her. Belinda ignored the woman. She removed the hat pins from her Venice bonnet. Smoothing the feathers before she set the hat on the dresser, she noticed that her fingertips were covered with a fine red dust.

Unnerved by the woman's continued stare, Belinda turned to face her. "Is something wrong, Mrs. Dobbs?"

"Yes, miss. Don't you like the room?"

"I beg your pardon?"

"The room, miss. Mr. Riverton went to great expense to furnish it with your favorite colors. But you've not said a word about it."

Hiding her dismay, Belinda had to swallow before she could answer her. "The room is lovely. I am sure that I will have everything I need."

Why? She had wanted to dismiss finding her favorite colors as an accident, but Mrs. Dobbs ended any chance of that. Why had Charles gone to the trouble of finding out her favorite colors? And why had her uncle—for it could be no one else—ever told him?

Belinda stepped aside to allow Mrs. Dobbs to fill the dresser drawers with her silk plaited stockings, cashmere hose and heavier cotton ones. She wanted to tell the housekeeper to stop, to return her corset covers, white lawn drawers, chemises and petticoats to the larger portmanteau.

She kept silent as the woman continued to fill the bottom drawer with nightgowns and matching wrappers.

When Mrs. Dobbs pursed her lips and made tut-tutting sounds, Belinda once again asked her what was wrong.

"These shirtwaists and skirts will all have to be pressed, miss. I expected a young woman like yourself to be traveling with your own maid."

"Were you? Well, as you can see, I am not." She wasn't quite sure what to make of the woman's audacity to voice such remarks to her. Belinda was not accustomed to explaining herself or her actions to servants.

But as the pile of clothing to be pressed mounted on the bed, Belinda realized that the gowns of dimity, dotted Swiss, poplin, cambric and corded silk, combined with the skirts and fine lawn shirtwaists, added to the woman's work.

"Mrs. Dobbs, there is no need for everything to be pressed. I will not be staying long."

"It's no trouble, miss. I shall tend to your clothing personally. And you're not to worry about a chaperon. I will serve—"

"Mrs. Dobbs, I do not require a chaperon. I am not fresh from the schoolroom."

"Yes, miss."

Irritated, Belinda glanced away. She had a feeling the woman was going to ignore her. But she had to remind someone else that she was not fresh from the schoolroom. The sheriff. That Kincaid man who had made a fool of her.

Eager to turn her back on the housekeeper, Belinda gave in to the urge to investigate the curtained alcove.

To her surprise the floor was tiled. A silk-paneled screen hid a large porcelain bathtub. A cupboard held an array of French-milled soaps, perfumed oils and lengths of linen toweling. Beside the tub stood a wide-topped stool and next to it a table.

Discreetly placed in the opposite corner behind a smaller silk screen, she discovered the covered chamber pot and slop jar. Like the china tray set on the dresser, these too were painted with pale pink roses.

Belinda found more of the china pieces on the wide marble-topped washstand. Ewer and basin, covered soap dish and drainer, water pitcher, brush vase and glass completed the set.

Belinda took advantage of the warmed water in the ewer to wash the dust from her hands and face. Mrs. Dobbs had been right to say that Charles had gone to a great deal of trouble and expense. Belinda was not happy with the answer she came up with to justify it.

With the aid of the gilt frame mirror above the washstand, she repinned her hair in a few places. Since she was unwilling to remain in the room with the housekeeper and couldn't hide in the alcove until the woman was finished, Belinda returned to the bedroom and announced she would be in the courtyard. She quickly waved off Mrs. Dobbs's suggestion that she accompany her.

Meeting the woman's eyes filled with censure before she closed the door behind her, Belinda heaved a sigh of relief. She took a deep, satisfying breath of clean air. There was no one in the courtyard as she walked toward the fountain, thinking of the housekeeper's remark about her traveling without a maid.

She was not going to explain that she wanted her mission kept secret. When she had received word about Robert's death and confirmation that his son lived, she knew it was imperative that she find the child before her cousin Albert. It was the only way to protect the boy and the trust her family had left to her. Albert was determined to wrest control of the family business away from her. She had always voted her brother's small block of stock along with her own. The shares now belonged to his son. If Albert had the boy he would force her to go along with his scheme, and once he was in control, Belinda knew she and her nephew would be in danger. Her uncle Phillip was the only one she trusted. He would not tell Albert where she was or what she hoped to accomplish.

Even her man of business had been told she was on an extended visit to friends who lived throughout the Southern states.

But Belinda could not deny her worry. Albert still might find out what she was up to. If he did, he would also find a way to stop her. He was a ruthless man. She had already dismissed one of the Irish maids after she caught the girl on her cousin's lap in the back parlor, whispering to him about her employer's plans for the day. And the stable boy. She could not forget letting the lad go for the same transgression. And the accidents...

She blocked the turn her thoughts took, remembering instead the other reason she traveled alone. She loved the freedom from the strict social laws that governed her life. There was no one to frown over, then whisper gossip about her behavior.

Like this morning when you gave in to the impulse to kiss a total stranger?

Wishing she could step back in time to recall the kiss was foolish. Wishing she could forget the taste of Conner's warm lips upon her own also appeared to be a futile exercise.

That only reminded her that she remained unsatisfied with Charles's vague replies about the Kincaid family, especially to those questions she had asked about the sheriff.

She was more than curious about him, she was intrigued. She had been distracted by his sensual nature, but he would not have the opportunity to fool her again. The man was a challenge and if she had time...

With no sign of Charles in the courtyard, Belinda decided to search for him.

She glanced down the archways that led to his suite of rooms. Not even the growing need to have questions answered would tempt her toward them. She had not forgotten what the housekeeper told her about Charles refurbishing the room with her favorite colors. Uncle Phillip had a great deal to answer for.

Belinda opened the door to the main hall. She paid immediate attention to a man's voice raised in anger. Charles's voice, she was sure. Allowing herself a few seconds' debate over the wisdom of staying or leaving, she proceeded down the hall.

"I told you," Charles reprimanded, "never risk coming here during the day. I don't care how important the information is. What if she saw you? What if she passed some innocent remark on to Kincaid?"

Belinda hesitated. Her grandmother's oft-given advice rang in her ears: Those who listen at keyholes never hear anything good about themselves.

From the sound of Charles's voice, the door wasn't quite closed, so she tiptoed down the hall. She didn't have the slightest doubt that *she* was the woman Charles had referred to. Anything that linked her with the Kincaids was information too important to dismiss. She would worry about her manners as a guest later.

Belinda flattened herself against the wall and glanced back at the door to the courtyard to make sure that no one was lurking about. She worked her way down toward the doorway by inches. What kind of information about the Kincaids would be important to Charles?

This is wrong! Belinda hushed her conscience. She would use every means at her disposal as a bargaining tool against the Kincaids. She would use whatever means necessary to keep the family's legacy intact and stop Albert's destructive schemes.

The door was partly opened, but not enough for her to see Charles or whoever was in the room with him. All she heard was the murmur of voices, then Charles spoke again.

"Now that you're finished marking the map, I'll get your money. Since the information you brought me is so valuable, I'll double your price this time."

The sound of a drawer slamming shut made Belinda risk a quick, more direct look through the opening. She saw Charles standing behind a massive carved oak desk, in profile to her. For a few moments he appeared to be staring down at his hand. He looked up, then came around the desk. The move put him out of Belinda's sight once more.

"Wait here until I send Mrs. Dobbs to you. I want to make sure that my guest doesn't see you."

Uncertain of what she had stumbled across, Belinda inched her way back down the hall. She had to find the map. An old ploy that often worked when she wished to excuse herself from unwanted company came to mind. She unhooked her eardrop and let it fall.

With a smile pasted on her lips, she called out to her host.

"Charles? Charles, where are you? I thought...oh, there you are. I thought you had forgotten me."

Charles came out of the room, pulling the door shut, and stood with his hands behind him, gripping the brass handle. "Never, my dear. Just a small business matter that required my attention."

Striding toward her, Charles offered her his arm. "Nothing would please me more than sharing your charming company."

"I am happy to hear that. I thought I heard you arguing..." Belinda focused an expectant gaze on his flushed face. Was it anger or excitement that added the color to his high cheekbones?

"Not at all. It's nothing to concern yourself over." He opened the door to the courtyard. With his hand placed at the small of her back, he ushered her outside.

"Ah, there is William with our repast. Forgive me, Belinda, but I took the liberty to have Cook make a small selection of native fare. If it is not to your liking, she can make anything you desire."

"I am sure that I shall enjoy sampling what you have chosen, Charles." As Belinda picked a seat facing the door, she caught the whispered exchange between Charles and his servant.

She barely glanced at the tray on the table between them, and urged Charles to fix a plate for her. She felt excitement mount when William went into her room to get Mrs. Dobbs. He left almost immediately to cross to the kitchen, and Mrs. Dobbs hurried along beneath the archway.

Belinda knew her timing had to be perfect. She counted to ten once the door to the courtyard had closed behind the housekeeper.

"Oh, dear," she cried, jumping up from her seat. "I seem to have lost my eardrop." Fingering the naked lobe, Belinda cast a frantic look around. "Please help me, Charles. These belonged to my grandmother. Uncle Phillip will be furious if I lose one."

Before Charles could rise, she dashed across the courtyard. Flinging open the door, she bit her lip to hide her smile. Her timing had been perfect. Mrs. Dobbs sent a startled look over her shoulder.

"My eardrop," Belinda called out to allay the woman's suspicions. She managed to note little about the person with the housekeeper. The figure was slightly built, darkly clad in a concealing jacket and hat, and Belinda couldn't tell if it was a man or a woman that Mrs. Dobbs ushered out the front door.

"There it is," Belinda announced, hearing Charles behind her as the housekeeper bore down on her.

Before Belinda could recover the eardrop, Charles scooped it out from under her hand. He glanced from the twinkling diamond-and-pearl drop he held to its twin.

"What an odd place to have lost this, my dear. Don't you think so, Mrs. Dobbs?"

Belinda caught the look the two exchanged. Her burst of excitement died.

Chapter Six

Conner didn't linger near the house once he made up his mind that he didn't want to see his mother. Minutes after Logan had left him alone in the barn, he rode out.

He waved to the men perched on the wooden rails of the corral watching a lone rider attempting to break a roan horse.

It didn't need much imagination for Conner to see himself being tossed high in the air then coming down hard in the saddle as the green bronc plunged and jumped to dislodge the man.

The horse was smart. When his crawfishing didn't work, he arched his back then threw himself against the railing.

Conner rode on, grinning when he heard the bets shouted, rider against horse, plenty of encouragement for the rider to haul the hell out of the crow hopper.

A feeling of regret rode on with him. There had been times in the past few months when he missed being in charge of the daily routine. Hot, sweaty, backbreaking and, in some cases, like when he was forced to shoot one of his animals for a broken leg, or snake bite, heartbreaking work.

It wasn't something he could admit to his mother or his brothers. Not when he had made it clear that he never wanted to run the Rocking K alone, that being a lawman was all he had ever wanted.

That had been the truth until this morning.

Now, with the problem that Belinda Jarvis had handed to him like a stick of dynamite with a short, lit fuse, he didn't want to be the one who had to explode it in his family's faces.

Yet he had sworn an oath to administer the law, to carry out justice fairly to one and all regardless of what last name they carried.

Riding out into open country, when he should be back in town sending telegrams off to confirm Belinda's story, was a delaying tactic. One he wasn't proud to admit that he'd used several times in the past. After his father died, men twice his age, having ten times more experience, spoke their piece, then waited for him to make a decision because he wore the boots of the ramrod.

The sunbaked earth, seemingly empty of life, called to him.

Conner heeded the call, needing the delay not only for himself, but to give Logan time to talk to his boys, and for tempers to cool.

Keeping his horse to an easy lope, Conner guided the animal toward the north corner of the Kincaid spread. The buttes and arroyos offered plenty of private places for a man who desired to be alone.

Minutes later, Conner left his gelding, Sour Mash, ground-tied below a rocky incline. He made the climb to the top easily, having worn a path over the years that he had come to this spot.

A large flat slab of rock offered him a seat from which he could see a good part of their land.

This was one of his favorite places on the ranch, the one he had escaped to most often when he felt hemmed in by all the demands for his attention. Especially in the years before Ty and Logan had shouldered their responsibilities as equal working partners in the family's holdings and all the worry and decisions belonged to him.

He tilted the brim of his hat back to wipe the beads of sweat on his forehead. It was long past noon, but the sun still beat strongly, sucking up every bit of moisture from land, animal and man.

A whisper of a breeze touched him, sultry hot, and died moments later.

He sensed he was being watched and slowly glanced to his left, then his right. A Gila monster's forked tongue darted out, testing the air not three feet away. The lizard was nearly two feet long, its pebbled skin a mottled brown and gold. Their name had come from the Spanish conquistadors who had first seen the large lizard near the Gila River.

Conner remained still. The lizard was venomous. It was unusual to find one out in the open while the sun blazed hot. He must have disturbed its resting place in the creosote bushes when he climbed up here.

The short-clawed feet held the thick body and even thicker tail away from the heated rocks. With a slow, almost waddling gait, the lizard made its way back down the incline.

Conner let out a breath he hadn't realized he had held.

Shifting his seat, he scanned the scattered brush below. Farther away were the glistening thin ribbons of streams and the dark brown smudges of cattle clustered on their banks where they'd come to water.

He caught the flash of sunlight reflecting off the rifle barrels of the guards he had ordered posted a few days ago, after another rustling incident. Four of the men he had chosen, with the agreement of Logan and Ty, he would trust with his life. The fifth, and the only one who had seen the map where each guard was posted, was Enrique. He was engaged to marry Santo and Sofia's daughter, Rosanna. And he was the one man they all suspected was feeding information to Riverton.

But no one had caught him doing it. Out of love and respect for Santo and Sofia, whom the Kincaids considered family, no vocal accusations had been made against Enrique.

Conner wanted proof, indisputable proof that would tie Enrique with Charles Riverton, before they did anything.

For now, all he had were suspicions, despite Logan's infiltrating the gang that had been robbing their mines of ore and payroll. His brother had almost lost his life, but the gang had been broken. They still couldn't prove that Riverton was behind them but the robberies had stopped.

Riverton either had enough money from the robberies to further his schemes, or the man was biding his time to lull them into a false sense of security.

But the rustling had continued. Logan had been the one to figure out how easily a Rocking K brand could be changed to the Circle R one. Conner had to quash any talk of a necktie party. He had patiently explained to their men that knowing their cattle were used by hot-iron hombres to run a maverick factory, and proving it beyond a shadow of a doubt, were two different things. The law needed proof.

When he'd been officially sworn in as sheriff at the county seat, Conner had come home with a personal warning to each man riding for the Circle R brand what would happen to him if he were caught altering the brand of any cattle.

He then ordered that every calf and cow found on Kincaid land have its right ear notched as another means of identifying the animal as Rocking K property. This added identification was not foolproof, but it was the best Conner had to use. That, and a letter he had sent as the new sheriff of Sweetwater to the stock buyers in the territory. He warned them to carefully check the brands of cattle purchased for shipment to the stockyards in Eastern cities.

Again, Conner knew this method of alerting the buyers that rustlers operated in his corner of the territory carried no guarantees that anyone would pay attention.

Conner couldn't blame the buyers. As fast as settlers were heading out to the territories to stake their twenty-five-cent-an-acre claims under the Desert Land Act, they were being replaced by immigrants from Europe. As the demands from the settlers to have goods available in the various territories escalated, new factories were built and more rails were laid to carry the goods west and, in return, they filled the demand for beef to be shipped east.

What man, receiving orders to fill, was going to look closely at the brands of cattle that he bought? Damn few that Conner knew.

He felt calmer for working things through, but had a feeling that the problem of the rustlers would take second place until he found a way to handle the new threat Belinda Jarvis had made to his family.

Despite what Logan's temper led him to believe, Conner was deeply torn over doing what his badge demanded of him, and being the eldest Kincaid brother. The caretaker...

And sitting there brooding wasn't going to solve it.

As was his habit, Conner once more sent a searching look over the land below him before he rose. His gaze passed over the long shadow thrown by the rocky incline where he sat back from the edge, then roved over the adjoining low buttes. They were empty of any signs of life. In the nearly cloudless sky he made out a pair of hawks floating on air currents too high to cool him.

A rhythmic muffled sound intruded on his thoughts. Conner looked down, quartering the broken land, his gaze probing every bush and rock.

The sound continued, drawing nearer, and he wished he had his field glass in hand and not tucked in his saddlebag. He wasn't alarmed by the sound, but a strange tension filled him as the sound grew louder.

"Bunch 'em up."

The hoarse male voice came from directly below him.

The only things bunched up around here were cattle and horses.

There were no cattle nearby, and the wild herds of horses rarely roamed this corner of the ranch. There wasn't any good water or grass.

No cattle immediately eliminated the chance that they could be Rocking K men. The order had been given to someone, so two or more were the odds against him.

He was prone on the flat slab in seconds.

As his body absorbed the heat of the rock, he broke out in a sweat. Calm replaced his tension. He had thought to put aside the problem of the rustlers, and now fate had handed him men to follow. He could feel the certainty of being right deep in his bones.

Conner identified the muffled sound. It was the slow plodding of horses' hooves that had been wrapped in cloth. When they were children, Santo had shown them the old Indian trick to avoid leaving tracks.

If these men hugged the deeper shadows cast by the rising buttes, odds were that the men posted as guards would never see them.

Conner was on his own.

"You go back with the boys," Santo insisted as Jessie finished probing his swollen ankle. He had refused to let her take off his boot, knowing, as she knew, that he would not be able to get it back on. He had been careless in his excitement of discovering evidence that a group of men had camped in the rear of the slot canyon for several days.

Rocking back on her heels, Jessie shook her head. "I can't leave you here and I won't send the boys back alone. What if the rustlers saw them? No, Santo, when Kenny brings the horses, we'll get you mounted and ride back together."

"You do not listen."

Jessie smiled. "So Logan often tells me."

Thinking of the pain to come when he tried to put his weight on the ankle, Santo closed his eyes. He

knew, and suspected that Jessie did, too, that his ankle wasn't sprained but broken. A stubborn woman,
she had refused all his sound arguments that she
should ride back to tell Logan what they had discovered.

"Santo." Jessie said his name softly, alarmed to see
the sweat beading on his leathered skin. His eyes
opened and focused on her. "It's more than a bad
sprain, isn't it?"

Reaching for her hand, he squeezed it. "I am a
careless old man."

"No. Don't say that. You're Santo the rock. That's
what they call you. Why I couldn't tell you how many
times I've heard Macaria mention that. She wouldn't
know what to do without you. And Logan—"

"Jessie. You chatter like woodpecker."

She glanced away for a moment, unwilling to let him
see what she was feeling. A strange tension beset her,
as if something was about to happen. She tried to dismiss it, but the feeling remained.

"You are frightened?" Santo asked. "Tell me
what—" He broke off and looked at the rock slide.
Marty was leading with his pony and Kenny brought
up the rear with the other three horses.

Jessie was already on her feet moving toward them.
She forced herself not to run when she saw the tears
glinting in Marty's eyes.

"J-Jessie, will he—"

"Santo is going to be just fine. We'll all help get him
home to Sofia. You know how she'll fuss over him."
She brushed her hand through his blond hair, smiling
to reassure him. Over his head she met Kenny's gaze.
The eyes of a man met hers. Sometimes Jessie found
it hard to remember that Kenny was still a boy. He had

been through so much and, like Santo, had become a rock to lean on.

Marty still had nightmares, less and less as the weeks passed, but half the time Kenny reached his room before she did.

"Jessie, I figured that my mare'll be best for Santo. I can get her to lay down so he can mount. Santo taught me how."

She stepped closer to Kenny. "I hope you can do it. He's in a great deal of pain. But don't let on that I told you."

"I won't. But Jessie, let's get going. I got a bad feeling about this place."

Kenny's honesty demanded her own. "So do I, son. So do I."

Less than a mile away, Conner had a few bad feelings of his own. He wedged one hand between his belly and the rock to cover his belt buckle. The other hand held the canted butt of his gun out of the way as he inched backward on the stone slab. He didn't want a whisper of sound to reach the men below him.

He had already dismissed the thought of firing his gun to attract the attention of the posted guards. Shots would give an alarm, but they would also send his quarry running for cover in any one of a hundred small canyons and washes that braided this corner of the land, before a man could come and help him.

He was on his own.

As he worked his way down the well-worn path, Conner hoped that Sour Mash lived up to his name and unsociable disposition, and didn't neigh a greeting to the animals passing so close. Or, if the gelding was in one of his real ornery moods, issue a challenge as if he still was the lead stallion of a wild herd.

Conner needed a solid plan of action. Beyond following these men, he had come up blank.

Easing alongside his horse, Conner cupped one hand over the animal's nose to insure his silence. He drew a mental map and saw a way that he could get ahead to set up an ambush if he moved out fast.

A deep-sided wash backed close to where he stood. Not wishing to make himself a target, he walked the horse down the loose scree slope before he mounted. He followed the wash as far as he could to where the land leveled off.

The rocky slope offered him a protective barrier as he leaned low, close to the gelding's neck, and gave the animal his head. Riding at a flat-out run, nothing moved on the heat-shimmering land ahead of him.

He slackened his horse's pace to cut into a slit that would lead him into Clove Bush Canyon, named for the spicy odor of the golden currant berries that grew in abundance there. From this slot canyon, he could reach a green-topped mesa and be waiting for the rustlers.

Berries? Conner shook his head, something nagging at him that he should remember. He didn't understand why the thought of berries surfaced now. Fruit wasn't going to help him set a trap.

He rode from the lip of the canyon into the deep, shadowy recess. This was one of the canyons that had been searched repeatedly in the past year as a possible hideout for the rustlers. The searches always came up empty, especially after several bad storms had sent part of the rock wall crashing to the canyon floor to erect a barrier that cut the canyon in half.

Conner let Sour Mash pick his way over the stone-strewn ground. The murmur of voices came from up ahead. He kicked free of the stirrups. In one smooth motion he slid from the saddle, dragging the reins behind him as he pressed tight to the rock wall.

He was trapped. The only way out was up.

Conner dropped the reins and grabbed his rifle, inching his way forward. He stared in stunned surprise when he recognized the first rider coming over the opening in the rock slide.

"Kenny? What are you doing here?"

"Santo's hurt," the boy called out, relieved to see Conner. "Me an' Jessie got him up on my mare, but he's in pain."

"An' me," Marty added, drawing his pony even with Kenny's horse. "I helped, too."

Conner shot a quick look at the opening of the canyon, then ordered, "Go back."

"Back? We can't, Conner."

Coming away from the wall, Conner's rapid, long-legged stride brought him to the boys. "Don't argue, Kenny. We got big trouble coming."

"The rustlers?"

Conner wanted to groan as he looked up at Kenny's eager face.

"What do you know about this? Never mind," he said in the next breath, "just do what I said." Conner started to turn back when he heard Jessie.

"Conner? What's wrong? Did something happen at home?"

"No. I was just—"

"Not that I'm sorry to see you," she interjected. "Santo's been—"

"Hurt. Yeah, Kenny already said that. Just turn around and go back into the canyon, Jessie. Find cover for you and the boys."

"But you don't understand. Santo's—"

"Jessie! I'm not Logan. Just do it!"

For a few moments, Jessie was shocked. Conner had never raised his voice to her, never ordered her, never snapped at her with temper flaring hot in his eyes.

Santo drew rein alongside Jessie. "Do as he said," he whispered to Jessie. Then he turned to Conner. "We found the place where men have camped. Four or six hombres, Conner. A few days, I think." Silently he cursed the weakness pain brought to his voice.

"We're wasting time. I want to set up an ambush for them."

"They're coming?" Jessie asked, darting a frightened look at first Marty, then Kenny. Guilt filled her. If she had listened to Santo, her boys would be safely away from here.

"I don't know how many," Conner said. "They've got our cattle. They wrap their horses' hooves which is why we couldn't track them. I want you and the boys out of the way. Logan'll kill me if any—" He broke off when he saw Santo sway in the saddle. "*Amigo,* how bad?"

"The ankle is broken. I will not be much use to—"

"Ain't to worry, Santo," Kenny interjected. "Conner's got me to help him. You said yourself I'm a damn fine shot."

"An' me, Kenny. He's got me, too."

"Yeah, he's got both of us."

"Then obey me. Get back on the other side." Conner stepped closer to whisper to Jessie. "I'm counting on you to keep them out of the way. I don't know what the devil I'm facing. If the odds are too high, Jessie, I'm inclined to let them go rather than risk anyone's life."

"But we need to catch them. Logan—"

"Is not here," he finished for her. Done talking, he hustled them through the opening and back into the canyon until he found the slit that led to the flat tabletop.

He sent Kenny through first, then Jessie, followed by Marty. All received the same instructions: dismount, lay the horse down and use the animal for cover. And keep quiet. He stressed that.

Conner eyed the narrow opening. Santo would have difficulty riding up. The trail twisted with rock that jutted out and if he caught his broken ankle he might cry out.

As if he had read Conner's thoughts, Santo spoke. "I will go with them. To remain puts you all at risk."

Conner couldn't argue. There was no more time. He heard the deep, sustained low of a cow. Handing his reins to Santo, Conner slapped the gelding's rump and watched them disappear.

He had a rifle, his handgun and surprise on his side. It had to be enough.

Chapter Seven

Belinda nearly jumped from her seat in the court-yard when the sound of a loud commotion penetrated the uncomfortable tension between Charles and herself. She welcomed the diversion, whatever its cause.

Charles had retrieved the eardrop, assuring her he would have the bent wire repaired. But he hadn't let her out of his sight since then. To allay his suspicions, Belinda had launched into her reason for coming there, leaving out her cousin Albert's threats. But she had not liked his avid interest when she'd explained how the Kincaids were involved.

Charles rose from his chair. "I can't imagine who is causing—"

"You can't go out there!" Mrs. Dobbs shouted as she bodily blocked the doorway.

"Riverton!"

Belinda did not need to hear Charles's muttered "Kincaid." She knew who it was by the imperious, commanding tone of voice.

"Mrs. Dobbs," Charles ordered, "please allow the sheriff to join us."

If Belinda had not been watching Charles, she would have missed the tightening of his facial mus-

cles. He was not, she surmised, happy about this unexpected visit. When she directed her gaze at the
doorway where two rope-bound men staggered out
into the courtyard, followed by a rifle-toting sheriff,
she understood why.

"Your men, Riverton," Conner stated. He prodded them forward with the barrel of the rifle. "This
time there's no question. I caught them rustling Kincaid cattle."

"That's a damn lie." Ned Askins lifted his head to
peer through his swollen eye at Packy Hanchett. "Tell
the boss what happened."

"He jumped us. Didn't have no cattle."

"Two against one, Sheriff. I believe my attorney-at-
law will once again have this case thrown out of court
when the circuit judge comes."

Conner longed to wipe the smug look from Riverton's face. He spared a quick glance at Belinda. The
fading sunlight highlighted the thick mass of her upswept blond hair. For a moment his gaze locked with
hers. He was surprised to find she didn't view him with
disgust. He knew he looked worse than his two prisoners.

"Why not save us both the trouble, Kincaid, and let
them go. You haven't got—"

"Not this time, Riverton. This time I have wit-
nesses. This time your men went too far. They put my
brother's wife and two young boys in danger."

"My Lord!"

"Shock you, does it?" Conner asked Belinda.
"Honey, I told you what you were dealing with."

"Get the hell out of my house! I won't stand for
your lies or insults, Kincaid. This time it's you who
went too far. I'll have your badge."

"You're the second one today who's made that claim and I'm still wearing it. Get your fancy-talking lawyer. These two'll be in jail."

"Charles." Belinda placed her hand on his arm. She felt the tension that hummed through him. "Is what he says true? Shouldn't you ask these men—"

"Don't interfere!" he snarled, shaking off her hand.

"That's a lady you're talking to, Riverton."

"I don't need the likes of you to remind me. Now get the hell out of my house, Kincaid. I'll see you in town."

"In case you figure to set up an ambush, Riverton, don't bother. I've already sent word that I'm bringing in two of your men. As a matter of fact, I have an escort of Rocking K riders waiting for me down by your gate right now."

Once again, Belinda found herself keeping a close watch on Charles. Blood suffused his face. She grew alarmed. Even Mrs. Dobbs dared not approach. Charles's hands curled tight at his sides, then as suddenly as it had come, the rage left him. Without a word he turned and walked rapidly toward his suite of rooms. Mrs. Dobbs hurried after him.

"You're not running, too?"

"No, I..." Belinda faltered as she looked at the sheriff. Dark, dangerous and disreputable looking. Why then did she feel drawn to him? She saw the bruise darkening on his cheek, and the place on his chin where blood had dried.

"You've been hurt, too."

Conner pinned her in place with a fierce look. "Just so you know. One of the boys who was in danger from Riverton's men might be your nephew."

"I realized that immediately. I—"

"Watch yourself about Riverton, Miss Jarvis." He herded the two men back into the hallway before she had a chance to answer.

Belinda darted around the table and chairs. "Wait. Please, wait."

He stopped inside the cool, shadowy corridor.

"The woman and boys . . . are they all right?"

Conner took his time searching her eyes for guile. He found nothing but genuine concern in her wide brown eyes.

"Yeah. They're all right. The Lord watches over fools and children."

"I'm not a child or a fool, Sheriff."

His gaze drifted lower to the tiny pleated front of her shirtwaist. The rapid rise and fall of her breasts increased as he watched.

"Really, I am able to take care of myself." Her voice unconsciously softened. "I know you are a Kincaid, but you never told me your first name." Belinda fought the urge to raise her hand to contain the quick beat of her heart. She felt breathless, as if she had run a long way. This time she could not blame the heat for his effect on her pulse. The sun had already begun its descent.

"Conner's the name."

"Conner."

There was something about her voice repeating his name, even though cool and guarded, that slid along his skin. It made him think of invitations, like the one to kiss her this morning. He didn't like the instant heat she drew from him, didn't like the awareness she created. It made him feel . . . needy and restless.

"Will you let me see the boy?" Even as the last word left her lips, Belinda knew he would deny her. She thought of what she had overheard, of the map that Charles had and how she could use it. Then she thought of what he had accused the two men of doing.

"I haven't had a chance to send the telegrams," Conner said, and, to his surprise, heard the regret in his voice.

"But you won't stop me?"

"Stop you?"

"If I ride over to the Kincaids'."

"That wouldn't be up to me. Logan's in charge of the ranch. Logan and my brother Ty. It would be better if you wait until I can take you there."

"When? Tomorrow? I know Charles will have a horse I can ride."

He didn't want to be pinned down. Looking at her expectant expression, Conner found himself reluctant to deny her. *And yourself her company,* a small voice nagged.

"Does he know?" Conner asked.

"Charles? About my nephew?"

"Yeah."

"I told him that's why I've come here."

Conner didn't like the coil of tension that tightened his gut. He dismissed it, believing it came from the minutes he had battled for his life against Charles's men. If Kenny hadn't had the presence of mind to fire a warning shot to distract them, Conner would've ended up dead. He was only sorry that one of the rustlers made good his escape from the canyon.

"Kincaid?"

Conner swung around fast, placing himself between Belinda and the man striding down the hall toward him. Joe Dacus was Riverton's ramrod. Conner was instantly reminded of a bull they'd had when he was a boy. Bribery and beatings couldn't rid that animal of its inborn meanness and they'd had to shoot it. Dacus had the same kind of meanness bred into his bones. Rumor had it that he'd boasted he would be the one to bring Conner down.

With a cocky stance, Joe tucked his thumbs into his gun belt. "Hear you're claiming you caught my boys red-handed?"

"It's a lie," Ned protested again.

"Shut up, Askins. I ain't askin' you."

"I haven't got time to waste jawing with you, Dacus. I've got prisoners to get into jail." Conner reached out with his left hand to grab Hanchett's shoulder. "Start walking. You too, Askins."

"Hold up, Kincaid. I ain't done talkin'."

"Perhaps I should get Charles," Belinda murmured from where she stood behind Conner.

"Don't bother. Dacus is going to move or I'll haul him in for obstructing justice. Only got one cell, Joe. Gonna be mighty crowded with three of you in there."

Conner lent his threat weight with a move that brought his rifle barrel up between the two bound men. His steady gaze left no doubt that he'd use it if he had to.

Dacus stepped aside. "This ain't over, Kincaid."

"Hell, no. Just beginning." Without turning, Conner said, "Miss Jarvis, it's been a pleasure to see you again. You remember what I told you."

A nudge started Askins and Hanchett moving down the long hall. Conner walked behind them. He could almost feel Joe Dacus's eyes boring holes in his back. He couldn't waver. One sign of fear and Joe would be all over him. He wouldn't take an easy breath until he was clear of Riverton's property.

"That son of a bitch—"

"No, Dacus," Charles softly said as he entered the hall behind them. "His mother, Macaria, is not the problem. Only her eldest son need concern you. I want—" Charles stopped when he saw that Belinda was still there. "My dear, I apologize for this intrusion. You will excuse me while I discuss this unfortunate matter with my foreman."

"Of course, Charles."

Belinda was only too glad to leave him. He had been distracted from his suspicions about her, which is what she wanted, but the map and the accusations that Kincaid—no, Conner—had made left her wondering what Charles was up to.

By the time she reached the privacy of her room, she was asking herself why she should care. The fact that Conner aroused these strange feelings of excitement should not have any influence on what she had to do.

Lighting the lamps on the dresser, Belinda looked at herself. She was lying. Strange as it was, she did care what happened to Conner Kincaid.

The moment Joe closed the office door behind him, Charles fired orders at him. "I don't want Hanchett or Askins to talk. Get rid of them and do it fast. If they bargain with Kincaid—"

"Boss, just tell me plain. You want them free, or you want them dead?"

Charles lifted the lid of the inlaid smoking box on his desk. He removed a thick cigar, one of the finest imported from Cuba, and clipped the end.

Striking a match, he held it up to the tip and puffed heavily until the cigar glowed. He tilted his head back, watching the smoke curl upward.

"Dead, Joe. I want them dead. If Kincaid went with them, I'd be the first to pay a condolence call." He eyed Joe. "Think you can handle the job? I believe we discussed a bonus awhile back. I'll double it."

"That's two thousand dollars, boss. Not that I need more to kill that gut-twisting bastard."

"Nevertheless, the money is yours. I will leave the timing and method up to you."

"Consider it done." Joe headed for the door. Charles called him and he stopped.

"One thing more, Joe. Find out if one of those orphan boys living with the Kincaids is Marston Jarvis. I have need of the information."

"You want him dead, too?"

"No. Just find out if he's there. I have other plans for the boy." *And his aunt,* Charles added to himself, then cursed Kincaid to hell and back for spoiling his plans for Belinda.

He fingered the eardrop still in his pocket. The image of her guilty look when he'd discovered it sent him to his desk. The center drawer was locked. He was foolish to think she'd overheard anything. She wasn't about to tip his hand to Kincaid.

And if she did... well, she could be involved in an accident. It happened all the time.

Like a snake, the thought twisted and twined itself in his mind. He knew the boy was more important to her than she'd let on. If anything happened to Be-

linda, her uncle would inherit. Phillip was an easy man
to manipulate.

Charles left the room at a run. He had to stop Joe.
He didn't want Conner Kincaid dead. Not yet any-
way.

Chapter Eight

Dawn was yet an unfulfilled promise when Conner suddenly awakened. He lay still on the single bunk bed in the jail cell, tense as the newly woven rope spring beneath him. Each one of his senses alerted him to danger.

It was no more than he had expected.

Earlier, escorted by four Rocking K riders, he had brought his two prisoners into town after dusk. At the last moment he had veered off from the path to the jail to ride back to Gladden's Tannery. There, in one of the empty storage sheds, his prisoners were locked up for the night. Riverton wasn't going to let these men talk. He would either free them or kill them.

He dozed off sometime after midnight, dreaming of a woman's wide brown eyes. He was fully awake now.

The bunk bed lay directly below the oilskin-covered barred window. Conner had not bothered to fasten the outside shutters. The window, placed high in the wall, allowed no one to see inside the cell, unless they stood on something.

Or sat on a horse.

He listened for the creak of leather, sounds made when a man shifted ever so slightly in the saddle. Over the beating of his heart, no sound reached him. But he sensed another's presence. Sensed it so strongly that he was forced to use every bit of willpower to stop himself from rising up and demanding to know who was out there.

A faint *thunk* made him think that someone had overturned one of the empty rain barrels. There was no scraping sound of the barrel being dragged closer to the wall. Whoever had the barrel was strong enough to lift and move it.

His rifle lay across his flat belly, his finger loose on the trigger.

He waited, pools of sweat forming in the small of his back, under his arms and behind his neck. It became difficult to keep his breathing deep and even as if he were still asleep.

Conner wanted nothing to alarm his rescuer...or his killer.

Inky blackness and sultry air pressed down on him. Conner kept his gaze pinned to the one lighter patch in the cell—the skin covering the window.

No breeze inched the loose skin away from the bars.

No whisper came to alert the supposed prisoners that rescue was at hand.

He strained in the darkness, listening, frustrated not to be able to see, to know, what was going on.

Was that a scraping sound? Of what? The *chink* of a spur hitting wood reached him, followed by a hissing.

What the hell was the bastard up to?

A rustling noise. A muttered curse.

Conner inched to the edge of the bunk.

He couldn't take his eyes from the window.

The tip of a knife blade lifted the skin from the center. His ears filled with the pounding of his heart, the increased surging flow of his blood. Blood that ran hot but couldn't warm his suddenly chilled skin. The sweat turned cold. Cold as the shivers snaking up his spine.

A bulky shape was being forced through the bars.

Instinct forced him to roll off the bunk. Conner obeyed. He hit the floor in a crouch and flung himself into the far corner.

Dark, writhing shapes fell from the window.

He heard the rattles. He barely registered a man's soft, coarse laugh.

Time ceased. He was locked in a nightmare. A boy again. Refusing to listen to Santo's warning. Sticking his hand down into the rock crevice. The stinging bite. The searing pain, followed by a burning sensation that rose from the fleshy pad below his thumb up his wrist, into his arm.

He remembered the slicing pain of Santo's knife. The bite of his teeth as he sucked, then spat out poison. Fast as Santo had been, the fever had still sent him to bed for days.

He hated snakes, hated and feared them.

It was a long time ago. You're not a boy. You're a grown man.

You've got a rifle. Shoot them. Shoot before . . .

Conner remained in the corner, pressing against the wall, too frozen to move. The dry, hollow-sounding rattles increased in volume until it was all he heard. He wanted to cover his ears, wanted to stop the sound, and he couldn't move.

Is this how it ends? Riverton wins.

No!

Then move.

He couldn't see where the snakes were. Fear clung like a second skin to his body. A small, sane corner of his mind kept urging him to move away from danger.

He imagined he saw the snakes. Slithering and sliding one over the other. Coiling themselves tight, shaking the death rattle in warning before a strike. Forked tongues darting out, testing the air, sensing human body warmth, seeking their prey. Thick, muscular length of diamond-patterned skin in sinuous motion.

Finding prey. Finding him.

How many?

Dear Lord! How many were there in the cell?

Sweat drenched him. His body was a quivering mass of bone and muscle refusing to heed his need to move, refusing to obey the scream in his mind.

His finger caressed the trigger of the rifle. The solid protection his weapon offered slowly penetrated the fear holding him captive. He managed to lift the rifle. He forced his left hand up against the wall. Fingers splayed open, palm pressing against the wood, this was his guide toward the cell door.

Toward safety. Toward freedom.

He had to remember that the rifle was loaded. Shells in the chamber, ready to fire.

He wasn't helpless. Not as helpless as Hanchett and Askins would have been.

Anger began to curl within him. An anger strong enough to trip through the fear.

If panic took hold, he'd lose his life.

Riverton was an animal. Only an animal would have ordered two men's deaths this way.

If one of them had been lying on the bunk when the snakes were pushed through the bars, the reptiles' repeated strikes would insure death before any cries for help were heard.

Conner couldn't let Riverton win.

Take a step.

The first step to freedom would be the hardest.

Take it!

His boot heel scraped against the rough plank flooring.

Conner couldn't think.

He wanted light. He needed to see. He had to have air.

There was a match case in his pocket. Long, wooden matches that would produce flare after flare of small bursts of light. He didn't dare reach for it. Delay would mean his death.

The wall of the cell seemed to lengthen as he inched his way out of the corner. He'd never reach the wooden door before he was bitten.

Fear had sucked every bit of moisture from his mouth. He couldn't call out. He couldn't swallow.

Sweat stung his eyes. He wouldn't move his hand from the wall to wipe it away.

"Where are they?"

The question exploded from his lips.

He froze. The rattles seemed louder. Nearer to him. So close, the sound filled his ears, his mind.

Conner worked the lever of the repeating rifle, firing blindly. The sudden volley of shots deafened him as he bolted from the cell.

He had to find the lamp. Light to see. He needed that desperately. The rifle barrel slammed against wood. With a crash the chair fell to the floor.

His harsh, gulping breaths filled lungs starved for air.

With one hand stretched out in front of him, Conner stumbled his way to the side wall. His hip butted against the chest. The good Lord had guided his footsteps, for he had lost all bearings.

Searching over the top, he found the cool glass bottom of the lamp. A moment later he threw the glass globe off. It, too, hit the floor with a splintering crash.

Match case in hand, he tore the top off with his teeth. The first match broke when he tried to strike it. Pounding filled the room. But he heard the rattle....

The sound came from behind him.

The rifle fell with a clatter. His handgun fit his palm like the grip of an old and familiar friend. He abandoned his attempt to light the lamp. With the pounding came the shout of his name.

Conner spun around. The door crashed open and blessed light flooded the room from the lamps held by the men crowding in one behind the other.

Conner had eyes for none but the coiled ring of death ready to strike him. He fired. Other bullets thudded into the floor, into the body of the rattler.

Rob Long, first inside, first to fire, reached Conner before anyone else. "What in blazes is going on, Conner?"

Conner sagged back against the chest. Weakly he waved his gun toward the back. "In there."

Doug Shelden kicked the dead snake aside. "Damn near seven feet long. How the hell did it get in here?"

"For Almighty's sake!" Tom Sweet yelled. "There's four more back here."

Rob had the presence of mind to take Conner outside. Mark Dryer, the editor of the newspaper, brought Conner a cup of cold coffee.

"It's all I could find. But I'd bet he could use a drink."

"No." Conner's hoarse whisper had Mark exchange a look with Rob. Conner wrapped both hands around the cup, sipping the liquid, bitter and cold though it was. He didn't think the dry-as-cotton feeling was ever going to go away.

Still hitching up his suspenders, Carl Gladden came up the street at a run. "Where the hell's the sheriff?"

"Over here, Carl," Rob answered.

"What was all the shootin' about? I ran over to the shed. Your prisoners are tucked all safe and sound inside. But—"

"Someone dumped a sack full of rattlers into the jail cell."

They all turned as Doug Shelden approached. "My boys are cleaning up the mess. Conner blasted them to hell and gone. Splattered those—"

"Conner?" Mark waved his hand in front of Conner's eyes. "Did you get bit? Lord, man, don't keep us waiting."

"Nothing bit me."

Another shot came from inside the jail. They all jumped.

"Steven!" Doug yelled to his eldest son, "What'd ya find?"

With his union suit front flapping over his pants, the young man revealed himself in the doorway. "Found one under the bunk, hiding in the corner. Did ya see the size of 'em? Two are almost seven feet long.

Whoever threw 'em in there didn't want to take any chances. No one would've lived.''

"Damn fine job, Conner." Walt Waterman slapped his meaty hand across Conner's shoulder. "Took a brave man to stay there and shoot a nest of rattlers. Don't know many that could do it. No sirree, ain't ashamed to admit I wouldn't stand there like a tethered hog in that cell. Lord have mercy, man, but—"

"Walter, shut up." Rob glared at the man. "Conner don't need you runnin' off at the mouth about how brave he is. We wouldn't elect a coward sheriff." He spotted his sister Deana at the edge of the crowd of women and children that had come from their homes. He stood close to Conner and felt the chill of his body.

"Deana, bring a blanket for the sheriff and some hot coffee."

"Who you got locked up, Conner?" Walt demanded to know.

"Hanchett and Askins from the Circle R," Carl answered before Conner even lifted his head. "Caught them rustling. Right on Kincaid land. Someone didn't want them to talk. And it don't take a prairie-dog-size brain to figure out who's behind this. Them men wouldn't have had a chance in hell to survive—"

"It's over. Conner ain't bit. His prisoners are safe and I'll stand coffee for everyone in the café." Rob grabbed the blanket his sister handed him. He tossed it over Conner's shoulders. Without making a big deal of it, he helped him to stand. Mark stood on the other side of Conner. Once more they exchanged looks. Without speaking, the two men closed ranks and, with Conner between them, the blanket hiding the supporting arms they kept around his back, they walked to the café.

"Shock," Mark whispered. "Seen plenty of it during the war. Let's get him upstairs, Rob. Tell those fools he's cleaning up or something."

Leaving Mark to support Conner, Rob blocked the stairway when Walt showed signs of following them. "Let him be. Mark's gonna see if he's been bit. You keep folks calm, Walt."

"He's a brave man, Rob. Damn brave."

At the top of the stairs Conner heard him. He didn't feel brave at all. Mark's whispered assurance that he'd have privacy to puke, collapse or whatever, sounded good. Conner wasn't sure himself what he wanted to do first.

He roused himself when Mark threw open the door. It was pitch black inside the room. "Light the lamp." He braced himself against the door frame until light flooded the room.

"Mark, make sure two men guard the shed. Arm them. Whoever did this could be watching. I didn't go through hell to lose those two to a bullet."

"I don't want to leave you."

"Do it!"

Conner threw off the blanket. He went to the front window and stood off to the side of it. With one finger he pulled back the edge of the starched lace curtain.

He could see a few men milling about in the street. The lanterns they held made them targets. The light shed didn't reach into the shadows of building fronts and alleys.

But Conner felt someone watching. Waiting.

Riverton couldn't stand failure. By tonight, he'd know that his killer almost got rid of Conner.

His mind shut down the memory of what he'd just lived through. He couldn't allow it to surface.

A slight sound had him spin around, his gun in hand.

"Oh, my word! Conner! It's me, Deana. I . . . you didn't hear me knock. I brought you hot water." She couldn't get the pitcher set down fast enough before she backed to the door. "I'll send Rob up."

"Deana, wait, I—"

Too late. She'd closed the door, leaving him alone. And when it came right down to it, that's the way he'd always been. Alone.

He stood there, a solitary man, watching the night sky give way to dawn.

Chapter Nine

Belinda came into town late the next afternoon.

Conner watched her ride in, seated sidesaddle on a high-stepping chestnut mare every bit as prideful as her rider. He admired Belinda's seat on the horse, her back straight as a fence post, head high, eyes straight ahead, gloved hands resting lightly on the horse's neck, holding the reins. She didn't carry a quirt. A sign of a woman fully in control of herself and the animal she rode.

She wore blue today. A fluttery light blue veil wrapped the flat-topped crown of her curled-brim hat. Not a feather or flower in sight. Her riding habit was a darker blue, like the sky at dusk, and not one ruffle, not a bit of lace relieved the tightly fitted basque or long riding skirt, yet she presented as feminine a picture as she had yesterday.

Still very much the lady. Still very much on his mind.

She kept the mare to the center of the street. Conner watched her, but he also recognized the young Circle R rider who kept pace with her about twenty feet back. Rich Dillion was a smart-mouthed, wet-behind-the-ears kid who reminded him of his brother Ty.

Although people had worked through the night to clear his office, Conner couldn't go inside. Slouched in his chair, hands resting on the flat plane of his belly, he stretched out his long legs in front of him. His hat canted forward, shielding and shadowing his face.

Belinda drew rein opposite to where he sat but made no move to dismount.

Conner noticed that Dillion slid from his horse in front of the mercantile, hitched his reins around the post and took up a watchful, leaning stance against the hitching rail.

A business call, Conner surmised.

"Good morning, Sheriff."

"Mornin', ma'am."

His greeting held all the welcome of a group of men interrupted by a woman while enjoying their after-dinner cigars and brandy. Belinda knew. She had done it.

"I enjoyed meeting your mother this morning."

As an attention grabber, this one hit with the force of being tossed on his rear by a sun-fishing bronc. But until he knew where and how she had met his mother, Conner did no more than cross one booted foot over the other.

"That a fact?"

"She joined Charles and me for breakfast."

"Must have been real cozy. You, Riverton and my mother."

"She is a lovely woman, and very young looking." Belinda leaned slightly forward to pat her mare's neck.

"Far too young to have a bastard like me for a son."

"You said that. I did not."

"Snippy, are we?" Conner tilted his head back to peer at her from beneath his brim. "Honey, you got a poor, short memory. Sure as I'm sitting here, you called me a bastard yesterday. Twice, if my memory serves." *Was it only yesterday? Feels like a lifetime ago after last night.*

"Are you interested in hearing what we discussed?"

"Figure you'll get around to doing that in your own sweet time, honey."

"I asked you not to call me that, Mr. Kincaid."

"So you did."

It wasn't the apology she wanted, but Belinda wisely understood it was all she would get from him. Her gaze lingered on the faded black twill pants hugging his long, muscular legs and lean hips. Afraid he would catch her staring, she glanced away.

"I suppose you told my mother why you're here."

"Charles did."

"Ah, yes, Charles."

The name spilled from his lips with a sneer, bringing her gaze back to him. Now that she had a moment to think about it, all his words were slurred.

"Have you been drinking, Sheriff?"

"Hell, no."

"A simple no would do. I asked because you appear to be in a surly mood. You have not asked me to join you. After meeting your mother, I know she taught you better manners."

"Brine, you strike me as an independent-thinking woman who'll get down off her high horse when she's good and ready."

"I cannot get down, you limp-witted fool, without help."

"That so?"

"Yes, that is so." She fumed as the moments passed and he made no move to get up.

Twisting and turning to look, Belinda saw no mounting block in sight. Not unless she rode back to the livery. He was more than likely to disappear if she did. Her gaze touched upon the young man whom Charles had insisted she needed for an escort. Escort? He had been ordered to watch her. She did not want him near her. She certainly did not want him to know and then report to Charles the real reason she had ridden into town.

Talking to the sheriff would not alarm anyone. But her patience was in short supply this afternoon.

"Conner."

The soft way she caressingly called him heated up the afternoon without a bit of help from the still-blazing sun.

"You tacking a *please* on that?"

"You are pushing your luck, Sheriff."

"Not me, ma'am. I'm just sitting here, minding my business. You're the one who's come calling."

The deep, lazy drawl slid inside her as sweetly and as potently as eating brandied cherries. Conner Kincaid irritated her. He challenged her. He gave her new and exciting feelings that constantly reminded her she was a woman. One too eager to repeat the experience of their first meeting.

As much as Belinda would enjoy having the verbal bantering continue, she was conscious of the time that passed and the man who watched her. Lingering overlong would raise Charles's suspicions that she had not come to plead her case once more, or deliver a message. She could not leave without accomplishing the real reason she had come to town.

"*Please,* Sheriff," she said in an effort to appease him, "help me dismount."

Conner thumbed his hat back. Her gasp was no more than he had expected. He'd gotten the same reaction from Deana when she served his morning coffee in the café.

He looked like the devil had worked him over. Conner made no apology for it. His eyes were as red rimmed as Seely Morehouse on a week-long drinking binge. They felt the same. Conner craved sleep, craved being rid of the gritty, burning sensation that hurt his eyes, but he didn't dare close them for fear of reliving those nightmarish minutes when he'd thought death had called up his number.

Belinda's gaze wasn't steady. It seemed to flit from each of his features. He rubbed the stubble on his chin with his thumb. He had started to shave only to abandon his straight-edged razor when the pallor of his skin showed beneath the two-day-old beard.

Far from being offended by his disreputable appearance, as she was sure he had intended, Belinda viewed Conner with deep concern.

Under the guise of patting her horse's neck again, she leaned forward.

"What happened to you?" Her voice had softened with an unconsciously made womanly plea to know what had hurt someone she cared about. Belinda heard it, but it was too late to recall the words, or the tone.

Conner appeared wolfish, as if something terrible had ravaged the night hours to deny him sleep. He claimed that he had not been drinking and she believed him. But what, then, had caused the haunted dark gleam in his eyes?

"Conner?"

"Don't you know?" Hard edged and blunt, he snapped the question at her. Coming out of the chair in a smooth, controlled rush, he stepped to the end of the planked walk and took hold of the bridle to watch her reaction.

"No, Conner. How could I know? Since I left town yesterday, I have been at Charles's ranch."

Without taking his eyes from hers, he stroked one long finger down the white blaze marking the chestnut's face. "I figured Charles had entertained you with the story. Over breakfast, or perhaps late last night."

"You are not asking me, but making an insulting guess. I asked you a civil question. It seems too much to expect you to do the same with an answer. For your information, Sheriff, the only time I discussed you was with your mother."

She attempted to jerk the reins, but Conner had a firm grip on the bridle. "Hold on. I had to know."

"Then ask me, Conner."

"I already did." His grin was cocky. "Do you always have such a snippety mouth?"

Belinda smiled in return, but it never reached her eyes. "No. Around you, it seems to come naturally."

"What else comes naturally, Belinda—" he paused, his gaze targeting her mouth "—around me, that is."

Throat and lips dry, Belinda slid the tip of her tongue over her bottom lip. She watched him come to her side and looked down into heated gray eyes that made no apology for the bold way he studied her.

She dropped the reins. She closed her eyes for a moment when his hands settled around her waist. The layers of cloth that prevented skin from touching skin were no barrier to the heat penetrating the tightly fitted basque, corset cover, corset or lawn chemise that she wore.

"Belinda?"

"What?" Her eyes flew open and her startled gaze met his.

"If you don't put your hands on my shoulders, honey, you could slip and fall when I lift you out of that saddle."

How did he do this to her? Conner made the world narrow down to the two of them. All she could think about was the warm, gentle ply of lips against hers. And when had she given him permission to use her first name?

"Stop this, Kincaid."

"Kincaid, is it?" Conner removed his hands from her narrow waist.

"What do you think you are doing? I thought you were going to help me down?"

"You said to stop. I stopped."

"That was not what I meant and you know it. Please, I do not have much time."

Conner lifted her from the saddle. Her hands rested lightly on his shoulders. He thought about sliding her down his body in a long, heated caress, for he realized since the moment she had arrived he hadn't thought of last night. He swung her to the side and set her down, quickly stepping back.

"I didn't think you were here for a social call. So tell me what it is that you want."

"Can we go inside your office?"

"No."

"No?" she repeated. From the way he set his jaw, she understood he was not offering an explanation for his refusal. Belinda glanced at the man across the street. He had not moved from his leaning stance against the hitching rail.

"Why did my mother visit Riverton this morning?"

Belinda did not immediately answer him. She busied herself gathering up the trailing end of her riding skirt and looping it over her arm. Then she looked at him.

"I will be more than happy to answer your question, if you answer one for me."

Conner's deep, knowing smile made lines crinkle at the corners of his eyes. He surveyed her from head to foot. "Still trying to bribe me?"

"No. A simple exchange is all I had in mind."

He leaned toward her, one arm extended. For a moment Belinda stared into his compelling, half-laughing, very watchful eyes.

"Don't be so distrustful. I'll escort you into the café. And we'll have a simple exchange of questions and answers, Belinda."

Again Belinda chose to ignore his deliberate use of her first name. She rested her gloved hand on the lean strength of his arm and stepped up to the planked walk.

They had gone a few steps when she stopped and looked down. "You're not wearing your spurs today."

"I took them off. Walking quiet keeps a man alive," he said cryptically, urging her forward.

"Your mother is upset over the shooting incident yesterday. That is why she came to see Charles this morning. I admire her forthright manner. She wasted no time asking him if he knew that his men had placed her family in danger."

This time Conner stopped before the open doors to the café. "That must be some question you want me to answer since you're volunteering information."

"You are a distrustful man, Sheriff. I need a favor, as well as a question answered. Think of it as a good-faith gesture on my part."

"You are a manipulating woman, Belinda Jarvis."

She looked up at him. There was laughter in his eyes, and no censure in his voice. Laughter escaped as she very politely thanked him.

Conner stepped back to allow her to precede him into the café. Once inside, he took her arm again to guide her to the table in the far corner.

Belinda started for the chair on the opposite side, but Conner held her back.

"Sit here," he said, pulling out another chair. "That's my spot back there."

It really didn't matter to her where she sat. She shrugged off his unwillingness to sit with his back toward the door as one of those vagarious male notions.

Conner took his seat. The position of sitting with his back to the wall gave him a clear view of the door. A careful man made every effort to protect his back and see what trouble came his way.

"Conner."

He looked to the side where Deana stood in the kitchen doorway. "Miss Belinda Jarvis, meet Miss

Deana Long. She and her brother own the café and
sometimes rent rooms to stranded travelers."

Deana nodded. She wiped her flour-dusted hands
on her apron. "You're staying out at the Circle R."

"Yes. Charles Riverton is a friend of my uncle."
Belinda did not know why she offered the explanation. It was not her habit to do so, but there was
something about the way the dark-eyed young woman
studied her that made her feel uncomfortable.

Conner glanced from Belinda to Deana, fighting the
damnedest urge to step in and offer Belinda his protection. The two women were almost bristling at each
other. He didn't understand why he felt the need to
protect Belinda. She had proved she was capable of
holding her own with him. He guessed she'd do that
with anyone who got in her way.

Giving himself a moment more, he tried to dismiss
the feeling. It wouldn't go away.

"Coffee for me and a glass of lemonade for Belinda."

Deana's brows rose at the use of the woman's first
name. Conner was always so polite, so careful how he
addressed a woman. It had taken months before he
stopped calling her Miss Long. Conner certainly had
changed his tune from yesterday when he had told her
brother that he'd better wear gloves to protect him
from the Eastern lady's thorns.

"Deana? The coffee?"

"Sure, Conner. But I wish you'd eat something.
You hardly touched your breakfast. I've got your favorite apple and raisin muffins."

"Fine. Add some of your molasses cookies, too."
He removed his hat and set it on the empty chair beside him.

Belinda toyed with the button on her glove. Without looking at him, she said, "Miss Long does not like me."

"That matters to you?"

"Usually, no. But she based her judgment on my being a guest—"

"Riverton's not well liked. By association, that dislike extends to you." He took her hand within his own, flipped open the button and began taking the glove off. "I apologize for Deana's making you uncomfortable."

"Does it have something to do with what happened to you last night?"

Conner tensed, then rubbed his index finger over the back of her hand. "Is that your question?"

Deana returned carrying a tray. She served Conner his coffee, black as he liked it, and left the pot and a plated filled with still-steaming muffins and large, soft molasses cookies. On a separate small plate butter was formed into a perfect mold of a pineapple.

"There's no jam," Conner noted.

"You never have any."

"But my guest might enjoy some, Deana."

"Conner," Belinda said warningly. "It is not necessary." She took a sip of the too-sweet drink, waiting, as Conner waited for Deana to leave them.

The moment they were alone again, Belinda asked, "Why do you refuse to tell me what happened last night?"

"I don't want to talk about it. Tell me what else my mother had to say to Riverton." She tried to withdraw her hand from his, but Conner shook his head. "Leave it. I like touching you."

"Has anyone ever remarked about your effortless ability to infuriate someone?"

"Is that what I do?" Laughter crinkled the corners of his eyes. "I thought I was picking up where we left off. You were volunteering to tell me about her visit. Remember, a simple exchange of information?"

Belinda attempted to ignore the small circles he drew with his thumb on the back of her hand. Conner seemed to find the repetitive motion fascinating, for his gaze never wavered from their joined hands. She tried not to read too much into his focused attention. After all, he wanted something from her. But a small part of her wondered what it would be like if Conner simply wanted her.

She mentally stepped back from where such thoughts would lead her. "All right, Conner, you win. Your mother was angry with Charles. She said it was the last time she could defend him to her sons. From what I observed, your mother did not believe his denial that he did not know what his men had been doing on your land."

"The Lord shows mercy at last. I'd given up trying to convince her that he's behind the rustling."

"Why?"

"Riverton courted my mother at the same time as my father. I guess he didn't like being the loser. She didn't have any contact with him, but then the rustling started. We had trouble with robberies at our mines. Logan rode with the outlaw gang in an effort to find out who gave the orders. They had too much information about what we were doing. Then Riverton bought up land as smaller ranchers sold out. The rustling got worse and he gets richer."

"It doesn't make sense. Charles is a wealthy man. I know about his business dealings with my uncle. Why would he need to steal your cattle or rob your mines?"

Conner looked up at her, studying her features. He found no guile in her dark brown eyes, only a steady and sincere regard. He weighed the chance he was going to take and decided how much to tell her. Half his mind conjured other pleasurable pursuits he could be indulging in with Belinda, the other half warned him not to trust her.

It was a little like being between a rock and a hard place.

"Riverton has lofty ambitions. Expensive ones. He's backing a man running for governor. I figure he's got an eye on the seat for himself. There are other pies he's helping himself to a large slice of. Railroads, for one. And running us out eliminates any opposition. Like you, my mother couldn't see that. But her thinking was clouded by memories. Maybe knowing that Jessie and the boys were almost killed by his men made her see Riverton for what he is."

His gaze lowered to their hands and Belinda's followed. She found herself in complete sympathy with him. She had had a difficult time trying to convince her uncle that his charming nephew Albert schemed to take over the family businesses. Phillip still had his doubts.

"You think Charles is ruthless?"

"Without question." Conner couldn't tell her he was sure Riverton was responsible for the death of Dixie's father, too.

"Your mother mentioned that you fought with your brother over me. I am sorry to have caused a rift."

"Logan'll come around. He's having a hard time now shouldering most of the work. Once Ty's got his house finished and his baby's born, Logan will go back to being the same easygoing, levelheaded man he really is."

Again he glanced up at her. "I can't believe she told you that. You made a hell of an impression on my mother. She doesn't discuss her family with anyone."

"But a small part of your family is the reason I came here, Conner."

"The boy."

"The boy has a name. Marston—"

"Why didn't you defend Riverton?" he interrupted to ask. "You were quick enough the other day."

Belinda was at a loss what to answer him. She couldn't forget that Conner still opposed her, and yet she found herself wanting to trust him. *With what? Your strange feelings?* No, she answered the little nagging voice, I know Charles paid someone to mark a map.

He hunched forward over the table, drawing her other gloved hand to him. "You didn't come all this way to tell me about my mother's visit, Belinda. What do you want from me?"

Belinda could not look away from his deep, compelling gaze. "I want..." She stopped, hesitating to ask her favor. He would want to know why.

"Go on, ask me. The most I can say is no. Pretty good odds I could say yes, too."

No laughter. No cynical expression. This was the Conner that Macaria told her about. The man of integrity, of compassion. From the gentle way he held her hands to the warm, steady regard of his eyes,

Conner called to her with an intensity she could not deny.

The feeling frightened her. She snatched her hands from his, dragging one hand across the butter dish in her hurry to escape his touch.

"Look what you made me do."

He looked from her butter-smeared fingertips to her face and grinned. "Guilty as charged. But if I'm the cause of your discomfort," he murmured in a lazy, drawling voice, "I insist you allow me to be the source of easing it."

Conner caught hold of her hand. She made no effort to pull away. He raised her hand to his lips, holding her bemused gaze with his.

"Conner," she whispered, "what are you..." Words failed her. She could barely swallow as sensations of warmth turned quickly to heat from the fingertips that he slowly licked clean of butter.

No man had ever dared what he was doing, and Belinda could not imagine any gentleman of her acquaintance calmly sitting in a café, seducing her. What was more startling was that she did indeed allow it.

"Conner. I...tell me...Conner, are you flirting with me?"

"Honey," he answered, eyes alight with amusement, "if you're asking, I can't be. Remember, I told you yesterday, if I was flirting with you, you'd know it."

"I wonder if I would. I have never met anyone like you. You make me so angry one minute, then in the next you..."

"Yes, I?" he prompted, giving extra attention to the fleshy pad below her thumb.

"You confuse me. What you make me feel confuses me."

"That makes us even. You're beginning to scare the hell out of me, lady."

Her heart began to pound in alarm. His look was sensual, caressive and openly speculative. "Conner, I—"

"I hate interrupting you, honey, but your guard dog is coming in. Better ask me quick whatever it was you wanted."

"Send this telegram." She fumbled to open one button on the tightly fitted basque and removed a tiny folded square of paper, shoving it across the table. The clink of spurs on the floor stopped somewhere behind her. Conner had palmed the note. "Please do this for me," she whispered, then raised her voice to add, "Since your mother kindly invited me to visit and meet the boy Marty, I accepted."

Belinda pushed back her chair and rose. "I realize you had other ideas, Sheriff, but I feel sure the boy is my nephew. I will ride out on Saturday to see him."

Belinda stepped away from the chair and turned to face her escort. "I am ready to return now. I hope you fetched my horse."

"Yes, ma'am. It's about time, too. Gone near to dusk. Ain't safe riding around at night in these parts."

Belinda did not dignify his warning with an answer, but she could not help but notice the warning glare Dillion shot at Conner. She brushed by the young man, then stopped when Conner spoke.

"Dillion, you make sure that Miss Jarvis gets back to the Circle R safe and sound. If I hear that one hair on her head raised in alarm, I'll come looking for you first thing."

Belinda shot a quick look over her shoulder at Conner. There was a dangerous glint in his eyes that targeted Dillion. When she glanced at her escort, his face was a thunderous mask. Conner had incited his temper.

"Come along. We cannot keep Mr. Riverton waiting for dinner," she said.

Conner watched them leave but made no immediate move to rise. He unfolded the paper Belinda had given him and read it.

Uncle Phillip, imperative you join me. Complications arise. Point to trouble. Your loving niece.

"Trouble?" Conner muttered to himself. "Who did she mean. Me or Riverton?"

He picked up the supple suede glove she had left behind in her haste and tucked it into his gun belt as he rose.

Walking to the door, Conner couldn't help but wonder what his mother had said to Belinda to suddenly make her trust him to send her message.

He wasn't sure if he should be grateful or mad as hell.

Chapter Ten

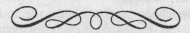

Riding alongside a silent Dillion, Belinda looked back once as they headed out of town. Conner stood in the doorway of the café, but offered no sign that he saw her.

She had to believe that he would send the telegram to her uncle. Charles had become a complication with his not-so-subtle innuendos that he found her attractive enough to offer marriage. Macaria Kincaid's arrival this morning had stopped him from painting a cozy picture of the empire they could have together.

Belinda shuddered at the thought.

"No need to be scared, ma'am. We'll take it nice and slow. Don't want anything to happen to you or the horses."

She did not correct Dillion's assumption that riding past dusk frightened her.

Very little air stirred. Belinda heard the high, whirring sound of the cicadas. The noise mixed with the shrieks of woodpeckers and the whistle of a rock squirrel. Being able to separate and identify the sounds no longer surprised her. She had listened and learned wherever her travels had taken her.

But with the coming of night noises, a subtle change could be felt. A feeling of tension and expectancy that was hard for her to define. The heat had barely diminished and the light behind the mountains deepened as the sky gradually shaded to pink. The land itself was draped in golden colors.

She wished that Conner was the man riding beside her. Deep inside, she knew he would share her wonder as the land came to life beneath the deepening shadows.

This was Conner's land. Harsh and beautiful, a constant circle of life and death. A land that had helped to shape a man into being strong and gentle, tender and hard.

Conner. His ravaged look lingered in her mind, while the things that Macaria had told her about him replayed themselves. His loyalty and love of family, his long-denied desire to be a lawman, his shouldering of a man's burdens before he had time to be a boy. These things, too, shaped a man. One that was beginning to consume her thoughts.

With a shake of her head, Belinda tried to stop the images of Conner that flashed in her mind. His most infuriating grin, the cool, hard stare, the lazy drawl of his voice. The angry Conner, whom she had pushed that first day by demanding that he arrest his brother.

Now she could understand how torn he had been—to follow his love of the law or hold to his love and loyalty of family.

"Ma'am, we'll be taking a shortcut back to the ranch over that next rise."

Dillion's intrusion put an end to Belinda's musings. She glanced over at his shadowed profile. "Do you think that is wise? I mean, it is growing darker. We should stay—"

"Ma'am, I know this land like I know the fit of my boots. Don't you worry none, ma'am. Just come along."

Belinda did not know where her reluctance stemmed from. She kept quiet, but the strong feeling persisted to hang back.

She remembered her earlier thought that tension appeared to come from the land itself as dusk layered a golden blanket, and shrugged off her reaction. Dillion had been sent to watch her, but the young man had been polite. Her reluctance to follow him was sheer foolishness.

Confident in her riding ability, Belinda loosened her hold on the reins to give the chestnut mare her head as she made her way up the small barren slope. Dillion waited on the rise for her, a dark silhouette against the sky.

Belinda drew rein alongside him. She held the reins with one hand, using the other to tuck stray tendrils of hair beneath her hat. To her dismay, she realized she had left her glove behind. It was not the loss of the glove that she minded, she had two other pairs for riding, but the fact that Conner had so bemused her she had not even noticed until now.

What Conner did to her was shameful. He made her forget . . .

A popping sound broke her thought. The chestnut mare whinnied in pain. The horse reared. Belinda grabbed for the animal's mane with her free hand to keep her seat.

Another popping sound broke closer to them.

Belinda shot Dillion a frightened look. "What—"
The mare's whinny cut off her question. Belinda tried
to calm the horse, but the maddened mare took a
plunging leap down the steeply slanted slope.

There was no time to think of Dillion. Belinda concentrated on staying in the saddle as the mare made
her rapid descent. Tossing her head from side to side
as the land leveled out, the mare took off in a ground-
eating gallop that sent Belinda's hat flying.

She had ridden hunters and jumpers, even raced
when she was younger and no one was around to tat-
tle to her grandmother, but Belinda had never ridden
a crazed horse across shrub-and-rock-strewn country.

Gasping for air, Belinda tried to soothe the animal.
Wind dried the moisture from her mouth before the
words formed. Her throat worked to bury the scream
that rose.

The muscles of her thigh, hooked over the sidesaddle's horn, burned, as did her arms, from the fierce
strength she exerted to hang on. If she could get the
mare to slow her pace, she knew she could regain
control.

Her heart raced in tandem with the sound of thundering hooves. The mare showed no sign of tiring in
her headlong flight. Belinda repeatedly yanked on the
reins, knowing that the harsh metal bit would tear the
horse's mouth. It was the only move she could make.
Fear prowled inside her, waiting for a breach in her
formidable strength of will. She refused to give in to
it.

She was not sure when she became aware of Dillion
racing alongside. He kept shouting at her, she could
see his mouth moving, but the wind tore the words
away before she made sense of what he said.

The fact that she was not alone helped steady her. Once more, she used her strength to gather the reins tight, despite the mare fighting her. A quick look showed Dillion inching ahead on the big bay that he rode. His arm was extended to catch hold of the bridle.

Even when he held the leather, it took minutes before the pace of both horses slowed. Guiding the mare, Dillion brought her around in an ever-tightening circle, until the powerful animals stood with sides heaving, but still at last.

Belinda could not move. A quivering began in her legs and rose to encompass her body. She felt chilled, then hot. Reaction set in. Fear found the chink it had been waiting for and attacked.

She lifted a shaking hand to push aside the tangle of her hair. Belinda had not felt the pins come loose. Like the animal beneath her, Belinda's chest heaved as she drew in great lungfuls of air, feeling as if she would never get enough. She swallowed repeatedly to alleviate the parched constriction in her throat.

"Here you go, ma'am. Drink a little at a time from my canteen," Dillion offered. "You ain't hurt?"

Belinda shook her head. She stared at the offered canteen. She wanted water, needed it to wash away the taste of fear, but she would have to release the reins to get it.

Dillion sensed what was wrong with her. He capped the canteen and slid down from his horse. Standing beside the mare's head, he held the bridle and kept his voice to a soft, calm murmur as he rubbed the mare's nose to quiet her. After a few minutes, he patted her neck, working his way to the side where Belinda held the reins.

"Let me have them, ma'am. It's all right now. You can let go. I won't let anything happen to you." His voice remained at the same low pitch as he coaxed Belinda until she released her hold on the leather.

"You drink up. Go on. I'll stand right here and keep this little gal still."

Belinda took tiny sips. The water was warm but slowly satisfied her thirst. She handed the capped canteen back to Dillion, who slipped the cloth strap over his head.

"Dillion, what happened back there? Those popping noises—"

"Someone used us for target practice."

"Target practice?" Belinda repeated. "Are you suggesting that someone deliberately shot at us?"

"Ain't suggesting. I'm telling you. The boss's gonna have Kincaid's scalp for this."

"Kincaid? You think the sheriff—"

"Don't think, ma'am. Know it for a fact. He's bound and determined to see the boss swing at the end of a rope. Everyone knows he'd do anything to prove the boss's behind his family's troubles."

Conner shoot at them? Belinda refused to believe it. The man was not a coward, and shooting at them in the dark was the act of a coward, no matter what Dillion said.

"See if the mare's hurt. She screamed with pain and I am afraid she may have been hit."

"Might be best if you got down, ma'am."

"I'm shaking so much that if I get down, I will not get back up. Walking does not appeal to cowboys, I am told."

"Heck no. Once knew a fella that rode his horse from the bunkhouse to the outhouse, and that weren't no more than ten, maybe twenty feet."

Belinda laughed, as he had meant her to do, but that laughter stopped when he found the bloody furrow where a bullet had grazed the mare's haunch.

"She'll be all right for you to ride her. But we take it slow and easy." He swung into his saddle, taking a moment to replace the canteen on his saddle horn. "I know you didn't like hearing what I said about the sheriff, but you'll hear worse from Mr. Riverton."

"It was a cowardly act. I cannot—"

"Meaning no offense, ma'am, but you don't have a notion of what you're talking about." He nudged his horse to set off at a walk. Belinda followed.

"See," he continued, "after what happened to Kincaid last night, he'd sink lower than a sidewinder to get even."

Belinda muttered under her breath. She did not like hearing Conner accused of being a coward. She wanted to defend Conner. An act that made no sense. He was a grown man who could easily defend himself.

A little interested prompting on her part would gain her knowledge of what happened to Conner last night. She could not forget the haunted look in his eyes.

"I am confused, Dillion. What exactly is the sheriff bound and determined to get even for?"

"The rattlers, ma'am. Instead of locking up those two hombres he claims he caught with Rocking K cattle in the jail, he was there himself. Someone dumped a sackful of rattlesnakes into the cell with him."

"My Lord!"

"Well, *He* musta been watching over Kincaid the way I heard it. Nothing happened to him. He shot the snakes and walked out without being bit."

You are wrong! she wanted to shout. Something did happen to Conner. A rush of compassion soared through her. The mare sidestepped, bringing Belinda's attention back to her. She murmured to the horse, patting her neck.

"You are claiming that the sheriff blames Ch—ah, Mr. Riverton for this?"

"Sure am. He's been after the boss since he bought the land and set up the Circle R. Kincaid was the big cattle king in these parts. Had the contracts for the Indian reservations, some army contracts, too. The boss gave better prices and took them away from the Kincaids."

"Revenge," Belinda said, mulling over what she knew. But if Charles was innocent, why would he have paid for a map that had something to do with the Kincaids? And who had sold it to him?

On the ride into town she had debated with herself about telling Conner what she knew. In part, her meeting with Macaria prompted the debate. The woman had assured her that, as painful as the decision might be to accept, if the little boy they knew as Marty was her brother's child, no one would stand against her. Learning that the boy still had nightmares about his parents' deaths helped Belinda to curb her impatience to see him immediately.

With Macaria as an ally of sorts, Belinda no longer had to use the information she had as a bargaining device. Yet she had not told Conner about it.

It was his own fault. The man reduced her to a mass of heated sensations with one lingering look from his gray eyes. It was a totally new experience for her and Belinda was not sure how to deal with it, or Conner. But she knew herself well enough to understand that she was drawn to Conner Kincaid as she had never been to any man before him.

Belinda had been so lost in her thoughts that she was startled when Dillion pointed out how close they were to the ranch.

"You intend to tell Mr. Riverton what happened?"

"Got no choice, ma'am. He's got to know."

"I wish you would not say anything. If what you claim is true, this will only fuel—"

"Pardon, ma'am. You heard Kincaid threaten me. See, he's got you thinking it couldn't be him, 'cause he warned me. But they're a tricky bunch over on the Rocking K. First thing I got warned about when I signed on was to watch out for them."

"Neither one of us was hurt, and you said the mare would be all right." But her argument was weak. Belinda had heard Conner threaten him, almost as if he knew...no! She refused to think that of him. Rubbing her forehead as Dillion held a quick, whispered conversation with the men guarding the gate, Belinda knew she could not sort it all out.

The moment they were clear of the gate, she pleaded with him again. "Let me tell Mr. Riverton what happened."

"You're welcome to say your piece, but it ain't gonna make no difference. Kincaid went too far. Now he's gonna pay for it."

Belinda saved her breath and further argument. She marshaled them for a confrontation with Charles.

But when they dismounted by the door, Mrs. Dobbs admitted them, and informed them that Mr. Riverton was not there.

"He was summoned away on business this afternoon," the housekeeper explained to Belinda when she asked.

"When will he be back?" Dillion demanded. "I gotta talk to him."

"He said he'd be gone a few days."

"It can wait until he returns." Belinda took hold of his arm and urged him to step aside with her out of Mrs. Dobbs's hearing. "I want you to keep quiet about this until he comes back. I grant you that your suspicions have a solid basis, but you do not know for sure that it was the sheriff shooting at us. Without proof, you have no right to make an accusation that could cause bloodshed."

Inside, Belinda was shaking, but she held a steady gaze on the young man's face, willing him to agree.

"I don't like it, but I'll wait till the boss comes back."

"Thank you, Dillion. I will not forget this." As he turned to go, Belinda added, "Please take good care of the mare. I do not want anyone else to tend her."

He tipped his hat and left.

"Will you still be wanting supper, miss?"

A reaction was setting in to the ordeal she'd been through and the thought of food made nausea churn in Belinda's stomach. "A cup of tea, Mrs. Dobbs. By the way, did Mr. Riverton leave a message for me?"

"Not directly, miss. He mentioned he hoped to be back from Tucson in order to accompany you to the Kincaids."

Belinda left the housekeeper. In her room she said a prayer that Charles's business would keep him away. She did not want him to visit the Kincaids with her. His presence would cause trouble.

She hoped Charles's absence would prove to be a blessing. She now had the opportunity to discover why he had paid to have a marked map of Kincaid property. She was not sure any longer why it was important for her to find it. An inner voice nagged that she had to. All Belinda had to do was avoid Mrs. Dobbs's prying eyes.

Long after the housekeeper had brought Belinda tea and bid her good-night, Belinda paced her room, counting the minutes until it would be safe for her to search Charles's office.

While she paced, she thought over what Dillion had told her about Conner. Would he use any excuse to take revenge on Charles? Would Conner attempt murder? She backed away from thinking of such a strong description of this night's incident. But Belinda could not lie to herself. If she had been shot, or thrown from a runaway horse, she could have died.

Had one kiss clouded all reason from her mind where Conner Kincaid was concerned? Or was she a pawn in a deep game played by Conner and Charles?

She had no answers. And it frightened her that she questioned her own judgment of whom to trust.

Chapter Eleven

For Belinda, Saturday morning arrived in a flurry of anticipation and dread. She was excited and worried about this first, and most important, meeting with her nephew.

She did not wish to appear intimidating to a little boy who had never met her. Memories of early years when she had been summoned into her grandmother's sitting room and faced that imposing grand dame made her determined that Robert's child would not fear her. Macaria had assured her that she would pave the way for this meeting. She had spent less time dressing for any number of evening entertainments, she reminded herself as she settled on what she would wear.

Comfort in the growing heat was a factor. Over her chemise she wore a light, open-weave summer corset. Her bodice of dotted lawn was decorated with lace inserts, Swiss embroidery and tiny tucks that fanned from the softly gathered neckline. A wide ruffle of lace formed the yoke. The lightest weight skirt she had was a black cotton printed with a tiny watered floral of rose, green and pale pink. The skirt, she noted thankfully, had been made to be worn without the cumbersome bustle.

Belinda coiled her hair into a simple chignon at her nape. She fixed the last hairpin in place and waited. Several worried looks were cast at the leather satchel filled with gifts that stood by the door.

She had had to rely on married friends' advice in choosing the toys. The painted iron soldier set came complete with tiny brass cannon. The wooden rescue hook and ladder wagon had four large draft horses to pull it and the inlaid game box combined fishpond, checkers and dominoes with a board to play on.

She strolled to the open doorway. In the distance the sky was overcast with dark clouds. She returned to her pacing, glancing time and again at the jacket she had set out. "Should I take it?" She fingered the material and decided against it.

Footsteps on the tiles outside claimed her attention. She was already pinning on the black straw hat with a modified brim when Mrs. Dobbs announced the arrival of the driver and buckboard sent by Mrs. Kincaid.

"I will be along in a few minutes, Mrs. Dobbs."

"Very well, miss."

Belinda, hearing the disapproving tone, stuck her tongue out to her reflection in the mirror. It was a silly, childish thing to do but it made her feel better.

She tilted the brim of the hat forward a bit more, and placed a last hat pin through the band that ended in a bow with a deep rose spray of tiny primroses. A dab of scent behind each ear, a little on the wrists, and she was ready for the black kid gauntlet gloves. Her eardrops were cameos, matching the one pinned to her neckline. Miniature pearls twisted with gold formed the frame.

"Reticule and satchel," she murmured, lifting them up. "Parasol, this time," she reminded herself, for her ride into town had tinted her skin to the same shell pink color of the cameo.

Mrs. Dobbs was nowhere in sight as she made her way down the long hall. It was just as well. The woman had had very little to say since Charles was absent, although Belinda could not fault her house-keeping skills. Mrs. Dobbs, thankfully, had proved to be a sound sleeper. Belinda had accomplished her goal, but it had taken two nights of trying before she managed to pick the lock on Charles's desk. She had yet to reach a decision of what to do with the map she had copied.

Stepping outside, Belinda frowned when she saw the old Mexican driver. Displeasure filled her when Dillion stepped away from where he leaned against the arch to take her satchel.

"What are you doing here, Dillion?"

"I'm escorting you to the Kincaids."

"That will not be necessary. As you can see, Mrs. Kincaid has provided me with an escort." Belinda glanced at the buckboard. It looked solid enough, but she was not sure about the driver, hunched over as if he were either drunk or asleep. The man wore a wide felt sombrero and striped poncho. He had offered no greeting and did not even bother to look up as she continued to argue with Dillion.

"Put my satchel in the buckboard," Belinda ordered. "Then go back to whatever it is you do. You are not coming with me. I am paying a social call and I will not have trouble with the Kincaids because you are there.''

"The boss said I ride when you ride, ma'am. Don't mean no disrespect, but he pays me and you don't. Them's my orders.''

"Dillion, I can take care of myself. And I care this," she stated with a snap of her fingers, "for your orders.''

"That's your right, ma'am. Don't change nothing. I'm coming with you.''

Belinda wanted to shout with exasperation. She did not want him coming with her for a variety of reasons. The one she had scarcely admitted to herself was the chance of seeing Conner there. She had not forgotten Dillion's accusations against him. Until she had the opportunity to speak to Conner about what happened, she wanted no trouble.

"You are a reasonable man. Compromise with me. You may ride with us as far as the boundary separating Mr. Riverton's property from the Kincaids. I assume you do have boundaries?''

"Sure do, ma'am. But I ain't so sure that's the right thing to do.''

Seeing that he was wavering, Belinda stepped closer to him and whispered, "Please understand, I am going to meet a young child today. He does not know me. If the Kincaids are annoyed or angered, they may not let me see if the boy is my nephew. Surely you can satisfy both me and your orders by waiting somewhere for my return?''

The young man scratched the back of his neck and looked around. "Well, since you put it that way, guess it'll be all right. But you can't tell anybody. It means my job, ma'am.''

"No one but you and I will ever know. I can promise you that."

A chortle that quickly turned to a cough made Belinda look hard at the old driver.

Once Dillion helped her up onto the buckboard's padded seat and handed Belinda her parasol, he went around to the driver's side.

"Old man, you take care driving Miss Jarvis, or I'll take it out of your hide. Savvy, *cholo?*"

Another fit of coughing attacked the old man.

Belinda wondered if Macaria had realized how sick the man was when she sent him over.

When Dillion pressed him for an answer, Belinda spoke in his defense. "Leave him be. I am sure that he will drive very carefully." She opened the parasol with a snap and sat up straight.

"All right. Go on. Just remember that I'm right behind you."

Holding the parasol with one hand, Belinda grasped the low wooden side of the seat. She could not help but notice the long, strong-looking fingers of the old man as he released the pole brake, made a clucking noise to the team of bay horses and snapped the reins to turn them in the circular driveway.

Smiling a secretive little smile, Belinda kept her suspicions to herself.

She glanced over her shoulder to see Dillion mount his horse. As they started out, she was thankful that he rode a short distance behind, far enough so that he could not overhear any conversation.

Belinda schooled her impatience until the buckboard cleared the gate. Dillion stopped to speak to the two guards and she quickly took advantage.

"I wonder why Macaria sent you along as my driver, Sheriff?" She stared straight ahead, feeling a little smug as the silence stretched. "Your ruse did not work."

"How'd you know?" Conner asked with a resigned note.

"Your hands gave you away. Although I admit I became suspicious when your laugh turned into a cough. What did I say that was funny?"

"I wasn't laughing at what you said, but your natural manipulating manner."

"I do not manipulate."

"Sure you do, honey. Not that—"

"I thought we agreed you would not call me—"

"Right," he said over her sputtering. "Like I was saying, I'm not objecting. I admire a woman who knows her own mind and knows how to get what she wants."

Belinda's mouth fell open.

Conner had to tilt his head to the side to peer at her. "Catch a lot of flies that way."

"You surprised me. I can hardly credit what I heard. I expected a man like you to—"

"Don't make assumptions about a man like me."

"All right, I will not. But you admitted that you admired me."

"Let me guess. No one ever said that to you."

"You ask too many personal questions."

"Helps pass the time if you answer me." But Conner already had the answer. "C'mon, tell me."

"My uncle made a similiar remark on a few occasions."

"Not one of your suitors?"

The wheels hit a rut and she was thrown against him. Conner moved like lightning to fling one arm in front of her so she wouldn't fall forward. For a moment, he had a glimpse of regret in her eyes, then she quickly moved to right herself.

He wasn't sure what the regret was for, some suitor she missed, or some suitor who had stopped courting her because he'd felt threatened by her strong-willed nature. He'd wager it was the latter, but he wasn't going to ask her.

Conner couldn't understand a man who wanted a clinging vine sort of woman. Life was harsh and uncertain in the territory. A man often left his home for days at a time, and needed to know his woman could not only protect herself but make decisions that often meant the difference between life and death.

Growing up with a strong-willed woman like his mother made him see firsthand the advantages a man gained with an independent-thinking woman. The good Lord knows, his sisters-in-law weren't shrinking violets. Ty and Logan wouldn't have it any other way.

But he couldn't help wishing that Belinda would toss off her restraint with him. He liked her better when she sassed him.

"You never answered my question of why you came for me, Conner."

"I sent your telegram to your uncle. Naturally, I read it first."

"Naturally," she repeated in a sarcastic tone.

"I had to see what you were up to. By the way, I received replies to the telegrams I sent."

"And you discovered that I told you the truth?"

"Yeah, but I'd already figured that out for myself."

"Then why did—"

"I had to buy time for Logan and Jessie to talk to the boys. You don't know what they've been through before they came here. These past months have been happy ones for them. The nightmares have stopped, most of them. And the boys are loved as if they were born Kincaids. That's why I gave you such a hard time."

"I see," she murmured.

"I hope you do. This isn't going to be easy on anyone. My mother talked to the boys, Logan and Jessie did, too. Kenny lied to protect the little one by saying they were cousins."

"Kenny is the other boy?"

"He looks like a boy, but he talks and figures things like a man. I can't wait for you to meet him."

There was a teasing promise in his voice that forced Belinda to look at him. Hunched over as he was, guiding the team through a shallow stream, she could not see much of his face.

"Conner, I have a feeling there is more to your coming to get me that you are not telling me."

"Smart woman." He thought about telling her that he wanted to be the first to show her the Kincaid lands, but not when he was forced to speak in a whisper so Dillion couldn't hear him. He had too much pride, just like the woman who sat beside him.

There were places he wanted to show Belinda, places that he'd never shared with anyone else. The thought that she would enjoy them, enjoy being with him, had planted itself in his mind and no amount of persuasion would remove it. Another one of those things that concerned Belinda that didn't make any sense to him.

But then, he reminded himself, he'd never lost sleep over a woman before she'd burst into his life.

"There's a rise up ahead. You'll have to tell your escort he can wait there. Once we cross over, we're on Kincaid land and I don't want someone taking pot-shots at him after he was so agreeable to you."

"He was more than that. He saved my life."

Belinda tilted her parasol so that her move to lean forward and look up at Conner's face wouldn't be seen.

"You know, lawman, you can catch a lot of flies with your mouth hanging open."

Conner closed his mouth with a teeth-snapping crunch. Belinda's soft, delighted laughter washed over him.

"I don't know what the devil's funny," he snapped from between clenched teeth. "How did he save your life? You get your fancy shoe stuck—"

"No, Conner. We were shot at the night I left you."

"Shot at?"

"I cannot wait until you take that ridiculous hat off. Maybe then you will hear me."

"Don't get testy. Tell Dillion to wait here, and then you're going to tell me what happened to you."

"I thought you might know all about it, Sheriff."

"What the hell is that supposed to mean?"

"Dillion," she called out, "I believe you know this is as far as you can ride with us. If I am detained, I shall make sure that someone informs you."

"I'll wait till sunset. If you ain't back, I'm coming looking for you."

Belinda sighed. She was not going to engage in an argument with him. Judging from the white-knuckled grip Conner had on the reins, she was going to have all the argument she could handle from him.

She gathered herself as the minutes slipped by. She knew Conner would wait until they were well away from Dillion. She had not meant to reveal the momentary suspicions she held about Conner being involved, but it had slipped out. Now she worried about paying the devil his due.

Chapter Twelve

Conner cautioned himself to wait as he guided the team over a flat stretch of land. In the distance an overcast sky threatened rain before the day's end.

He had chafed at the added delay driving the buckboard brought, but in view of what Belinda told him, he was glad the trip to the house would be longer.

Why would anyone shoot at her? How could a lovely, educated woman like Belinda have enemies that wanted her dead?

Her accusation that he knew something about the shooting rankled. He'd never hurt a woman in his life, and he wasn't going to allow that remark to stand. He wanted time, uninterrupted time, to question her.

Abruptly Conner swung the team. He headed toward the stand of cottonwood trees on Ouajaia Creek.

Belinda tightened her hold on the ivory handle of the parasol. The change in direction meant Conner was not going to wait. Why did the thought of being alone with him set her heart thumping so fast?

The air was warm. Crystal-clear water tumbled over a rock-strewn bed. Cottonwood trees, blooming with new spring growth, proudly displayed their lush foliage.

Conner led the horses into the thick, hock-high grass and stopped. He shoved the pole brake in place. Flies gathered, buzzing the horses, the droning heard over the soothing sound of running water. He whipped off the sombrero and poncho, tossing them into the bed of the buckboard. Tunneling the fingers of both hands through his thick hair, he glanced up. The overhanging branches laced together to form a bower, as private a place as a man could want.

But he wasn't here to court Belinda. A sharp reminder he needed to remember.

She set the closed parasol on the seat between them and sat quietly in profile to him.

Conner leaned back, flinging one arm over the back of the seat behind her. Two inches separated her very straight spine from his fingers. For a moment he was tempted to slide his hand up her rigid spine right into the wealth of blond hair so neatly pinned beneath her hat.

What happened to remembering you aren't here to court her?

"Well, Conner," she said very softly, "you are not yelling. I expected that at the very least."

"I don't want to yell at you."

"You want to argue?"

"Nope. I want to know why you accused me of knowing you'd been shot at."

"Dillion thought it was you. He told me what happened at the jail the night before. He said you would do anything to place Charles in jail. Even killing me."

Conner didn't move. His fingers curved around the wood of the backrest in a fierce grip. "And you believed him?" Rage shook his voice.

"I never said that."

"But you had your doubts, didn't you? Don't bother to lie to me."

"I have no intention of lying to you about this or anything else, Conner."

The absolute conviction in her voice cut through his rage. "I couldn't have shot at you. I left town right after you did. Only I went in the opposite direction to take my prisoners to Estralla. The sheriff over there is a friend of mine who hates rustlers more than I do. He lost his wife and two sons when they tried to stop men from stealing their cattle."

"I am sorry."

"Why, Belinda? You don't know him."

She stared down at her folded hands. "It is the polite thing to say. The right thing."

"Always so contained, always doing the *right thing.* Tell me, Belinda, what's the right thing for you?"

"There you go, asking personal questions again."

"It seems the only way to get you to snap the leash you keep on yourself."

"I do not keep a leash on myself." She rounded on him. Her gaze clashed with his. The look in his eyes was sensual and caressive, openly speculative. She was the one to look away. If you left town right after I did when did you send my telegram?"

There was an edge in her voice that made Conner think she fought not to reveal how important that telegram was to her. "I sent it first. It doesn't take all that long to walk two doors down from the café. This isn't the city, Belinda, where they line up waiting to use the telegraph."

"So you keep reminding me."

"Maybe," he admitted after a few tense moments, "it's a reminder for me."

Belinda's gaze strayed to the long length of his muscular legs that moved beneath taut black cloth as he shifted his seat and angled his body into the corner.

Conner gave in to the need to touch her. His hand moved from the backrest of the seat to trace the line of tiny tucks up the back of her shirtwaist. The thin, soft material allowed him to feel the warmth of her skin and the betraying tremor his touch caused her.

"Belinda, look at me."

"Your mother must be wondering where I am."

"No, she won't. She knows you're with me. Safe as a babe in its mother's arms. Just as safe as you want to be."

Safe? It was not the word she would use to describe how she felt. Being with Conner in a seductive mood put her in mind of walking around a quicksand pit. Dangerous. Very dangerous. One slip and . . . *and you do not want to know?*

Belinda fought to hush temptation's voice. Safe was the very last thing she wanted to be with Conner, but she could not tell him that. Conner would grab hold of such an admission and believe it granted him all sorts of liberties. Forbidden ones. *Delicious ones?* Conner's light, caressing touch played havoc with all her good intentions.

"If you won't look at me, Belinda, at least talk to me. Tell me where you were when the shooting began."

This was safe. Without hesitation she told him, striving for a controlled delivery, but as she recalled those terror-filled minutes, she heard the betraying quiver in her voice.

Conner resisted the urge to gather her close to him, to stop her and swear that she'd never face such fear again. He had no choice but to let her finish. Alarm grew as he puzzled the why of it. Added to his confusion was wondering where the fierce protectiveness for Belinda came from.

He knew what his brothers called him behind his back, and never in fond terms: Conner the caretaker. He never denied it. There wasn't a place in his memory when he'd ever turned from an animal or a person in need.

And Belinda struck him as a needy woman, more than she was aware of being.

He had to be ruthless in shoving aside his personal musings. Someone had shot at her. He refused to even consider that Dillion had been the target. It still didn't make a lick of sense to him, unless . . .

"And what did Riverton say when you got back to his ranch?"

"Charles was not there. He had been called away to Tucson on business."

"How convenient."

"Sarcasm does not become you, Conner. Why would he want me dead?"

"Why, indeed? Why would anyone want to kill you?" He watched her so intently that he caught the telltale tightening of her lips. "You know, or at least suspect someone, don't you?"

"No one knows that I am here."

"That doesn't answer me."

She closed her eyes and her cousin Albert's face came to mind. Was he so desperate to stop her that he would send someone to kill her?

Conner decided to allow her to keep her secrets for now. But the thought still rankled that she had entertained the suspicion that he was behind the shooting.

"Belinda, why did you suspect me? And don't tell me it's because Dillion said it."

"Because of the boy. You strongly opposed my being here. You did not want me to meet him."

He wanted to shatter that calm, cool facade, until he saw the betraying tremble of her mouth. The silence grew, and with it, tension wove itself between them. Conner fought with himself to concentrate on what she had said, not think about the smooth pale sheen of her skin or the way her mouth had fitted his as if those lips had been shaped for his.

He hadn't stopped touching her. It was only a move to torment himself, but he couldn't seem to stop. She'd made no protest, and he could feel the tremors deepen with every slow, sweeping caress of his hand against her back.

"C-Conner?"

Instead of answering her, he gazed down at her hands, nervously twisting in her lap. He reached out with his left hand to catch hold of one of her gloved hands. He wasn't smiling when she threw him a startled glance, he merely lifted the hand to his lips.

"What are you doing?" The heat of his mouth touched her skin through the fine kid material. All her senses came alive in a way that both excited and frightened her. "Conner, we should—"

"Get rid of these damnable gloves and do what's best for what ails you. And me," he noted in a hushed, intimate voice. He grinned to see her brown eyes widen, but not with alarm. Working the glove free from her hand, he tucked the offending material into his pants pocket.

"I'm getting a collection of these gloves, for all the times we—"

"I intend to leave here as soon as my uncle arrives."

"I know." He held her gaze with his, hearing again the regret in her voice and not the words of caution.

"Then why—" She stopped herself, no longer wishing to hear his answer.

"Start something that can't go anywhere?" he finished for her. He kissed her fingertips, watching her eyes, and the flare of sensual curiosity that mixed with an innocence he hadn't noticed before. "If I knew why, Belinda, I'd stop myself."

"Can you?"

"I don't believe I want to."

Conner studied the arch of her brows, and the sweep of her lashes, noting again the contrast they made to her blond hair. He gave in to the urge to run his finger down the straight shape of her nose, then drifted lower to trace the line of her mouth.

"Maybe I'm curious," he mused. "And then, it might be something more."

An expression of uncertainty flitted across her face. Poise deserted her. The blatant appraisal in his gray eyes challenged and aroused her. Belinda had never been so aware of herself as a woman, a desirable woman if she judged by Conner's darkening gaze. The small net that temptation had presented rose up to ensnare her. Under its blossoming, she lost the will to fight. All the trappings that had been her protection drifted away in a moment, just as they had the first time she had met Conner Kincaid.

His fingers caressed her cheek. Heat trailed behind his lightest touch. She held her breath, waiting, as he slid his fingers around to slowly curve over her bare nape and, just as slowly, giving her every chance to stop him, he drew her toward him.

Belinda managed to lift her hand. Hesitantly she placed it on his chest. The incredibly soft blue cloth of his shirt, pulled taut over muscles rigid with tension, invited her touch. The rapid beat of his heart assured her that Conner was not immune to the sensual heat that built between them.

"C-Conner, you... you cannot go around satisfying every bit of curiosity you have. Such indulgence is considered..." He drew her nearer. "Is..." Their breaths wove together in an erratic, highly charged cadence.

"Is what? Sinful?" He laughed softly at her frown. "Funny thing about curiosity. I never did learn not to satisfy mine. What about you, Belinda? Aren't you a little curious?" She was staring at him with a bemused expression. "Yeah. Just a little bit curious."

Tunneling his fingers beneath the thick, silky coil of her hair, he murmured in an intimately hushed voice, "So let's explore that something."

Conner gently tilted her head. "Yes, perfect." The angle allowed him access to her slightly parted mouth. "Yes," he repeated as she closed her eyes, "let's see if it's sin or bliss."

Drawn against him, Belinda's hip butted the heavy muscle of his thigh as she half reclined on his side. "Your gun... do you ever take it off, Conner?"

"When I make love to a woman. If I reach for the buckle, run like the devil's chasing you.

Run? She did not think her legs would hold her to stand much less run away. She felt the mere brush of his mouth against her cheek. He was going to kiss her and she had not wished for...*A lie.* Yes, she answered the little nagging voice, it is a lie. His lips grazed her temple. Warmth trickled down inside to weaken her knees. She did not move when his light, teasing caress roamed across her forehead down to the corner of her eye. Her lips parted a little more, waiting, eager now for his kiss.

The wait was maddening. Such a tiny space separated his mouth from hers. She licked her lips as her body pleaded with her to close the distance. As if he had sensed her thought, Conner's fingers tightened on her neck.

"Conner?" The whisper was half plea, half demand. He was so close, holding her, yet making no move to end her torment. Their breathing was harder, coming faster, and she felt as if she were unraveling inside.

Her hand measured the increased beat of his heart, which more than matched the throbbing ache filling her. Belinda inched her fingertips upward to his shoulder. She held power and male heat that tangled with the faint scent of bay rum. She longed to be bold, to slide her fingers into his thick hair and pull his head down to seal their mouths together.

His teasing kisses continued. He was not a lawman, but an outlaw intent on stealing her very reason. No gentleman skilled in the social arts, but a man too skilled in the arts of seduction. Without touching his mouth to hers, Conner had aroused her until she was melting inside for want of his kiss.

He moved then, his lips brushing lightly against hers, barely touching them. It was not nearly enough. It was not a wicked kiss, but a sweetly coaxing one. Not a kiss of demand, but one designed to expand the need building inside her.

"Does your mouth always tremble when a man kisses you?"

"Does it? No man ever—"

"And none will," he finished. Conner felt her hands tighten on his shirt. His mouth covered hers. Belinda had done the impossible. She'd gotten under his skin, snapped the patience he'd spent years honing, and she'd made him hungry.

His hunger turned the kiss hot, then hotter, harder and hungrier. He nibbled her lower lip, drawing it into his mouth. She pressed snug against him, her breasts flattening against his chest, her hip pushing against aroused flesh and the muscular thigh he moved to accommodate her.

Using one hand, he pulled the pins from her hat, then the hat itself tumbled backward. His hand worked into the thick coil of hair, using it to tilt her head back as his kisses moved from her mouth to her jaw, down the length of her neck. The high collar of the shirtwaist prevented him from exploring the pulse at the base of her throat.

The harder slant of his lips moved insistently back to her mouth. Belinda tried to separate the sensations, but she yielded to the slow stroking of his tongue and, with a jerky sigh, she offered her mouth without restraint. The giving made her bold. She traced the breadth of his shoulders. The strength of the muscles bunching in his arms made her weak and wanton. His low groan mingled with her sigh.

Belinda was overwhelmed by the intensity of his passion. This is what other women whispered about, this was the desire that overcame all reason.

She found that she wanted to know more, to feel the fluid heat that surged through her as he claimed the dark recess of her mouth. She could feel the hard rise and fall of his chest; it sent a pulsing beat deep into her body until she could hardly breathe past the wild pounding of her heart.

Her hands tangled into the thick hair at his nape, savoring the softness under her fingertips. She felt his hand at her throat then, sliding hungrily up and down. He shifted beneath her, bringing her head back against his shoulder. The kiss deepened, going on and on, until she was near to fainting when his mouth reluctantly lifted from hers.

Conner looked into dark, luminous eyes filled with desire. Slight tremors had racked her body at the start of the kiss, but powerful shudders had replaced them. He had felt each and every one of them, for they acted as a caress against the taut hunger that held sway over his body.

Her lips were a natural rose color, but now they were reddened and swollen. He licked the corner, soothing and enticing her at the same time. At least he had discovered he wasn't kissing a timid virgin. She had not protested when he slid his tongue into her mouth, but she'd been darn shy to return the pleasure.

Pleasure, as he had long ago taught his brothers, was given to a woman first if a man wanted to find any for himself.

Still, a nagging doubt rose in his mind. Belinda hadn't stopped him, but she seemed unsure of herself. Her eyes drifted closed and she seemed perfectly content to remain sprawled on him in an abandoned posture oblivious to the true state of affairs—his state to be accurate. Conner's curse was silent but potent just the same. Her lips curved with a lazy, almost sinful smile. A smile that enticed him. It was the smile of a woman who knew exactly what she wanted. Conner knew he was more than ready to satisfy that want. He hurt he was so ready. He couldn't ever remember feeling a need to have a woman as strong as the one surging inside him for Belinda.

But Conner had it ingrained to always listen to the voice of reason before he acted. He wasn't being given a choice now. It raised a clamor that he couldn't continue to ignore.

And reason said that Belinda didn't know what she was inviting with that smile. He'd likely shock her to the tips of her high-buttoned shoes if he reached behind him and tossed his poncho down on the grass.

Wouldn't he?

The little doubt played havoc with his mind. He swore harder, silently, damning himself and his conscience for not letting matters take their natural course.

"Conner? Is something wrong? Did I do—"

"Wrong? What could be wrong?" Anger directed at himself laced his voice. He could feel her slight withdrawal from him, although physically she didn't move.

"I asked you first. One minute you were kissing me senseless, and the next—"

He took her mouth in a quick, hard kiss. It seemed the easiest and best way to keep her quiet. But when he attempted to end it, Belinda held him in place.

"Kiss me, Conner. My curiosity is not nearly as satisfied as yours seems to be."

Soft and sultry, the words were whispered against his lips. Conner was no saint. He never claimed to be, never wanted to be one.

"You don't know what you're asking, Belinda." He ran his hand up her side, his thumb stopping at the curve of her breast. "I'm a man, not a boy. I won't stop with kisses. I won't stop at all."

"You are very aroused, Conner."

"Yeah, that about describes the state I'm in." He closed his eyes briefly, unable to believe that he was having this conversation with her.

Belinda used one finger to rub the outer rim of his ear. He muttered something that she did not understand, something that sounded like an imprecation to the devil. She smiled and snuggled closer.

"Conner, if I am the cause of your...er... discomfort, then let me be the source of easing it."

His first reaction was to set her on the opposite side of the buckboard seat. What the hell had he set free?

"Belinda, are you flirting with me?"

"If you need to ask," she murmured with regret, then sighed, "I must not be doing it right. I had hoped—"

"Never mind. You're doing just fine. As a matter of fact, if you do it any better, I'll expire right here."

Her sinful smile was back in place and Conner gave in to the need to kiss her again. Virgin or not, it no longer mattered to him.

He tamped down frustration, tempered his passion that had built too high, too fast, and settled down to give her as much or as little loving as she wanted to take from him.

Pleasure for a woman first, he reminded himself.

But Conner had a last sane thought before he lost himself in the hungry little sounds Belinda began to make. The lady confused the hell out of him.

Chapter Thirteen

"What can be keeping them?"

None of the family assembled in the garden had an answer to Macaria's question. She had asked it so many times in the past hour that she was not offended when there was no reply.

Kenny and Marty were playing with their pet ferret, PeeWee, and Jessie smiled when they saw she looked at them. A glance at her husband showed him still by the back gate. Ever since Macaria had told them about Belinda Jarvis's visit today, Logan had withdrawn from her. He had to know how painful this was. She loved Marty as much as he did.

"Come sit with us, Jessie?" Dixie called out.

"I'm too restless to sit." But Jessie softened her refusal with a smile as she looked to where Dixie sat beneath the shade of a lemon tree, her hands folded over her distended belly. She appeared the picture of contentment with Ty standing behind her chair, gently rubbing her shoulders.

Logan moved outside the gate and Jessie gave in to the need to talk to him alone. Things could not go on the way they had been. Behind her, she heard Ty stop the boys from following her.

He headed for the pond, where the sweeping branches of the willow offered concealment.

"Logan?"

"Go back, Jessie. I'm not fit company for man or beast."

"You think I don't know that?" She stood behind him and reached up to touch his collar-length dark brown hair. "This is painful for me, too, Logan. I don't want to lose Marty. I don't want to lose you, either."

He spun around, disbelief flashing in his dark blue eyes. "Lose me? Where did you get such a damn foolish notion? You couldn't lose me," he whispered, taking her into his arms. "Never, Jess. Do you hear me?"

"I hear you." She wrapped her arms around his waist. "You're so distant with me. You won't talk to me. I want to know what's bothering you besides the thought of losing our boy."

Logan smoothed one hand over her head, pressing her against his chest. He loved her tawny-colored hair down, and they compromised with Jessie wearing it in a long single braid.

"Talk to me," she pleaded.

"Honey, it's you. You're bothering me. Now don't get all het up and tighter than a newly woven rope, Jess. You think I don't know that you're not happy here?"

"But—"

"No, let me finish. You wanted to know what's bothering me and that's it. I see how you look after coming back from the house Ty and Dixie are building. I know you want a place of our own. Things just got out of hand and there's been no time. I only want you happy, love. And now this thing with Marty..."

She pushed away a little bit, just enough to cradle his cheeks with her hands. "Logan Kincaid, I love you. I won't deny it's been hard for me to share your mother's home, not," she quickly denied, "that she and Sofia have not made me feel welcome. But there's just too little for me to do. I felt shut out of your life, Logan.

"With Ty and Dixie wrapped up in their own dreams and you so busy all the time, no one needs me. Not even the boys."

"Jess, oh, Jess, how can you think I don't need you." He lowered his head, his loving gaze holding captive her wide, golden brown eyes as he took her mouth in a soul-searing kiss.

And when he lifted his lips from her, he whispered, "Don't ever tell me again that I don't need you, Jessie. If I didn't have you, I couldn't have made it through these past few months. Just hang on with me a little while longer until Ty can take over his share of the work again. Then I swear to you, love, I'll make it all up to you."

They held each other tighter, giving strength to face the wrenching loss that soon would come their way.

"Jess, I'd give everything I own to see you happy. I can't stop us from losing Marty, but Jess—" he leaned close to whisper in her ear "—let's make a baby of our own." His hand covered the lush fullness of her breast, measuring the rapid beat of her heart that matched his. "Say yes, Jessie. Tell me that's what you want, too."

"How can I say anything else? I want your baby, Logan. I want us to have our family, too."

Logan wrapped his arms around her waist, desire hot in his gaze as he looked down at the joy filling her eyes.

"We can't start now, but damn, woman, I sure want to."

Jessie laughed. "Ah, but my fine young stallion, who taught me that anticipation heightens all the senses?"

"I did. More the fool for ever telling you that."

Once again, Jessie rested her head against his broad chest. "Where do you think Conner and that woman are?"

"I'd like to think my brother remembered he's a Kincaid, not the sheriff, and lost her somewhere in the back of beyond."

"Logan? You should pity poor Conner, love. He's done so much for the family, and now he is the one who's forced to make the choice of being honorable, despite his knowing that it will hurt us. Conner always does the right thing. But you can't be angry with your brother for that. And he's alone, Logan. There's no one to share his burden with."

"Ah, Jess, you're a generous woman. More, much more generous than I deserve. Conner's always had the hardest road to walk. But it hurt me, Jess, really hurt me to hear him say that he'd take sides against me."

"Hush." She set her fingertips against his lips. "You know that isn't true. Conner has sworn to uphold the law. It's what he's dreamed of doing. What you and Ty agreed to help him do. You can't condemn him."

"Don't get angry with me. I've conceded that his is the difficult choice."

She turned within the gentle cage of his arms so that she faced the pond. Logan tightened his arms around her waist. "We mustn't forget that Marty, too, has a difficult choice to make. I don't mind admitting now that it was hard to forgive Kenny for lying to us about the boys being cousins, even though I understand he did it to protect Marty. Jess, I think Marty's already made up his mind. He doesn't want to leave us. Twice now, I've heard him call you Ma. Don't tell me it didn't please you all to pieces to hear him say that."

"It did. I can't lie about that. But I worry that she won't let us keep him. I wish Conner would get here so this will be over with soon."

"Conner'll come, Jess. I just hope Riverton didn't cause any trouble for him." Logan's voice was even, and he didn't feel a twinge of guilt in keeping secret the news that Hazer had brought back along with supplies from town. No sense in Jessie and his mother getting all upset, or Dixie, who had been ordered to remain calm. But he knew what it cost his brother to shoot his way out of a jail cell filled with rattlers. Even Ty didn't know how much Conner hated and feared snakes.

The memory of this secret shared with Conner went a long way toward softening Logan's feelings about his brother. And he found himself repeating to her, "He'll come. If I know my brother, nothing short of a bullet or a dust storm will stop him."

It wasn't a dust storm but one of passion that prevented Conner from moving. The buckboard seat had been abandoned. Belinda was too aroused to be shocked to the tips of her high-buttoned shoes when he tossed the poncho down on the thick grass. She wasn't wearing the shoes, or the silk stockings that had covered incredibly long, shapely legs. Draped alongside the stockings on the side of the buckboard was her skirt and his gun belt. She hadn't bothered to run when he reached for the buckle.

He stared down at her, at the play of weak sunlight and shadows from the laced branches overhead on her flushed cheeks, the slender bridge of her nose, on her ripe, sweetly giving mouth. Against the dark, rough-woven cloth, the spilled waves of her blond hair cushioned her head. Her expression was curiously beseeching.

Conner refused to be rushed. He fell to his knees beside her. "Are you sure, lovely lady, that this is what you want?" He called himself a fool, but he wanted no recriminations later. He couldn't forget that she was a woman who knew what she wanted and how to get it. Still, he had to be sure.

She trailed fingers lightly up his powerful thigh. "How can you still doubt that I want you?" She was mesmerized by the desire in his eyes, by his touch, and by the strong feelings that sprang to life at his nearness.

"We're going to be very late," he noted. His hand moved to the tiny buttons at the neck of her shirt-waist and began opening them with unhurried fingers. All the time, he watched her for a sign that this wasn't what she wanted at all.

"Late?" she repeated in a dazed whisper, resting quietly beneath his hands.

Conner smiled. Forgetting the purpose of their being together should have flattered his male vanity, but small doubts cropped up over her falling into his hands like a ripe peach.

His fingers slipped under the fragile lawn to lightly stroke her slender neck. "Rose petals," he murmured. "Velvety soft, fine as silk." He was being offered the most delectable body of a woman he desired and he'd be a fool to refuse the gift, to deny giving the lady what every sultry sigh asked him for. Yet again, the dark voice of reason asked why. Why him? Why now?

He trailed one finger over the soft rise of her breast. The thin chemise with its feminine, delicate lace edge and tiny pink ribbon tie contrasted sharply with the darker skin of his callused hand. It was no obstacle at all to his sudden need to touch her silken flesh.

Conner slid one hand beneath her back, bringing her up slowly toward his mouth. Her lashes fluttered, her head fell back, lips parting in unmistakable signs of surrender. His thumb and forefinger touched her nipple through the sheer fabric. He thought about taking the generous shape of her mouth beneath his, but contented himself by watching the flush of sensuality mantle her cheeks. Slowly then, patiently, and very, very gently, he teased each crest into aching hardness.

Belinda rewarded him; softly moaning, she arched her back for more.

Her eyes were half closed, her breathing hushed as he finished opening the buttons and slid the soft cloth from the waistband of her skirt. She felt fragile under his hands. As he drew the cloth aside, Belinda roused herself, drawing her arms up to shield her breasts.

"Don't tease me, honey." His arousal was aching now and, control or no, he didn't care to wait too much longer. "If you are, I'll promise to pay you back later." Promise was hot in his eyes. He lifted her hand, bringing it to his lips. A faint floral scent rose from her wrist, as delicate and tantalizing as the woman who wore it.

"Lovely Belinda, don't hide from me." He kissed her palm, gliding his open mouth across to the fleshy pad below her thumb. Conner bit her very gently, smiling as she rewarded him again with a soft moan.

"Come, let me see you. I want that. I want to touch you," he whispered in a soft, intimate voice that brought forth a betraying tremble from the woman in his arms. He nestled her hand beside her head and lifted the other one with a brushing motion that peaked her nipples. "I want that very, very much." A kiss to her fingertips, and this hand too was rested against the wealth of tumbled blond hair.

Compelled by a desire so powerful the world shrank to Conner's touch, Conner's voice, Belinda felt helpless as she looked up into eyes smoldering with passion.

"I knew you would be like this." There was a breathless quality laced in the words as she continued to stare up at him.

"Like *this*?" Conner said softly, encouragingly.

"Yes, like this."

His male vanity was pricked to the core. Had she so many men that she compared him to others? He thought it was his curiosity that had paved the path to this point, that, and his lovely lady's own.

"You must tell me, *querida,* what *this* is." Gentle derision underlay the encouraging tone. "Slow, Belinda? Tender?" His gaze drifted down to the rapid rise and fall of her breasts.

Her thought flashed back to that first morning. *Slow as molasses on a winter morning.* She had wanted so badly to stop thinking about him and his slow idea of pleasure. Badly? Not true, she decided, or she would not be half-undressed, more than willing to surrender to him.

"Tell me," he ordered in a low, heated voice.

"Experienced," she confessed.

Her wide brown eyes were guileless as they gazed up into his penetrating gray eyes. He lowered his head with a deliberate slowness to kiss her.

"Experienced," he repeated softly, brushing her mouth with his. Polite, savagely civilized, Conner traced the shape of her mouth with his tongue. "I admit, the matter has never been called to my attention, but I appreciate the confidence."

"I said the wrong thing."

"Never, lovely lady. Say whatever you please. I certainly will."

"Honesty was something I thought you would welcome, Conner."

"I do. Experience and honesty. Is that what the charming Eastern society lady is looking for? A tumble in the wild with a cowboy makes fine conversation over afternoon tea. Doesn't it?" He teased her lower lip with a nip of his teeth, soothing it with his tongue.

"No. Yes. You confuse me, Conner. I did not lie when I said I wanted you. I never said those words to another man."

Conner held himself still. He had stripped away her habitual restraint and poise. No guile in her eyes, no coy confession, but truth. And still the dark voice of reason plagued him again.

"Never wanted to say them, Belinda, or never had the opportunity?"

His indulgent, waiting smile beckoned for the truth. Again. Would he leave her nothing secret? Bright with desire and ruthless with impatience, she knew he would stop and walk away if she did not answer him. And the aching fullness that he aroused would remain just that—aching. A moment more of uncertainty held her.

"Conner?"

His thumb touched the corner of her mouth. "No lies. No pretense. You wanted honesty. I demand it."

"Both then. I never said the words to another man, never wanted to, never allowed any man close enough to make me want to say them."

She whimpered softly when his mouth took hers, but tenderness turned hard, possessive, and this time her lips parted of their own accord when his tongue sought entrance.

But Conner wanted more than acquiescence as he swept the sweetness of her mouth. He wanted the passion hot, unfettered, and belonging only to him.

Her tongue played softly against his, twined and teased then danced away until he coaxed it forth again. His hands moved beneath her, lifting her up, one hand sliding down to discover the smoothness of her back, pressing her closer.

His mouth left a fiery trail down her throat, his teeth lightly nipping her satin-smooth shoulder. She trembled at the restrained hunger of the small bites, and her arms rose up to grip his strong shoulders. He guided the soft thin lawn cloth from her shoulders, down her arms, over her small hands, freed it completely from her body and tossed it aside.

"Lovely, lovely lady."

She basked in the rich, heated approval of his voice, in his eyes. He made her feel beautiful and desirable. And Belinda, who never allowed anyone to rule her, allowed Conner the freedom to tease and torment, please and pleasure them both with his maddening slowness.

He removed her arms from his neck and lowered them to her sides, then grasped the thin straps of her chemise to slide them down her arms. The fragile garment was never meant to be removed this way. Conner opened the tiny pink ribbon tie and returned to tug the fine cotton over the ripening swell of her breasts. The bodice tightened, resisting his effort as Belinda did not.

"Conner, must you...must you take it off?" she stammered, moving her legs restlessly, anticipating yet suddenly shy.

"Desire, love, is such a hard, hard mistress. Fickle as the wind, but we'll manage to outwit fashion to satisfy her. And you. Most especially you." He gently eased the fabric under the perfectly formed breasts. "There," he whispered in a rough-soft voice into her ear.

Belinda gasped as the lace edge slid over her nipples, leaving desire racing through her body. The silk of his hair brushed her sensitive skin that neither sun nor man had ever seen, much less touched. She felt poised on the fringe of the unknown, heated and tutored to his lightest touch, about to surrender what she had always guarded.

Sheer insanity.

It was her last thought as he slowly drew the tip of her breast into his mouth and teased her so gently with his teeth and tongue that she was sure this time she would faint from the exquisite pleasure he gave her.

Warm, sultry air, crushed spring grass and the heated scents uniquely Conner's made a heady blend as she drew ever-deepening breaths. She was pressed back down to the coarse-woven poncho beneath the weight of Conner's body. His lean hips moved rhythmically against her in a slow dance of persuasion.

She could feel the length of him, his aroused masculinity settling against the apex of her thighs, feel him seeping into every pore, every nerve ending, until she knew only him. Deepening kisses snapped the bonds of her passion. Her hands glided up his arms to clasp his neck. She laced her fingers together as she melted into his powerful frame.

Even as she gloried in the sensations filling her, she longed to touch him as he was touching her. Her fingertips pressed into his shoulders with need. She feared making the wrong move and having him stop the delicious pleasure spreading through her body.

Her body trembled beneath him. Conner arched his neck as her tentative touches grew bolder. He whispered encouragement as an overwhelming sexual response welled up inside him. He no longer asked himself why—all he could think about was having Belinda's lovely long legs wrapped around him.

She was incredibly responsive. Adding to his pleasure, allowing him to temper driving need to return its full measure back to her. The fragile cloth was no barrier to the heated kisses he trailed across her waist and down the flat plane of her belly. He held her hips, stilling their restless twisting as he freed the tie of her petticoat and added moist kisses to already dampened cloth. A few gentle sweeps and turns and the froth of cotton and lace lay pooled at her feet. His mouth touched dewy warmth and the welcoming heat brought a sheen of sweat to his body.

The blaze of his body bathed her heightened senses. She reveled in the urgency and swiftly moving passion that drove Conner and swept her along in its tide. She answered his needs with dampening flesh and soft cries, and found her own needs sharpened with a greediness she had never known.

His whispers laced over her skin, dark, liquid words without meaning to her, but the hushed delicacy of his voice sent a fresh surge of desire to coil deep inside her.

Her heart beating wildly, Belinda cast caution to the wind. She worked her hands down between them, and began pulling at his shirt. Conner proved accommodating. A string of kisses that had her tossing her head from side to side preceded his upward rise until his lips closed over hers.

Driven now, she yanked at the cloth until she could slide her hands beneath it. His back was damp, like the touch of satin and steel, marred with tiny scars, hard and very alive while soft, so soft, to her caressing hands.

The heat of him invaded her on every level of feeling, from the thin layer of skin to the hidden corners of her mind. Conner stole doubts and filled her with drugging sensations. Her senses were drawn to wherever he touched her with his mouth, making her believe each place was where she craved him most, until he moved on to the next, and the next.

Raising himself slightly, Conner looked down at her. Her eyes were bright, the longing in them clear for him to see. He came to his knees, slowly unbuttoning his shirt. If he had harbored any doubts that Belinda wanted him, they instantly disappeared beneath the bold appraisal and blatant approval in her eyes. He blessed every deity and spirit he had ever called upon for the rich bounty waiting before him.

The opened shirt revealed dark hair covering his chest, arrowing down to his waistband. Belinda, no longer unsure of herself, gracefully sat up and stilled his hands.

"Let me," she murmured, leaning close to scatter kisses as she drew the shirt from his shoulders, down the tense, muscled length of his arms, over his strong hands.

Her head tilted from side to side as she explored the texture and taste of his skin, her long blond hair brushing against him like the softest, finest silk. He shuddered in reaction and felt the smile that curved her mouth. He closed his eyes and gave himself over to the heated and satisfying torment. Her lips closed over one brown nub, and a soft cry of surprise drifted upward when she discovered his flesh was as hard and responsive as her own.

Conner's spread thighs welcomed her closer. He raised his hands to her slender hips, pulling her snug against his violently aroused flesh. Patience strained, he felt the tiny string of kisses she trailed along his waist, and he gently urged her head up until he gazed into her passion-drenched eyes.

"To satisfy your evident curiosity, lover," he murmured, taking her hands and placing them on his shoulders, "I've a most pressing matter that desires your complete attention."

She leaned into him, drawing his lower lip into her mouth with the edge of her teeth. She rubbed the tip of her tongue over it, sighed, then released his tempting mouth.

"Ah, pressing matters require one's complete and most immediate attention." Belinda laced her fingers behind his neck, her forehead touched his and her lips curved in sinful anticipation.

"Accommodate me, love." He tumbled her onto the ground. Smoothing back the tangled waves of her hair, he grazed his lips against her cheek, then to the lobe of her ear. A delicate and delightful cry suspended talk as he paid homage to her daintily shaped ear and was rewarded by a plea he no longer could deny.

With a sure touch he loosened the ribbon holding her drawers and then sought tantalizing feminine heat. "My compliments to your modiste," he whispered, touching silken curls through the slit in her drawers. He touched layered softness and honeyed warmth. She writhed helplessly against him. "Very accommodating for a man's pleasure."

"And a woman's," she returned in a barely audible voice. A shuddering moan escaped her lips. "Conner," she cried out. In moments she was quivering, gasping with rapturous sighs.

Passion-glazed eyes touched upon his smile. "I commend your style. Please," she said with a capitulative sigh, "more."

His laugh was soft and knowing and he touched her again.

It was deeper this time and pleasure flowed in torrents through her senses. She had never thought there could be such thrilling excitement from a man's touch, as pleasing and as effortless as Conner brought forth from her. Belinda lost herself in enchanted ecstasy.

She barely felt the drifting downward glide of fine cotton against her legs. But she keenly felt the loss of his body and made a fretful sound when he moved away.

"A moment, no more. I'd ask for your assistance, love, but you're trembling so badly, I fear it will only prolong my...er...discomfort."

"Take your time." Belinda could afford to be generous, she was lost in the throes of her release and powerless to move. But she wondered if it would hurt the first time. She heard the soft thud of his boots fall to the ground, then the rustle of cloth sliding against skin. Nothing could make her open her eyes, nothing but the returned coil of tension that held her in thrall, demanding that she look at him.

"Sweet heaven." Prayer and plea, her gaze lifted to his eyes.

Indecision clouded her gaze. With suffocating patience dredged from deep inside himself, Conner had to address the issue. Although he could never recall having ever, ever referred to his sex as an issue.

"Don't worry," he promised, all rich, heated indulgence again. He joined her on the makeshift bed. "We'll make a perfect fit."

Belinda stretched her hand to touch him. "Show me. Come show me, Conner."

Past the point of preliminaries, Conner moved her beneath him, and nudged wide her thighs. His mouth took hers with a greedy, hungry kiss as he pressed against damp heat below. His smooth, gliding progress, aided by the gentle movement of her hips under him, came to a halt.

He remained poised motionlessly for a few moments, allowing her this small grace, but the cost to himself was measured in excruciating frustration. He thrust forward again, and she moaned, her fingertips digging into his shoulders. Determined then, neither brutal, nor overly gentle, encouraged greatly by her pleas, he broke the fragile barrier.

Startled by the pain, she screamed, her eyes snapping open to target his.

"It's over, love." He kissed her and murmured in the soft liquid language of his mother's people, whispering endearments and dark, heated words that by inflection if not meaning, brought forth her eager caresses.

She saw in her mind's eye, in that instant he had stood before her, tall, heavily muscled chest, lean through torso and hips, his erection bringing forth a silent plea for mercy, even as the fire between her thighs burned hot.

The slow way he moved inside her, withdrawing carefully, only to begin the slow thrust again, formed another plea in her mind. She never wanted this to end. Soft moans and sighs of pleasure seeped from her parted lips and she clung to him, losing the shyness, instinctively undulating her slender hips to draw him deeper. Arching against him, passion driving her as it drove him, Belinda felt a gathering storm that only moments later shattered her. There was a few moments' respite, then once again the exquisite rhythm started and Belinda relinquished the last ladylike tenet that had guided her. Her ardor was as wild and fierce as the man who showed her the pain was truly over, and only pleasure remained.

Conner was driven by the knowledge that he'd never felt this fierce, reckless desire for any woman before her. She was fire in his hands, and the world hurtled away as he brought her to peak after peak, finding himself as insatiable as his lover until once more he felt the tiny convulsions begin for her and he met them with his own pulsing spasms.

There were moments when time stood still, before he lifted himself to his elbows, his breathing harsh, his body bathed with sweat. He kissed her reddened lips and she stirred beneath him, opening dreamy brown eyes as she reached up to cradle his cheek.

"Curiosity..." Her whisper trailed off, he was still hard within her.

"Replete. And yours?" he murmured with a half smile.

"Sinful bliss."

"I try."

"You succeed...."

Chapter Fourteen

"Hairpins for my lady. As many as I could recover." Conner's voice was indulgent as he dropped the pins into the depression made by the cloth draped over Belinda's slightly parted thighs.

Belinda sat on the tail of the buckboard, fully dressed, an accomplishment—from a hasty wash in the cold water of the stream to buttoning the last button at her neckline—that Conner had made into love play. Replete, as she believed he was, in passion's aftermath, she leaned forward to kiss his lips and murmur her thanks.

Conner broke the kiss before he lost himself again with this incredibly responsive woman who puzzled and disturbed him. "The lady entices," he whispered. He placed his hands on either side of her hips, fingers spread and pressing into the hard, rough plank wood of the wagon's bed.

"The lady is delighted to know she can."

"No regrets?"

She returned his serious regard, understanding at once that he was not teasing now. She bit back her first response, an unqualified no. While she had no regrets for what happened between them, for Conner was all that she had secretly dreamed of finding in a lover, she also sensed the underlying and unasked question of why she had chosen him. Especially when she had clearly stated that nothing could come of it. *And why not?* Belinda hushed the little nagging voice. The reasons were complex and she was too confused to sort them out now, not when Conner loomed so close, his chest bare, gray eyes probing her own, and the taste of him lingering on her lips.

His knuckles whitened with the force of pressing against the hard wood. Abruptly he straightened and turned away.

"Your silence is as eloquent as your love talk. Don't dally too long, *honey,* it's close to noon." He stood there, tunneling the fingers of both hands through his thick hair before he walked a few steps to pick up his discarded shirt and the poncho from where they lay in the grass.

The soft, indulgent-speaking lover was gone and the hard-bitten lawman had returned. Belinda opened her mouth to call his name, but the rapid beat of fast-moving horses arrested her attention. Conner was already gazing toward the rise they had traveled down.

"Belinda, get up on the seat."

The quietly given order puzzled her. "Why, Conner? Who is coming?"

"Do it. Now." He spun around, tossing the shirt and poncho into the buckboard's bed behind her. Belinda hadn't moved. Normally Conner wouldn't worry about riders approaching, but they weren't that far onto Kincaid land. The skin on the back of his neck prickled with alarm. He grabbed her by the waist, lifted her high and carried her to the front of the buckboard.

"What is wrong?"

"Sit." He ignored her repeated questions that swiftly became demands to answer her. From beneath the seat, he removed his gun belt and rifle. "Hold this."

Belinda stared at the rifle, then glanced to see him strapping on the belt, leaning over to tie the leather thong around his thigh. Every move was calm and controlled. She had a feeling that Conner did not want to alarm her, but his manner gave lie to that.

Mentally Conner dismissed the chance of outrunning four riders in the buckboard. If those were Rocking K men they would have hailed him by now. The silence meant they were Riverton's men or strangers. All he could think about was getting Belinda safely away.

It wouldn't be her they were after, but him.

"Can you drive the team?" He took the rifle from her.

"I imagine I could." She stared at him. She sensed the impending danger as well as he did, yet his voice had been politeness itself. "Conner, I am not going—"

"Take them," he ordered, handing her the reins as he released the pole brake. "For once in your spoiled life, do what someone tells you. Get out of here and don't come back."

"Who are those men?" she demanded.

Conner stepped forward and slapped the rump of one of the bay horses. The wagon lurched forward. Belinda was thrown back against the seat.

"I am not leaving you alone!" she yelled, sawing on the reins. She threw a quick look over her shoulder. The four riders were closing fast. Though soft, Conner's vehement swearing—mostly directed at her for disobeying him—filled the air.

"I never take orders well, lawman," she muttered as she urged the team around in a wide circle. How could that impossible man think that she would ride off and leave him at the mercy of strangers? She no longer had a question in her mind that they meant to do Conner some harm. If they were Charles's men, her presence could prevent Conner from getting hurt.

The riders had slowed their horses to a walk, as if they had nothing to fear, when Belinda pushed the pole brake in place, but did not let go of the reins.

"Do you know them, Conner?"

"Riverton's men," he answered tersely. He recognized the Circle R ramrod in the lead.

"What do they want? I thought you said we were on your land."

"Dacus can't read, even if it was posted. I want you out of here, Belinda, before they come closer. They won't ride after you. Go on," he ordered. "Leave me."

"No."

Her single, softly spoken denial sent a shaft of anger shooting through Conner. And hot on its heels came fear for her. She didn't know what men like these were capable of doing.

Conner had no illusions that they were coming to pay a social call. He'd end up using his gun. It was a gut-deep instinct that he didn't argue with.

He kept his eyes on Joe Dacus, riding a showy black, white and brown spotted paint horse with a distinctively marked black mane and tail. The horse and the fancy silver-worked bridle made the man an easy target even at this distance.

Temptation beckoned to Conner. One bullet and he'd have his revenge. He wasn't thinking as the sheriff who had sworn to uphold the law but the man who had narrowly avoided losing his life in a nightmare that still lingered.

He had no doubts that Dacus had been the one who let the snakes loose in the jail cell. It couldn't have been anyone else. Riverton paid his men well, but Dacus was the only man on his payroll he would trust to do murder for him.

Conner willed the tension to leave him. He blocked out the sound of the tumbling water, the horses munching grass, but he couldn't find a way to block out Belinda's voice.

"Conner, the man riding in front, he is the one you fought with at—"

"Yeah, that's Dacus in the lead. Riverton's ramrod and hired gun. And right behind him is Dillion, your most *agreeable savior.*"

"He did save my life. You heard him promise to wait for me. Why would he be riding with them?" She knew there was bad blood between these men and Conner. She had never seen the other two riders around the ranch and Conner did not seek to enlighten her.

A strange fear took hold of her, settling marrow deep. A cold hard knot coiled in her stomach. The fear grew as she understood that the men moved slowly toward them as if they knew no one could see them. But the fear was for Conner, not herself.

"They cannot stop us from leaving, Conner. Dillion and Joe Dacus know that I am Charles's guest. They would not dare—"

"Dare? They'd dare anyone, anything. I tried to tell you to get away. They'll be all over us like buzzards on the dead if I get up on that seat with you to make a run for it. I know what these animals are capable of doing. Ah, hell! Just keep quiet. If you think being Riverton's guest will protect you, it won't."

"I could not leave you." Belinda's whisper was lost beneath Dacus's shout.

"Kincaid!" He drew rein about twenty feet away. "I've been hoping for a chance to get you alone."

"If you wanted the pleasure of my company, Dacus, you should've sent a note. But I'm not alone. Riverton's lady guest is with me. And you're too far a piece from your home range."

Worried and tense, Belinda shot Conner a reproving look. Dacus's voice was gloating and goading. There were four of them and Conner dared to taunt him.

Conner stood away from the sheltering cover of the cottonwood trees. A hazy sun glinted off the barrel of the rifle he held loosely cradled in his arms. Even without his shirt on, he appeared dark and dangerous. He stood five feet away from her to the side of the buckboard.

Belinda thought of the small two-shot derringer in her reticule. Palm sized, the small gun made a deadly wound at ten feet. Not that Belinda knew for certain. She had never had occasion to use the gun beyond practice fire.

"Conner," she whispered. "Give me your rifle."

"Stay out of this, Belinda. If they see you with a weapon they'll take it away from you. A discriminating society lady like yourself wouldn't like their hands all over her body." *And I'd kill the first man that tries to touch you.*

His rebuke and reminder that his hands had been all over her stung. She only wanted to help him. "You have a deplorable sense of humor, lawman."

"It wasn't meant to be funny."

Soft and deadly, his words sobered her. "I am sorry, Conner. I have made it worse for you by staying."

He didn't respond. He wasn't going to lie to her and he couldn't take the chance of turning to look at her. Her realization of the danger she was in had come too late.

Hard, lean and calm, Conner watched the four men come in closer to form a loose half circle in front of him. He felt Belinda's burning gaze on his back. Sweat trickled down his spine and flies buzzed around his head. He did not move.

"That's about as close as you're coming," Conner stated. He wished he had put on his shirt, knowing the conclusions these men drew from finding them together, him half-dressed and Belinda with that glorious blond hair tumbling to her waist. But like her realization of danger, it was too late to do anything about it.

From the heat crawling into each man's eyes, a flash of regret came to Conner from what she would be forced to listen to, despite her status as Riverton's guest. And if he allowed them to goad him into a fight, he could get her killed.

Joe Dacus leaned forward, his forearms crossed over the saddle horn. Conner likened him to a bull. The man was stocky but not fat. He was a vicious fighter, having learned his dirty tricks on the Galveston waterfront before he started to hire out his gun.

"Taking a free ride with the boss's fancy piece of goods is gonna cost you, Kincaid."

Conner could have shot him for the way he leered at Belinda. The others laughed. Conner didn't say a word, nor did he move his gaze from Dacus. One move... just one move toward her...

But Dacus didn't make a move. He knew that's what Conner was waiting for.

"Real nice little piece of land, Kincaid. Good for a little bird-nesting. Didn't know she went for the Adam an' Eve bit. Why, hell, Kincaid, I don't even blame you none. If I'd known her plumbing wanted priming, I'd've been first in line."

Belinda's shocked gasp fell in the silence that followed. Conner wondered how long it would take her to understand the insults that Dacus uttered.

Conner's gut clenched with the effort he forced from himself not to answer the goads. It was the foolish move that Dacus waited for, but in order to protect Belinda, he had to allow the insults. *Don't move.* But he wanted to... Lord, how he needed to wipe that leering grin off Dacus's face, then go to work on the others.

Though four against one weren't the worst odds he'd faced, one bullet would remove him from any chance to protect Belinda. The bone-deep knowledge held him still.

Thumbing back his high-crowned, sweat-stained hat, Dacus barked a short, ugly-sounding laugh. "Riding ramrod for Riverton means I got to straighten out the boss man's problems, Kincaid. You've become a big one, like a real hard thorn in his side and a burr under my saddle." He scratched his beard-stubbled chin and spat to the side. "Yes, sirree. The boss ain't gonna like hearing you stretched your leather with her."

"Stop it." Dillion eased his horse up alongside Dacus. "We didn't come down here to insult Miss Jarvis. She ain't done nothing. And Riverton's gonna be madder than those damn snakes you keep if she tells him what you've been saying. And we don't need to hang around his land while you set spit to the wind needlin' Kincaid."

"*Miss Jarvis,* is it? Shut your mouth, boy. Ladies don't go around tumbling the likes of Kincaid. Why, boy," he said, his eyes burning with hate as he targeted Conner, "don't you know he's still got to hunt up his backbone. The way I hear it told, Kincaid left it in his jail cell a few nights back."

Conner didn't hear Belinda's outraged cry on his behalf. His unblinking stare never wavered from Dacus's face. Around the rifle, his fingers clenched with the need to rearrange the ramrod's features. In his mind, from the dark corner where it should have stayed buried, the terror of being alone in the jail cell rose up. He saw himself, sweat drenched, plastered against the wall . . . afraid.

Dacus had been the one who let the snakes loose. And from his word, the bastard had stayed around long enough to see the results.

Conner didn't know where he dragged the strength from to block the nightmarish vision from continuing. He had no time to be grateful, for a high-stepping roan brought one of the other men in closer.

"*Amigos,* this man is mine. His brother left me to die. Without a weapon, he left me in the desert. I will be the one to return the favor, *sí?* Then, we will show the lonely *señorita* she does not need this *cholo*. She will have a fine, brave caballero in me.''

"What you got in mind for him, Billy Jack?" Dacus demanded to know. He didn't turn to look at the man at his side. He didn't dare lift his gaze from Kincaid. He knew how good the lawman was with both the gun tied down low on his thigh and the rifle he cradled loosely in his arms. And it bothered him that Kincaid stood calm and quiet in spite of his goading him.

"You are foolish to continue, Mr. Dacus," Belinda called out. She was proud that the fear coiling through her was not revealed in her voice.

"Belinda," Conner warned.

"No. This has gone far enough. Charles is going to be furious when he hears what has happened."

"How's that, lady?" Dacus spat again. "We ain't done nothin' but fun some with the sheriff here."

"Your idea of fun is appalling. You have insulted me and goaded Sheriff Kincaid beyond any man's bearing."

"Lady, I don't know them fancy words you're spitting like some prissed-up schoolmarm, so shut up."

Belinda hit back every choice name that rose up to call Dacus. No one, not even Conner at his most arrogant, had dared to tell her to shut up. She did not understand why Conner stood there, refusing to answer one goad.

Her gaze strayed to find Dillion staring at her. He shook his head in warning. Belinda, ever headstrong, ignored him.

"Dillion, you must ride back to the ranch. Surely there is someone this . . . this man will listen to."

"Ma'am, I—"

"Boy, since you're so damn worried about *Miss Jarvis,* you get to shut her mouth and keep her the hell out of the way, or I'll do it."

Dillion heard the underlying threat in Dacus's order and nudged his horse forward. He neck-reined his horse so that he was even with Belinda.

"I tried to tell you," he whispered. "The boss pays my wages. I can't go against the ramrod. A man that rides for a brand owes that brand his loyalty."

"Loyalty?" She hated looking away from the whispered conversation between Dacus and Billy Jack, but Dillion had given her a means to end this.

"You call ignoring or partaking of the plans to hurt Conner being loyal? All right. You claim to be loyal to the one who pays your wages. I can pay you more money than you would make in a year riding for Charles. Stop them and name your price."

His face took on a stubborn cast. "Don't expect you to understand, being you're a woman and all. Just set quiet. I ain't gonna let them hurt you."

I am not worried about myself, but Conner, you fool! She could not say this to him. He believed the lies that Dacus had told him about Conner. She could not.

"Who is the other man?" she asked him.

"Webb Fulton. Him and Dacus are tighter than a cow and its hide. Dacus saved his life. Webb'll do anything Dacus tells him."

"Such loyalty should be commended but somehow is less than reassuring." Her sarcasm made no impression on Dillion.

Conner heard the whispered conversation going on behind him. He didn't dare turn around and blister Belinda the way his tongue burned to do. She had managed to split them up. Now he had to worry about Dillion behind him.

The man whispering to Dacus was the half-breed that Logan had told him about. He had ridden with the outlaws, robbing their mines. Pity that Logan hadn't killed him. Billy Jack Mulero, a mixed breed of Mexican, Apache and white, was as vicious as any the territory had bred. Conner carefully searched for a sign that he'd been chewing mescal. Logan had warned him that when he had the powerful drug in him, Billy Jack got wild and unpredictable. But his scrutiny revealed no bloodshot eyes or fitful moves, sure indicators.

Billy Jack not only relished taunting, especially when he had others with him, he had a fondness for women. Jessie had been one of his victims, saved from rape only because he'd cornered her in a mercantile, not out in the open. *Like here.*

His stomach hollowed at the thought of Belinda being at his mercy. Dacus laughed at whatever Billy Jack said. Conner didn't dare move closer as he cursed his luck that the unpredictable man was back in Riverton's pay.

He knew what it felt like to be between a rock and a hard place. They wouldn't kill him, not unless they planned to kill Belinda, too. But from the look of the two of them, he was going to end up hurting. If he opened fire, he'd get two of them. But he would put Belinda at risk of taking a stray bullet from Webb, before Conner got off another shot.

And there was Dillion . . . the wild card in a stacked deck.

Conner started backing up. He cocked the rifle.

"While you're jawin', he's gonna make his move," Webb yelled. He spurred his horse forward to cut off Conner's retreat. To enforce his move, he drew his gun. "I say we shoot the bastard an' be done with it." Webb shot a look at Belinda. "She ain't gonna talk. Not if she knows what'll happen to her."

"And who's gonna tell her? You, Webb?"

"You won't be talkin' so big, lawman, when we get done with you."

"I figure the way Dacus is going, I'll likely die of boredom right where I'm standing." Dillion's horse started to lip Conner's skin. He shoved the animal's curious nose away just hard enough that the horse pranced back a few steps.

"Conner?" Belinda murmured.

"When I fire, move."

"What are you telling her, Kincaid?" Dillion demanded. He walked his horse forward until Conner was forced to move away from the buckboard.

"Kincaid ain't gonna die of boredom. Billy Jack's convinced me he's got a right to Kincaid. His *amigos* are rotting in prison because of Kincaid and his damn interfering brothers." Dacus looked at Billy Jack and grinned. "He's all yours."

While Dacus talked, Billy Jack had uncoiled the rope that hung from his saddle. "It is beautiful, *sí?* By my own hand came my *reata*. In my country, *señorita,* the *vaquero* must be skilled with his *reata*." He shook out the loop. "It will give me great pleasure to see this lawman run for me."

"You heard him, Kincaid." Dacus spurred his horse closer to cut off any chance of Conner's retreating to the trees. "Drop your shooting irons and start running."

"Stop them, damn you!" Belinda cried out. She was close enough to grab hold of Dillion's arm. "Did you hear me?" she demanded, panic filling her voice. "I'll pay you five thousand dollars." She shot a frantic look at Conner. He was maneuvering away from the buckboard, but Webb and Dacus kept pace with him. Why was he not shooting at them?

"Ten thousand, Dillion. Twenty thousand," she offered in the next breath. The young cowhand wasn't responding to her. Money was the only weapon she had to help Conner, but for the second time in her life, Belinda found a man immune to bribery. What was an admirable trait in Conner, she cursed in Dillion.

She nudged the edge of her reticule with the toe of her shoe. Desperate to do something to help Conner, she slid to the edge of the seat, and, keeping an eye on Dillion, who was closest to her, she leaned over to pick it up. Cringing at Billy Jack's taunts of what he was going to do to Conner, she tried yanking the drawstring open with one hand.

"Don't get any ideas of using that tiny peashooter, Miss Jarvis. You'll end up hurt."

"How did you know?"

"Mrs. Dobbs told the boss she found it in your room. Best hand it over to me."

"Like hell I will!"

"Then toss your fancy bag in the back of the buckboard. That way you won't hurt anyone, and no one hurts you."

Belinda swore under her breath. Dillion faced away from her as if she were no longer a threat. The string was tangled and she left it on the seat. Still watching Dillion, she eased the pole brake forward. She offered a quick prayer that Dillion paid no attention to her now.

Billy Jack swung the wide loop of his rope back and forth. His voice had taken on a singsong quality as he taunted Conner in a mixture of liquid Spanish, English and another, guttural language. In horror, Belinda listened to his regretful indecisiveness of whether to hang Conner or drag him behind his horse.

She knew Conner had to make a move soon. Her timing had to be perfect to get away. This time she would obey him.

Nerves stretched tight with tension, Conner watched Billy Jack's eyes. He closed out the sound of his voice. He knew firsthand what skilled hands and a rope could do. But he watched his eyes, for that is where he'd have his clue to Billy Jack's move on him.

Saddle leather creaked with a shift of Dacus's body at Conner's side. The three men were avidly watching and listening to the half-breed as he continued to toy with the rope.

Within the cradle of his arms holding the rifle, Conner tightened his finger on the trigger. Shooting was no longer a choice. He had to cling to the hope that Belinda whipped those horses the moment he fired, or had the sense to duck beneath the seat so she wouldn't get shot.

He wanted to warn her to be ready. Wanted to kiss her lips for luck. Wanted to take time back and wish her safe at his home.

Billy Jack stopped talking.

His gaze locked with Conner's.

A second later, Conner dropped to the ground, rolled over and fired.

When the shots exploded from Conner's rifle, Belinda slapped the reins against the horses' backs, better prepared this time for the sudden lurch as the horses raced out of the clearing.

Dacus slumped forward. He grabbed his mount's neck to keep himself in the saddle. He screamed when Conner's second bullet ripped into the same shoulder the first bullet had grazed.

"Get that bastard and kill him," Dacus yelled. He didn't give a damn about the boss's orders to wait. He'd find a way to make this unexpected chance to get Kincaid and the woman work for him. "Go after her," he ordered Webb and Dillion.

They took off at flat-out runs to chase the runaway buckboard.

That left Conner and the crazy Billy Jack.

Chapter Fifteen

Conner fired at Billy Jack, but he moved in the saddle like water flowing over rock, spurring his horse to circle behind Conner. The ever-threatening rope still swung at his side.

Without the buckboard in the way, Conner had freedom to dodge the first throw of the rope.

Dacus let loose a string of curses, charging his horse at Conner.

Conner fired again, missed Dacus and levered another bullet into the chamber. He darted one way, then spun and ran to avoid the rope and Dacus's repeated charging.

Safety waited for Conner if he could back up to the massive cottonwood trees. Billy Jack's rope would tangle in the branches if he attempted to lasso him.

Dacus was shrewd. He had already figured out what Conner attempted to do. He kept his cutting horse on a short rein. The animal had won him plenty of gold dollars on payday because of the horse's ability to wheel and turn right on one of those shiny gold pieces. The animal's sharp maneuvers kept Conner from gaining the trees.

Conner didn't know how much longer he could keep this up. He tried to block his worry about Belinda. The image of her wouldn't leave him.

The momentary distraction allowed Dacus to come up behind him and land a vicious kick to Conner's lower back. Conner spun around to fire again. The repeating rifle was empty.

The ramrod charged him again. Conner used the rifle like a club. He landed a solid blow on Dacus's good arm. The whir of the rope warned him. Conner ducked and dropped to one knee, ripping off the rope that Billy Jack had thrown before the breed could pull it taut.

Dacus's showy paint barreled into Conner, knocking him off balance. The ramrod grabbed for the rifle. Conner released the gun. Despite his leather gloves, Dacus cried out when his hand closed over the hot metal of the barrel.

Occupied with Dacus, Conner was left vulnerable. It was all Billy Jack needed. He rode in close, his throw short, but he and Dacus had Conner squeezed between their horses.

Dacus slammed the rifle butt into Conner's shoulder. Billy Jack kicked his boot free of the stirrup. He backed his horse up a few steps and used the sharply pointed rowel end of the spur in a raking motion across Conner's bare belly.

Conner grabbed for the boot. Dacus hit him again with the rifle, sending Conner to his knees.

Their muttered swearing came to Conner from a distance. His vision blurred. His breath labored from pain. He brought up a hand covered with blood…his blood.

The whirring sound of the rope warned Conner. He struggled to his feet, swaying as pain spread from the blows he'd taken and the long bleeding furrow that marked him. Shaking his head to clear his vision, he still saw a double of Billy Jack riding toward him. Conner ducked to the side. The bite of the rope settling around his body, locking his arms at his sides, told him he'd made the wrong move.

"Ride him, hombre," Dacus muttered. He swayed in the saddle cradling his doubly wounded arm. "Ride the bastard to hell and gone. When you finish him off, meet me back at the ranch."

Those were the last words Conner heard. The rope tightened and his feet flew out from under him. Conner hit the ground with a bone-jarring thud. The breath was knocked from him. He barely managed to get his hands around the rope.

Billy Jack, shouting a wild Apache yell, set his wicked spurs against the horse's sides. The animal reared, whinnying at the pain, then bolted, dragging Conner behind his flying hooves.

Conner's world shriveled to one of pain.

Belinda barely kept her seat. The horses had taken the bits between their teeth, racing along the uneven ground with jarring results. Flecks of sweat flew from the horses and hit her repeatedly.

Behind her still thundered the sounds of pursuit. She had prayed that the two horsemen would give up the chase.

She tried not to let panic take hold, but fear of what was happening to Conner, once the echoes of firing faded, brought a stomach-clenching terror to the surface.

Wind whipped her hair. She tasted bile. She could not summon a clear thought when she desperately needed to form a plan.

Every bump of the wheels threatened to topple her from her precarious position. She heard someone shouting at her, but could not make sense of the words. Racing along at neck-breaking speed, she racked her memory for the map she had copied faithfully, diligently recording every painstaking detail.

But even as she recalled a rough idea of the layout of Kincaid property abutting Riverton's, the landmarks, if there were any, passed by her in a blur. She had no clue to where she was.

She was lost, hopelessly lost, in a barren land filled with rocks and brush that threatened to overturn the buckboard with every passing second.

But you are not lost. All you have to do is slow the horses, let them catch up with you. Dillion promised he would not let them hurt you.

No!

They will take you back to where Conner is.

I cannot trust him. Not anyone. But the devil's nagging battered her resolve.

She could not summon hope of rescue. Nor could she scream. There was not enough moisture in her mouth or parched throat.

And she knew there was no one to hear her.

Suddenly she saw that both Dillion and Webb rode on either side of the buckboard. They were keeping pace with her, but they used the long ends of their reins as whips to spur the horses to greater speed than her team.

Trapped, she felt a silent scream well up. She had no experience to draw upon to help her. All she could do was cling to her determination not to be caught by them.

Conner, she knew, would never forgive her.

If he still lived . . .

Dillion pulled ahead of the buckboard's bed, leaning out to the side from his saddle. He tried to grab the reins from her.

Belinda's arms, shoulders and back burned painfully from the effort she made to saw back on the reins to turn the team into the path of Dillion's horse. He would have to veer away to avoid a headlong spill.

She felt her team's maddened pace slowing. And with it, her strength ebbed. She willed the horses to hurry and complete the turn. Conner's warning of what they would do to her drummed in her mind.

A loud crack sounded.

Belinda's first thought was a shot. The next moment she understood it had come from the buckboard. The rear wheel hit a sizable rock. She slid sideways on the seat, slammed against the backrest. The reins ripped free of her grip. Pain seared her palms. She scrambled to hang on to the seat, anything she could grab. Her tangled hair blinded her. The cracked wheel hit another rock and shattered, tilting the buckboard. Thrown off balance, Belinda found the breath to scream. The team gamely dragged the buckboard. Belinda fell forward and hit her head. She lost her grip, felt herself sliding but could not stop her fall.

Webb had cut off the buckboard's team, slowing their pace, when he saw it was too late. The woman tumbled out of the seat and lay sprawled on the ground. Dillion was already off his horse, running toward her when Webb yelled at him.

"Leave her!"

"She might not be dead." Dillion had stopped to stare in disbelief as Webb rode to where he stood. "You're crazy if you think I'm gonna leave her for the buzzards."

"Think about saving your own skin. The Kincaids'll come looking for them. This ain't the way it was planned, but the result is the same."

"What the hell are you jawing about, Webb?"

"This is what the boss wanted. Her dead, and Kincaid blamed for it. Let's get back. I need to tell Dacus what happened. We'll come back an' dump Kincaid near her."

"Riverton wanted her dead?"

"That's what I said. I don't draw wages to ask questions. Mount up, boy. We're goin' back."

"I ain't leaving—"

"Then I'll send you to push grass up from the other side." Webb reinforced his threat with his drawn gun. "Don't make me shoot you, boy. Orders are orders. You don't like 'em, pack your war bag an' draw your wages. There's plenty more who'll ride for Riverton."

Dillion eyed the gun, then looked up into Webb's eyes. He had no doubt the man would shoot him where he stood.

"Calm down, Webb. Just calm down. I ain't aiming to get myself killed. I'll ride with you." He threw a last, regretful look at where Belinda lay so still. "Don't make a lick of sense to me," he muttered, grabbing hold of his reins. The horse danced around in a half circle while he managed to get his boot in the stirrup. "I could've sworn the boss wanted to marry the lady."

So could I. Belinda's thought remained just that. She lay still, eyes closed, stunned from her fall. Listening to them ride away, she knew she should move. But the shock of hearing that Charles wanted her dead left her numb with a chilling fear. Why? Her death gained him nothing. Only Albert would benefit... Albert?

Could Albert and Charles conspire to kill her?

"Conner." His name escaped her lips as a moan, and a plea. He had tried to warn her about Charles. She turned to her side, wincing as a sharply pointed rock dug into her hip. She felt a mass of aching bruises and pain. *Move.* But when Belinda opened her eyes, the sky swirled above her.

You will not panic. You will not faint. This will pass. The sane voice of reason helped steady her. She rested, waiting, and hid from the pain messages her body sent, hid from the terrifying thoughts of what had happened to Conner.

"I will not die," she whispered. "Albert and Charles will pay. I swear they will."

Brave words. They were all she had. Her money meant nothing in a land where lizards and snakes reigned. Her social position would not help her stand and find Conner.

A dark well drew her toward it. Belinda fought not to give in to the siren's call. She had to rouse herself. She had to move.

Time ceased. She thought she heard Conner calling her. Impossible. They were going to kill Conner.

Whoso sheddeth man's blood, by man shall his blood be shed. Some preacher had read the words from his Bible. Conner knew it wasn't man who had shed Billy Jack's blood, but his horse. Blessings for him. The animal bled from his heaving sides where the rowels had cut his hide one time too many. Conner still wasn't sure how or when the horse had thrown the half-breed. But he would never forget hearing the man's neck snap when he fell.

As soon as he could breathe without pain, he'd say a prayer. And then he'd get rid of the rope around him.

He assessed the damage to his body. Nauseated, giddy from loss of blood, every twitch of his body had him believing there wasn't a bone that hadn't been splintered in the minutes he'd been dragged behind the horse.

Pain intensified. It interfered with his thinking clearly. Conner dragged his head up. A wavering vision of the roan, standing quietly, watching him, dived in and out. Pain smothered thought.

''Belinda.'' Her name fell from his lips, plea and moan. He tried to focus on her, knowing he had to help her.

He forced himself to his knees, an appalling feat of will, for the crushing agony tore at his mind and a black oblivion whispered enticingly to give in. He yanked the rope off, swallowing a scream. He called Belinda's name again, a frantic sense of panic evoking another cry to her, for her, Conner no longer knew. With unknown dread, her name hovered in the pain-racked corner of his mind.

''Got to get . . .'' *Save your strength.*

Panting, he held himself on his knees, his head down, drawing in great labored gasps of air, absently watching the blood dripping from his chest and belly.

He shook his head to clear his vision and forced himself to think.

The Lord watched over fools. He'd also blessed him with a horse and, if he could crawl, he'd have Billy Jack's gun.

Conner grunted deep in his throat. The pain swamped him. He compelled himself to move. He had to find Belinda. But he remained on all fours, swaying back and forth, then rocking when agony hit in a fresh wave. He clenched his teeth against the shock.

Time had no meaning. He didn't know how long he stayed that way before he found the energy to crawl. Spasms dragged along nerve ends, forcing him to stop until he controlled the shuddering.

He had to stop thinking about pain. He *had* to. Drawing his mind to Belinda, to the time before the attack, and keeping his thoughts firmly on his eager, generous lover, Conner forgot the sweat that poured profusely as his body fought shock and his formidable strength of will held off the darkness.

His progress was measured in the inches he crawled. He could see a looming boulder, his goal, his means to stand.

Move or you'll die right here. Just move. Again. And yet again.

When Conner's strength was about to quit, guilt, battering to be free, rushed to fill his mind and spurred his effort to stand.

Guilt over lingering with Belinda. If he hadn't encouraged her they would have been at the ranch…she safe, and him still curious. Too high a price, that damn curiosity.

As guilt quit aiding him, he opened his mind to the shame that hid there. He'd let them beat him. He'd let them take an innocent woman. *Hell of a lawman. Hell of a man,* a devil's voice goaded. *Quit and they win.*

Where was she? What had they done to her?

That spoiled Eastern darling. Disobeying his order. Telling him she couldn't leave him. Damn her! Damn her!

Conner thought he blacked out. He came to, smelling fear. His own.

"Belinda." Her name was a weak cry. His heart beat so thunderously he could taste the drumming in his mouth. The sound filled his ears. He called every spirit he could recall from Indian tales, he prayed to God and nearly jumped out of his skin when he felt the warm, questing breath of the horse touch his shoulder. He turned to the animal, grabbing hold of the bridle, inching along until he clung to the saddle horn. The canteen butted his chest.

He struggled to force his fingers to uncap the canteen. Warm water dribbled down his throat, dripping on his chest, but he tasted life, better than brandy, more than quenching his thirst. The simple act of drinking water lent him hope that he was going to survive this and get on the horse to find Belinda.

His hand closing over the rifle stock jutting from the leather scabbard on the other side of the saddle sent a fresh burst of strength into him.

He'd find Belinda, then they'd pay with their lives for hurting her.

He felt cold as he hauled himself into the saddle, a chilled-to-the-marrow cold that filled him with icy rage. He drew out the rifle, resting it across his thighs, not knowing if he'd be able to lift and fire it. Conner tangled his free hand into the long mane. As he did so, a boiling tide of anger rose, building in momentum to a violence he had never before experienced.

His family joked about his legendary temper and what happened when he lost it. No one, starting with Riverton and ending with every man he'd hired, would be laughing when he was done.

Conner gently pressed his knees against the horse's sides. It was in the Lord's hands if the animal threw him, too.

At first he whispered sounds more than words, then promised apples and grain and hay and pasture in an unbroken supplication to soothe the animal.

He snarled the second the horse nervously pranced in place, then moved out at an easy canter.

Conner never looked at the body he left behind. Billy Jack would have done the same for him.

And he needed to search for signs of Dacus and the other men as he rode back to find Belinda.

Chapter Sixteen

Within an hour of Phillip Jarvis's unexpected arrival, the Kincaids' concern with Conner's delay turned to worry. It was left to Macaria to welcome him. She had seen the admiration in his eyes each time he looked at her. At another time, Macaria would have pursued the mutual attraction. Now she had to stop him from arguing with Logan as he handed out rifles to the search party.

"I don't give a damn if you're her uncle. You ain't riding with us," Logan insisted. Now that he had settled on a course of action, he had no time to waste on Belinda's uncle.

"It seems you've stepped into Conner's boot real nice, Logan," Ty commented, grinning as he slapped his brother's shoulder. "You sound just like him at his most arrogant."

Logan grunted in reply, then tossed rifles from the gun cabinet in the office to Ty. He in turn passed them out to Hazer, Blue Dalton, Moddy Helms and Glenn Casey. Large as the room was, it was crowded now. Logan took out a rifle for himself.

"You have not given the new repeating rifles to my son, Raphael, and Enrique?" Santo asked. He had hobbled into the room on crutches the moment he had learned there was cause for concern. His broken ankle was healing rapidly, but Santo knew this was one time he could not ride with the men he had raised like his sons.

Logan shot a quick look at Ty, then at his mother. "I want Raphael and Enrique to stay here at the house with you, Santo. They can be your legs if the rest of the men need to be rallied. I wouldn't put it past Riverton to ride on us."

What Logan didn't say, couldn't say to the man who had been like a father, was the distrust he held for both Raphael and Enrique. The trouble with cattle-rustling had started soon after Raphael brought Enrique to work for them. Logan knew it would break Santo's and Sofia's hearts to know their son was suspected of betraying the Kincaids to Riverton.

"No one will question Logan's orders," Macaria said, regal in posture and bearing as she came to stand beside her middle son. She lifted her worried gaze to his face. "No one but your mother may do so. Allow Phillip—"

"No, *Madre.* I can't watch out for him. You heard what Casey said, shooting down by Ouajaia Creek. Maybe it has something to do with Conner being delayed, and maybe it doesn't. I can't imagine why Conner would be anywhere near there. I'm not taking chances by hauling some pilgrim along while I find out."

"Macaria," Phillip said softly, "do not beg for me."

"Since when did you and my mother get cozy enough to use first names?"

"Logan! You will not question me, my son."

"Nor I," Phillip added in that same soft tone, but a hard look at Logan conveyed the message that he meant it.

"I don't have time to hear this," Logan declared, but his mother's hand gripping his arm said otherwise. He didn't like the way Phillip stood alongside his mother, nor did he understand why she allowed it. Phillip's black boots gleamed, his black box suit, white shirt and string tie made his dress the most formal of the men gathered in the room. He was as tall as Logan, slimmer in build, his craggy features tanned in a face framed by black hair threaded with gray.

"Logan, I realize my unexpected arrival at this time is not something you wish to deal with, but I am as worried about my missing niece as you are about your brother. I insist you allow me to accompany you. And I assure you," Phillip said, leveling a hard, steady look from almost black eyes, "I am well versed in the use of firearms."

"Well versed in firearms? What'd ya do...shoot ducks on Lake Michigan?"

"Logan! I have taught you better than to insult a guest in my home."

"*Sí, Madre.* Jeez, listen to him," Logan muttered, disregarding every politeness his mother and Sofia had drummed into him. He turned aside and opened the large drawer of the cabinet to remove boxes of cartridges.

Phillip leaned over and took one for himself. "Ah, .44-40 center fire. Good. I shall be able to use these as extra ammunition for my Colt." He opened the two buttons of his box-style black jacket, pushing the material behind the holstered gun belted around his hip.

"I didn't know you were carrying—"

"I shall recommend my tailor, if you'd like. Even a city like Chicago can be dangerous to traverse at night."

"Fine. You got a weapon. But—"

"Don't worry, Logan," Phillip interrupted again, then smiled. "I do know how to use it for more than shooting ducks in a lake. I rode with the First Illinois Sharpshooters under Brigadier General Jacob Ammen during the war until a bullet curtailed my military career."

Logan didn't have any more time to argue with him. He didn't like giving in, but he couldn't refuse his mother's silent plea. He offered a curt nod of acceptance and moved to where his Jessie waited.

"Hey, sunshine, keep those rascals close to the house. I don't want you chasing after them. You're too precious to me."

Jessie nodded, her expression solemn. "Keep your head down, outlaw. I don't want anything to happen to make you forget your promises." Her smile was forced, but then so was Logan's as he looked away. Hidden by Jessie's skirt, his fingers entwined with hers.

"Listen up. I want you men to understand that there will be no quarter given if Riverton's men attacked Conner."

The men didn't murmur assent. Their eyes, hard and bright with the promise of violence, spoke for them.

Macaria held Logan briefly. Touching his cheek, she whispered, "Go with God, my son." She moved away, going to Ty to whisper the same to him.

Logan gave Jessie a quick, hard kiss, then looked at his boys. They quickly came to stand with them.

"Kenny, you're near a grown man. I'm trusting you to keep Jessie and Marty safe for me."

"Ah, jeez, let me come with you. You know I can help. I was with you with those outlaws and—"

"And I remember nearly losing you, son." He leaned over, his tone confessional. "Jessie'd have my hide to tan if anything happened to you. It's a man's responsibility to care for those he loves. You're my oldest boy," Logan said with pride, "and the responsibility is yours when I'm not here."

"All right."

It was a grudgingly given agreement, but Logan took what he could. He wouldn't embarrass Kenny with a hug, but he squeezed his shoulder before he hunkered down in front of Marty.

"You promise me to obey everyone bigger than you?"

"I p-promise. You promise me you w-won't let them hurt Conner?"

"'Course he promises," Kenny answered for Logan. "His word's good as any pa's."

That was his Kenny, Logan thought, heart-punching a man when he least expected it. "Kenny's right. No one's gonna get hurt. Now give me a hug for luck."

Marty flung his skinny arms around Logan's neck and whispered, "Conner was gonna bring me my badge today."

"And you'll have it from him." The guilt feelings over his fight with Conner and parting in anger could not be held at bay any longer. Logan welcomed the stinging reminder they brought. It was another spur to make sure his brother would be found. *No matter what it took.* Logan rose to his feet with Marty in his arms. "Remember, no sneaking off." He set the boy down next to Kenny, who immediately put his hand on Marty's shoulder in imitation of Logan.

"Ty."

They all turned to face the doorway where Dixie stood, Sofia beside her. Macaria broke off her whispered conversation with Phillip.

"I told you to rest," Ty said, striding across the room to his wife. He handed the rifle to Sofia and took Dixie in his arms. She was warm and sleepy eyed. A close hug wasn't possible, so he stepped to the side, resting his hip against hers. His hand caressed her distended belly.

"Angel, don't you ever listen to me? You need to take care of yourself and our little one. And don't," he murmured in her ear, "dare have this baby without me." Like his brother, Ty gave his wife a quick, hard kiss.

Dixie cupped his cheek. "Remember that I love you. Come home safe to me. As for the baby—" she glanced down to pat her tummy "—I hope your order to wait was heard."

"Bet on it, love."

Ty turned to call Logan, his throat closing with emotion when he glanced back at his wife's eyes. He feared this latest upset would bring on her labor.

Ty took his rifle from Sofia. "I leave her in your good hands."

"*Sí, corderito,* I watch her and the *bebé.*"

He shook his head, then smiled, as Sofia had meant for him to do when she called him lamb, her childhood nickname for him. Seeing the smile widen on Dixie's lips, he kissed the old woman's cheek and whispered his thanks.

"Where's Rosanna? She's the only one missing."

"Ah, that one," Sofia answered, shrugging. "She is here, then she is gone. You go with all our prayers."

"Then let's ride. Logan." Ty's gaze fell on two sullen faces—Enrique's and Raphael's. It was all he could do to turn away when he longed to take the two of them behind the barn and beat the truth out of them.

He spun on his heels and walked down the hall. The men filed out after Ty, Logan in the lead, Phillip bringing up the rear.

Macaria hesitated, then went after them.

In front of the house, Jed Henley, one of the old-time hands, stood with the horses. "Handpicked each an' every one of 'em," he told Logan.

"They look good, Henley."

"Phillip," Macaria said, as the others began to mount. "Wait a moment, please." She beckoned him away from the others.

"Will you send me off with good wishes and a kiss, too, Macaria?"

"This is not why—"

"Don't ask me to stay now."

"No, it is not of this I wish to speak to you. I . . ." She chided herself for hesitating, but his dark eyes staring into her own made her forget the words. She had to look away to say her piece. "This has been a shock for you, to come so far to find your lovely niece missing from Charles's, then coming here to discover that she never arrived for her visit with the child."

"He is my great-nephew, Macaria. Marty, as you call him, is a miniature replica of his father, Robert."

"We do not dispute this." Eyes flashing, Macaria's regal manner came into play. "There are the child's feelings to consider before a decision of what to do can be reached. We love the boy."

"I see for myself how much, but—"

"But you distract me. I wished you to know that you must not place blame on my eldest son, Conner. He is a man of honor, one who would give his life to protect someone entrusted to his care. Conner is like our ironwood trees, hard and strong. If Charles has betrayed my friendship and past feelings for him and hurt my son or your niece, he will pay. If Conner breathes, he will make Charles pay."

"An admirable man, your son. I shall look forward to meeting him. But there is something you must understand, Macaria." He took her hands within his, holding them and ignoring the question in her eyes.

"Charles is my longtime friend. If there is any paying to be done, Charles will pay me first. My nephew Albert disappeared from Chicago a few weeks after Belinda began her travels to find the boy. I had to follow Albert.

"Belinda is unaware that Charles and Albert have been communicating for some time. I should've warned her instead of thinking I would find him first. I sent her here, to Charles, believing she would be safe with him. But the letters I discovered written between them alarmed me. Belinda tried to warn me about Albert. I wouldn't listen to her. Now, my disregard of her strong feelings may have put her life in danger."

"We do not know this, Phillip. There is hope. Always there is hope."

Phillip shot a quick look over his shoulder, hearing a low-voiced taunt from Logan. "Your son scowls at me for delaying them."

"Then I send you off with the same words I gave my sons. Go with God, Phillip."

"Hey, pilgrim," Logan yelled, annoyance tinged with a growing anger in his voice. "We're riding now." He suited action to word, neck-reining his horse toward the open gates. "Henley, bar them after us. No one is to leave here, understood."

"I'll be up in the tower myself to make sure of that," the man replied.

Phillip cast Macaria a last look, then mounted the fresh horse and followed the others out of the wooden gates set in the adobe walls that surrounded the house and outbuildings.

Logan turned to see that Phillip had indeed joined them. He looked at Ty, riding alongside him. "I'll have a talk with him when we get back."

"We'll both have a talk with him. But let's choose our words carefully, brother. Ma wasn't exactly making sheep eyes at him but that may be due to being worried about Conner.

"She's gonna be a grandmother, for pity's sake."

"Come to think of it, Logan, Ma ain't that old."

Logan looked forward. "We can always turn Conner loose on him."

Ty laughed, softly though, thinking of Conner's anger and disbelief when their mother informed him that Charles had once courted her and planned on doing so again. But the laughter quickly faded.

"First, Logan, we need to find Conner."

As one, they spurred their horses into a ground-eating pace. The others followed suit.

All but Phillip. He raced his horse at a flat-out run until he drew even with the Kincaid brothers.

The two of them, Logan and Ty, shot the man intense, hard looks, but Phillip's grim demeanor warned that he would not tolerate staying behind the pack.

Logan shrugged, tugged his hat brim down low and concentrated on the task at hand. Ty mimicked his brother's moves, and settled deep in the saddle.

Phillip's lips broke into a brief smile. Grudgingly given, it was still acceptance of his place to ride in front with them.

Nearly an hour and a half later, they approached Ouajaia Creek, which lay at the far boundary of the ranch, close to Riverton's property. Logan had not raised the question of why his brother Conner would have taken this route, it wasn't the most direct way to get to the main house. He recalled how hard his brother had tried to convince him that he didn't find Belinda Jarvis attractive. *Damn you, if all this was your dallying with some woman.*

But the itch at the back of his neck—a sure warning of trouble—gave lie to his thought about Conner.

Logan ordered a lower pace as they neared the area, then halted the group before they rode for the shade under the big cottonwood trees.

"Ty, you and Hazer read what happened here, before we churn up the ground."

"Let Ty do it alone," Hazer said, reaching for his canteen. "Santo taught him as well as he did me. Ty's eyes are a hell of a lot younger than mine." His gaze locked with Logan's, then shifted to Ty. "We don't want any mistakes."

Logan removed his short-crowned Stetson, wiped the sweat from his forehead and resettled his hat on his head, all the while he looked at the ground. He heard the sounds of canteens being uncapped. The hazy af-

ternoon sun showed no mercy in relieving the stifling
heat.

"Ty—"

"I'm gone." Ty slid from his saddle, then started
walking a slow circle well back for the trees. He went
down to the creek, squatting to study the muddy bank,
then rose to begin quartering the area. Neck bent, eyes
cast to the ground, Ty moved slowly.

Impatience marked the cast of Phillip's features,
but he remained silent. Not so Logan.

"Talk to me, little brother. I've got an itch that
wants scratching real bad."

"The buckboard came in here. Set for a spell." Ty
hunkered down in the thick grass. He didn't see the
need to tell anyone that the crushed grass he ran his
fingertips over had come from cloth pressed by a
heavy weight. It didn't take the sense of a week-old
kitten to figure out that Conner and his society lady
had found a way to communicate after all.

He stood up, avoided looking at Logan and continued. "Three or four riders. Kinda hard to tell, the
earth's pretty tore up. I can't swear that our buckboard was here, it could've been someone else driving
a wagon without weight. But if I had to guess, I'd say
Conner stopped here. It's funny about the way the
ground's tore up. Almost as if a horse was racing and
turning—"

"Like a cutting horse?" Casey asked.

"Yeah. Just so. That doesn't make sense. But I'd
bet money there's been some kind of a scuffle here."

Ty bent over and picked up a small object between
his thumb and forefinger. "Lady's hairpin," he said,
walking over to show Logan.

When Ty stood next to his brother's horse, he held his open palm up to him. "What do you make of that?"

"Blood, Ty?"

"That's what I figured. Damn it!" Ty looked away. The angle at which he stood gave him a clear view of the furrow of flattened grass. "Logan," he said very softly, waiting until his brother directed his gaze to what Ty saw.

"Something dragged?"

"What the devil are the two of you whispering about?" Phillip demanded. "Remember, my niece is supposedly with your brother, although how anyone could mistake an old Mexican man for—"

"Conner's the sheriff and there's bad blood between him and Riverton."

While Logan continued to explain to Phillip, Ty started to follow the furrow, careful to walk along the edge of it. Several times he bent down and picked up something, until he was satisfied and returned.

"Whatever was dragged behind a horse was bleeding." Holding up long, thin reddish hairs, he showed them to each man, then to Logan. "What do you make of these?"

"Horse or human. If it's horse, could be from a roan's mane or tail."

"Yeah, but look at the way the hairs curl. Don't know many men who braid their horses' tails or manes. Now if they were weaving a rope—"

"A hair rope?"

"Logan, I don't know what else it's from. Found them by the furrow." Ty glanced at the other men. "Any of you know who braids rope from horsehair? Seen any of Riverton's men with one?"

"There was a fella over at Rosie's saloon when I was in the other day," Hazer said, kneeing his horse to move closer to the brothers. "A mean-looking breed. Bragged he could lasso anything with his *reata*. Claimed he made it himself. Didn't ever say he worked for Riverton."

"Half-breed, Hazer?" Logan asked, thoughtful.

"Sure looked like one. A little 'Pache, Mex and white. Don't see many in these parts. Leastways I ain't seen one in Sweetwater before this."

Billy Jack. The name popped into Logan's mind and wedged deep. His gut instinct said he'd come back.... *I should've killed him when I had the chance.*

"What makes you sure they didn't hang the man?" Phillip asked. "Those trees would be a temptation if men—"

"I'll look." Ty stepped away, his head tilted back, searching the branches for any visible torn bark. He got a cold knot in his stomach thinking about Conner and a rope and Riverton's men.

"Hazer," Ty called.

"I'm already there, Ty. Don't look like one of these was used for hanging. Not recently."

Shaking his head, Ty walked back and mounted. He waited for Logan to make a decision.

He didn't wait long.

"We'll split up. Ty, you take Moddy, Blue and Casey with you. Follow that rope trail. We'll ride after the buckboard tracks. Three spaced shots means you found something. We'll do the same."

Logan looked at Phillip. He gave the man points for not questioning him seven ways to Sunday. "You stay close to Hazer and, before you get your back up, understand that it's for your protection. I don't know what we'll find waiting for us. You don't know the land, and Hazer can ride it blindfolded." Logan hesitated, then added, "That all right?"

"You're the man giving the orders, ride on."

They did, with their rifles across their thighs, eyes peeled for trouble.

Chapter Seventeen

A hot, stiff wind blew down through the flat, and Belinda turned her face from its furnacelike blast. She swayed on her feet, stubbornly working another strap of the buckboard's traces free from the horse. A large pair of birds circled above her, gliding on the wind currents. She did not look at them often, fearing they were buzzards and not hawks.

Finding Conner was her only thought. She had stopped thinking about water minutes or hours ago. She was numb to pain. Her breath sounded ragged in her ears against the utter solitude of the empty land about her.

"Damn you!" Once again her fingers slipped from the leather, the small cuts bleeding freely. Her head fell forward and she rested it against the warm, broad animal's side, too exhausted to cry. Drums beat in her head, at least she thought they sounded like drums. Rolling her head from side to side, she moaned as the pounding continued.

Belinda did not know how long she stood there, staring without focus. At first, the shadow cast on the land that fell across her narrow range of vision did not penetrate her dulled senses. She thought it a mirage.

She had seen a few in her travels when the heat waves danced between ground and sky. But there was something about this shadow that forced her to lift her head.

A dark form slowly moved toward her.

"No!" The defiant utterance was louder and more forceful in her mind than in speech. But it rallied her to yank the small derringer from the waistband of her skirt. She was not helpless. Moving proved an effort, but she managed to get to the back of the buckboard where the axle rested on the ground. It was not the best of shelter, but all she had. Crouching there, waiting with labored breath, she gave in to fear again.

More than the thought of buzzards circling above, she had feared that someone would come back for her.

The roan Conner rode whinnied to the placidly standing horses. It roused Conner from his stupor. He had taken a longer, circular route to avoid the creek and the men who might be hunting him. Somehow he guided the horse, always heading in the direction he'd last seen Belinda driving the buckboard.

Despite the aches of his body, Conner sat erect in the saddle. A few times he'd come close to passing out, falling forward over the roan's neck, instantly in agony when his cut and bleeding chest touched the saddle horn.

Seeing the team of horses and the crazy angle of the buckboard sent a fresh surge of fear through him. He'd found something, but he wasn't sure he wanted to ride any closer.

A hoarse cry hovered in the air, sending Belinda to huddle against the side of the buckboard. She could not tell if it was human or animal. One of the team's horses nickered a greeting. She cursed the Fates that had stolen the few more minutes she had needed to have a horse free. She could have been riding for safety, not cowering like a weak-kneed ninny, wondering if she would have the courage to shoot.

The thud of something knocking against the other side of the buckboard made her hold her breath. If she was very still, if she did not breathe...her thought ended abruptly.

The hoarse cry sounded like her name.

Belinda was afraid to hope, that fragile feeling had taken a battering. She closed her eyes and prayed.

The noises—creak of saddle leather, the plod of hooves—came nearer. Her prayer was, of necessity, brief. Yellow was a coward's color, and she had never worn any shade of it well. Cocking the derringer, she gripped the wood edge with her free hand and inched her way upward to peer over the side of the buckboard.

The sight of the lone horseman brought tears to her eyes. "Conner?" she whispered. He turned to look at her. "Oh, my sweet Lord, what did they do to you?"

His upper body was a mass of cuts and bruises. The pants, or what was left of them on the side facing her, were shredded, and she could see more wounds on his skin. She covered her mouth with her hand to stop a scream.

"You're...alive." The two words cost Conner a lot of pain. What he could see of her showed that Belinda had not fared any better than he had. Her shirtwaist, torn and filthy, hung from her shoulders, the sleeves in tatters. A bruise marred her forehead. A ragged piece of lace held her hair away from her face.

She had never looked more beautiful to him. "Alive," he murmured.

"Of course I am. I come from good German stock, Conner."

"If I...if I didn't hurt...I'd laugh."

"Be my guest, Kincaid. I could do with a few laughs."

He eyed the small gun. "Don't...shoot."

"What?" She looked down at the derringer she still held and tucked it into her waistband. "I thought you were one of them coming back."

Ten questions popped into his mind, but the effort to ask them was beyond him at the moment.

"Is there water in that canteen?" She thought he nodded, it was hard to tell, but she moved away from the buckboard to stand at his side and grab hold of the canteen.

"Your hands are all—"

"I've been trying to work the straps loose so I could have a horse to ride." Belinda took a long swallow of the warm water. It was wet and she wished for a barrelful. Not knowing how long it would take to get to the Kincaid ranch, she recapped the canteen.

"Take more."

"No, thank you. Would you like—"

"No."

Belinda was not thinking, her need to touch him took over. She laid her head against his thigh, careful not to press his injured flesh.

Conner felt the heat of her tears. "Don't," he whispered, forcing his hand to release the reins and touch her hair.

With his touch came a torrent of words, telling him what had happened to her, the broken wheel, and the fear for him that had overridden all else.

Conner hated being so helpless. He could only sit there, letting her pour out her fear. He couldn't lift her into his arms and hold her close the way he longed to do. He couldn't get down and press her body close to his, silencing her torrent of terror with kisses that celebrated life and mocked their escape from death. If he got down, he'd never get into the saddle again. He could feel his strength ebb by the moment.

The sobs had quieted, the words at an end, and still Belinda remained as she was, clinging to him. "Conner," she said in a broken, sniffling voice, "I do not want you to die."

"You won't . . . die."

Belinda struggled to lift her head and look up at his face. He misunderstood her. His gray eyes were glazed with pain. She wiped at the tears still bright in her eyes, sniffling and wiping her nose in a most unladylike manner. She was amazed to see what might be a grin on Conner's lips.

He couldn't tell her, but the thought of her unconscious move to wipe her nose and how appalled she would be if he could say something to tease her, did indeed bring a grin to his lips.

"You won't die."

"Not me, you thick-headed lawman. You. I do not want you to die."

"Can't." He swayed slightly. "Got to...get home." He cast a worried look around. The sun would be going down soon, and with it, the heat would be lost. He could feel a chill in his body.

For a few seconds all he wanted to do was revel that she was alive. But he hadn't come looking for her to end up dead if Riverton's men did come back. He still couldn't understand why they'd left her. She had been vague recounting that part of her ordeal. More questions that would have to wait. He had to get them both out of here.

Conner looked at her hands. She'd hurt herself trying to free the horses. He wasn't going to give her any more pain. Gathering what was left of his strength to talk to her, he fought off the black oblivion that beckoned him.

"Listen," he began. "Climb—"

"Don't talk. I can see for myself how much it is hurting you."

He closed his eyes, willing his lovely, stubborn lady to listen and do, without an argument. The Lord smiled. Belinda mutely listened to the haltingly given instructions. She climbed on the precariously tilted buckboard, grabbed his shirt and the poncho, then reluctantly, for the fear of causing him pain made her awkward, she managed to settle herself behind him. She brushed her lips over his skin, then slid the shirt over his shoulders. Lightly and very gently, she smoothed the soft cloth down his back. The poncho was too bulky to set between them, so she wore it.

Conner felt her light kiss and even gentler touches. They humbled him. After all the anguish he had caused her, Belinda still found him worthy of her tender attention. His guilt acted as a barrier against the pain constantly renewing itself.

He made a vow. He'd get her home where she would be safe, then out of his life.

"Conner," she whispered, "I will hurt you if I put my arms around you."

"Do it."

His order had no force behind it. Belinda raised her hands. Wherever she placed them, she would cause him pain.

"Bel—"

"All right." She tucked her fingers into the waistband of his pants. Not the most secure grip, but one that satisfied her.

"You'll fall—"

"I will not. I would not let go of you were we to swim a river, climb a mountain or traverse hell itself." Her firm tone softened when she added, "Take me home, Conner. Take us both home."

Belinda wished she could share with Conner her guilt, which weighed heavily upon her. If she had been stronger, if she had not given in so easily to the intense desire to have Conner for a lover, they both would have been safe.

She had to swallow the sobs burning her throat. Blinking rapidly, she managed to stop the tears again filling her eyes. She was selfish to think of telling him. This was her burden, and hers alone to bear.

Conner had paid with his blood, and she could not even help him. Her skills with injuries extended to using muslin soaked in beaten egg whites to wrap a sprained ankle.

The easy canter of the horse brought twinges to her bruised body that were minor when measured against Conner's tense body shaking with agony caused by every lengthening stride of the animal.

She felt her payment had just begun. Even the pride she had harbored for not crumbling—as so many women of her acquaintance would have—died slowly with every step bringing them closer to his home.

Then shame replaced pride.

His family would soon know that she had not obeyed his first order to leave when he knew there would be trouble. They would all blame her for not riding to them for help. Help that might have prevented some of Conner's injuries. A little devil's voice reminded her that even if she had left him at first, she had no idea where the Kincaid ranch was. Belinda ignored it. She wanted to punish someone for the way Conner was hurting. She was the only one available.

Her grip tightened on his pants. She gazed at the rolling terrain broken by a few red rock outcroppings. An occasional towering saguaro cactus or a clump of the thorny low-growing ocotillo bushes broke the view as they followed a dried-up streambed.

They were both sweating. She wanted to ask Conner how he had managed to get free of Dacus and Billy Jack. What had they done to him? The many cuts and bruises on his body suggested they had beaten him. Such violence was beyond any she had known. And her questions remained unasked. Conner had had enough trouble speaking a few words to her.

She might be a stranger to violent acts, but an icy rage filled her when he could not stifle a groan. Right now, she could shoot those men for what they had done.

All that should matter was Conner—alive and warm, and able to take them home.

But did he blame her?

The growing tension gripping Belinda's body shifted through Conner's layers of pain. The reaction from being terrorized had finally set in. He had believed it too good to be true when she sassed him back at the buckboard, and her complete silence since they had started riding proved to him she realized how badly he had failed to protect her.

His first failure had been forgetting he was a lawman. Hell, he thought, he'd forgotten everything in his desire to have her. Bitterly he recalled something he had always taught his brothers when they were much younger. Please and pleasure a woman and she'll always invite you back to her bed a second time.

He was lucky she still trusted him enough to ride with him. But then, he'd not given her much choice.

He couldn't even blame her for hating him.

And she did blame and hate him, didn't she?

The question burned to be asked. Conner denied himself the pain or the pleasure of her answer.

Thoughts of Belinda had to be put aside. He had to figure the best trail home. The shortest and easiest ride would take them past the creek and eventually Billy Jack's body.

This was a sight he could protect Belinda from seeing, and spare himself the reminder of his shame and failure.

The responsive roan didn't break stride when his light touch guided the horse to a westerly direction. The terrain would be rough, but gentler on her peace of mind.

And his own.

Conner's murmur of home roused Belinda as they climbed a rise and she had her first sight of the sprawling ranch below them. It was a welcome sight to her dulled senses.

"Beautiful," she whispered, knowing it was more. This was the haven they both needed.

Set in open country with a wide, winding stream running past, the grand Spanish-style house was graced with ancient cottonwood trees that offered shelter and shade to those within the thick adobe walls.

Belinda shook off her exhaustion. She gazed at the stream and the dam that created a fair-sized pond. The image of a young boy laughing and swimming there stole into her mind. She smiled at the whimsical thought that it could have been Conner she saw.

Corrals formed an irregular pattern around a long barn. Horses, hides gleaming, tails high and ears pricked forward, raced back and forth in their fenced pastures as they rode by.

She saw the men stop their work, to look, then the whispers turned into shouts.

Conner did not acknowledge them. Belinda felt as if all his concentration was directed at reaching the massive wooden gates set in a high adobe wall.

Her head tilted backward as her gaze tracked the rise of a high windlass, still and silent until the need for water would set it in motion. There was a tower, too, and she spied a man within its open archway. He shouted something, then disappeared.

Men began to gather from the smaller buildings and other corrals. There was an undercurrent of violence to their whisperings as they caught sight of Conner's injuries.

The closer they rode, the more the scent of lemon trees in bloom filled her with a message of comfort and haven to be found within these walls.

Belinda had a feeling that Conner's thought mirrored hers, for the tension seeped from his body as they halted in front of the gates.

She heard the shouting behind the gates grow louder, and moments later both gates swung open to admit them.

She saw Macaria rushing forward.

"*Sangre de Cristo!* What have they done to my son?"

"*Madre*... our guest ..."

Conner slumped forward. His fall was stopped by two young men.

Belinda scooted back to allow them to lift Conner's body from the horse. Macaria followed them as they carried Conner into the house.

"Ma'am, allow me?"

Belinda saw only broad shoulders and a kindly face as the man lifted her to the ground. She straightened her skirt and, when she looked up, a young woman walked rapidly toward her.

"You must be Belinda. I'm Jessie, Logan's wife. Come into the house. We've all been worried about you." Jessie didn't give her a chance to refuse. She gently took her arm, then slid hers around Belinda's waist, murmuring small comfort sounds. At the door, she turned. "Henley, send someone to fetch Logan and Ty. If I know my mother-in-law, she'll want a war council."

"War council?" Belinda asked, wondering where were the accusations that this had been her fault.

"Don't let Macaria's gentle manner fool you," Jessie replied. "She'll demand blood for this outrage against her son. She'd do the same for the others, for any of us that carry the Kincaid name."

At a cry, Jessie looked up. "Rosanna, bring hot water to my room for Belinda. I know your mother will be with Conner."

"And the boy, Marty?"

"He's with Kenny and my sister-in-law Dixie in the garden. Children have a sixth sense when it comes to adult trouble. He'll wait, but he is curious to meet you."

There was that word again—curious. Belinda never wanted to hear it, ever. "I had gifts," she murmured in a distracted manner, for they passed the open doorway to what she assumed was Conner's room. Seeing Macaria bent over him on the bed, Belinda gripped the doorway, wanting to go in but afraid her intrusion would not be welcomed.

Next to Macaria, an older woman stood holding a basin, and behind her, a white-haired man balanced on a pair of crutches while a stream of rapid Spanish flowed back and forth between the three of them.

"That's Santo and his wife, Sofia, with Macaria. It was their son Raphael and their daughter Rosanna's fiancé, Enrique, who carried Conner." Jessie took her hand to urge her to leave.

"Please wait. I must know how Conner is."

It was Santo who heard Belinda and hobbled to the door. "Pardon, *señorita,* it is not wise to come in now. *La patrona,* she is like the mountain cat with her cub, snapping and snarling." He saw the deep concern in her eyes. "Go with Jessie. You too are in need of care. I will come to you when there is word of Conner."

She had to be content with his assurance. Belinda was not aware that she was crying. She felt Jessie's arm around her shoulders leading her away, never knowing that Jessie forgot that this was the person who had come to take Marty away from her and saw only a vulnerable young woman who needed her.

"Conner will be fine. Why, when I met Logan, I thought he was going to die. I never knew anyone who healed so quickly. And Dixie will tell you the same about Ty." As Jessie opened the door to her and Logan's bedroom, she kept up a constant stream of stories about the three brothers. She decided there was no point in telling Belinda about her uncle's arrival now.

Belinda would find out soon enough that her cousin was somehow involved in Charles Riverton's shady dealings.

Chapter Eighteen

A hot bath, clean clothes and Jessie's gentle attentions to her small cuts with a soothing ointment helped restore Belinda's flagging spirit. She wanted to ask how long it had been since she had arrived with Conner, but Jessie had left her supposedly to rest. Instead, she nervously paced, barefoot, dressed in an assortment of Jessie's and Macaria's clothes.

What could delay Santo's coming for her? Surely they all knew how Conner was by now? Back and forth over the flowered carpet she walked, and the questions became her only thoughts.

The rocking chair in the corner, near the side table stacked with books, drew her attention. Belinda smiled as she saw they were a series of boys' adventure stories. Trailing her fingers over the gold-embossed spines of *The Castaway, Lost in the Cañon, Treasure Finders* and *A Young Hero,* she knew that Conner had not lied to her about Marty being loved. There was a Bible, a book of poetry by Tennyson and his *Idylls of the King.*

She could imagine Jessie seated in the rocker with Marty and...Kenny, that was the other boy's name, the lamp glowing warmly while she read stories to them.

It was the image of a family. Could she offer the boy the same? Belinda thought of her days, from breakfast in bed with the morning's paper, calling cards and correspondence that required her attention, to the evening social functions after a day overseeing business matters.

What would she do with a little boy who had enjoyed the freedom of land without end to ride and play in?

There were parks and riding paths, lessons from a variety of tutors in deportment, music, studies, even sailing. But they would not be things she could teach him. And their uncle—a great-uncle to Marty—had his various clubs to occupy his days. How much family life would they give him? The tiresome Sunday dinners that she remembered as a child? The birthday parties where attendance was mandatory, despite a dislike for the children who had always made her feel the odd one out.

Was she being fair to the boy to take him away from the home the Kincaids provided? And the love. She could not forget that. Rubbing her forehead, she knew the issue had somehow become confused with her own mixed-up feelings about her life and Conner. What happened to the conviction that taking Marty back to Chicago with her was the right thing, the only thing to do?

How could she force a child into a way of life that she had been only too glad to escape from?

Belinda turned away from her questions, and the corner that brought them to mind. The swirl of her skirt hem caught a basket, spilling the contents. She picked up a child-sized sock with the egg-shaped wooden darner wedged into the toe. More evidence that Jessie mothered her nephew.

The tiny neat stitches halfway through the tear served to remind her that she had never learned to sew a fine seam. Not for lack of trying on her part, or her grandmother's who had hired a constant stream of expert needlewomen to teach her their arts.

Exhaustion and fear made her feel vulnerable, and this homey example of womanly skill mocked her. She replaced the sock and moved the basket back against the wall.

For a moment more she stood there, fighting other unhappy childhood memories from coming to the surface.

Harsh as the reminders were to her, she could not deny they served to keep her from worrying about Conner.

The soft knock brought a sense of relief. Hearing the masculine voice that called her name sent Belinda quickly to open the door. "Uncle Phillip? What are you doing here?"

His immaculate boots were as dusty as his suit, and a look of fatigue crossed his features as he drew her into his arms.

"Thank God you're safe, my dearest. When we found—"

"Wait. Wait," she repeated, pulling back within his embrace to look up at him. "First tell me what you're doing here? You couldn't travel this quickly in response to my telegram."

"I never received it. I left home a few days after you. Let me get your things. I assumed they were yours. We recovered them from the buckboard."

Phillip released her, lifting up the satchel and her reticule he had set aside. Following Belinda into the room, he placed them on the bed.

"They were—are gifts for Marty," she said with a distracted air. "Please, I do not understand—"

"All in good time, my dearest. I want to know that you're really all right. Those men that attacked you—"

"Truly, I am fine. A little tired and concerned about Conner's injuries. But never mind me. I think I need to sit down. Seeing you is a bit of a shock." Belinda suited action to words and sat on the bed.

Phillip came to sit beside her. He took her hand, noted the ragged edge of her nails, the broken blisters and cuts, but wisely kept silent.

"Belinda, I'm afraid I have another shock for you. Albert has disappeared."

"Albert? When? Where? What happened to him?"

"Gently, my dearest," Phillip said, easing her fierce grip from his arm. "Several weeks after you departed, I came across some correspondence between Charles and Albert. Wait, let me finish before you ask questions," he cautioned.

"Albert had been paying off a crew at the stockyard to handle cattle that Charles shipped. None of the invoices showed on company records. Needless to say, I went to his rooms to confront Albert only to be told that he had left for an extended trip. His housekeeper was most reluctant to allow me access to his library, but you know how persuasive I can be when I set my mind to it."

"Yes, oh, yes, I have seen your charm, Uncle." But there was no censure from his niece.

"That's when I discovered that Charles had been writing to Albert. What disturbed me greatly was the frequent mention of your name, along with questions about your likes and dislikes—"

"The colors," Belinda interrupted to say. "I thought you were the one who told Riverton what my favorite colors were. He had his guest room redone to please me."

"Riverton? Since when did Charles become Riverton, Belinda?"

She withdrew her hand from his. "Since his men tried to kill me and Conner."

"You don't know for sure—"

"Yes, I do, Uncle. You were not there. I was. Joe Dacus is the foreman for the Circle R. Rich Dillion was ordered to be my escort. He was there, too." She could not sit still a moment longer. Pacing again, she asked, "You never explained where it was that you lost Albert."

"As I said, I was disturbed by the tone of Charles's letters. I left immediately when I found reference to a meeting in Tucson. He disappeared and I thought it best to find you."

"Tucson? Riverton was summoned to Tucson on business, his housekeeper claimed. Obviously they were meeting there. Uncle Phillip, there is something else you should know." Belinda paused with her back toward him. He was upset and she would add to it, but they had never lied to each other. To her, keeping the incident of someone shooting at her from him was the same as a lie. So she told him, in as calm a voice as she could muster.

Phillip waited until she was done. "I should have listened to you about Albert. I had no idea how desperate he'd grown to have you out of the way. I can almost understand how perfectly you fell into his schemes with this trip to find the boy. Accidents happen all the time to people traveling to the territories. Who would question your death by an unseen shooter?''

"Who indeed?''

"Belinda.''

She turned to see Jessie in the doorway. "Conner? Is he—''

"He's asking to see you.''

Belinda ran from the room, flying down the hallway only to stop before she reached his door. She wiped damp palms down her skirt, smoothed back the drying curls of hair that had slipped free from the combs Jessie lent her and took a deep breath. She slowly released it as she stood in the doorway.

Vaguely aware of others in the room, Belinda had eyes for no one but Conner. He was swathed in a sheet, only his head visible as she approached the foot of the bed. His gray eyes appeared dark and unfocused as he whispered her name. She went around to the side of the bed, ignoring the straight chair near the bed, and fell to her knees.

"Are you . . . all right?''

"Fine, Conner.'' She was shaking with a wealth of emotions she could not begin to name. "Please, I know it hurts you to speak. I had to see you, see for myself that—''

"I'm fine.'' His attempt to smile failed. He slipped his hand from beneath the sheet to touch the curling ends of her hair. "Stay.''

"Yes. I would not wish to be anywhere else.''

His eyes closed and his hand fell back to the bed. Belinda leaned forward to rest her forehead against his hand. She could not explain to herself why his simple request meant so much, or that the promise to stay had come from her heart.

Someone cleared his throat behind her, soft whispers followed but Belinda did not acknowledge them. She heard one set of footsteps cross to the door, moments later another set followed. She sensed she was not alone with Conner, but the effort to move was more than she could make. There was comfort to be had by touching him, by listening to his even breaths as sleep claimed him.

The soothing scent of herbs rising from the heat of his body infused her senses. Her eyes grew heavy. Belinda turned, sinking to the floor, her cheek cradled by Conner's hand, and healing sleep claimed her as well.

"She'll have a crick in her neck by the time she wakes," Logan said to his mother.

"Leave her. She will not thank you for disturbing her now. Go to your wife, my son. I will keep watch over your brother."

"Not too long, *Madre*. We need to make plans. Conner said it was Dacus who came after him. We can't let him think he's getting away with this."

Anger and pride mixed in Logan's voice. Macaria took his hand and lifted it to his lips. "Soon. I will join you and Ty."

He took his dismissal with good grace, knowing that his mother would leave when she was sure that Conner wasn't going to have a fever from his wounds.

Logan went down the hall to his bedroom and found his wife talking with Phillip.

"How is your brother?"

"He'll pull through. I can't convince my mother yet, or your niece, but Conner's tough, hard as ironwood."

"Your mother said the very same thing about him." Phillip rose. "I'll excuse myself and give you both some privacy." At the door, he turned. "I would like to talk to you, Logan, about what Conner told you."

"Just let me get cleaned up and I'll join you in the office." Logan glanced at Jessie. "Are there any spare bedrooms left for Phillip to have?"

"I'm sure your mother or Sofia—"

"They're both busy, honey. You're the lady of the house for now and your guest—"

She smiled. "Of course, I'll take care of him."

It was almost two hours later when Logan and Phillip met again in the office. Ty had volunteered to keep the boys occupied by taking them down to the long barn where a mare was about to foal. To make up for all the attention Marty had been getting, it was decided that whether filly or colt, the mare's offspring would be Kenny's to name and raise as his own.

"I had Rosanna fix us something to eat," Logan said, taking one of the large leather chairs and indicating the other for Phillip. On the table between the chairs were plates of corn bread, *bolillos,* crunchy hard rolls, steaks and ham slices, fried chilies, and beans.

"Beer, wine or—"

"Whiskey, bourbon if you have any," Phillip said, heaping a plate full for himself. He had not realized how hungry he was. Phillip stopped long enough to nod his approval at the bottle Logan displayed before he broke the seal to pour them both a drink.

"No matter the crisis, I've never lost my appetite." Phillip sniffed then swallowed a healthy drink from his glass. "Can't beat Kentucky bourbon."

"I agree. But Phillip, the crisis hasn't passed yet. There's still the matter of Riverton and his ramrod. They need to pay for this outrage against Belinda."

"And your brother?"

"Conner? For what they did to Conner, they're dead men." Logan tossed back the half glass of bourbon he had poured for himself. "And if you don't believe me, wait till you hear my mother say it."

Phillip set his glass and plate aside. He studied Logan for several moments, then smiled. "I'm relieved. I thought you were going to ask me what my intentions are toward your very attractive mother."

"Don't think I didn't want to do just that. My mother would have me roasted, slowly, over the spit outside if she ever found out. No, Phillip, I just wanted to warn you that she's no docile Eastern lady. You haven't seen mad till you've seen her in a temper. Conner's got one just like it."

Far from discouraging him, Phillip's eyes gained a decided twinkle. "Consider me warned. Now, tell me what your brother said. Despite witnessing what I did, it's still difficult to believe Charles sent his men after my niece. Belinda mentioned that he made overtures as if he wanted to marry her and take over her money and stock in our family businesses."

Logan made a decision. He liked this straight-talking man, and he proceeded to tell him all of the suspicions that the Kincaids harbored about Riverton.

It was an emotional delivery, for Logan left out nothing, not even his part of riding the outlaw trail in an attempt to bring the outlaw gang to justice.

Neither man noticed that Macaria, having left a sleeping Conner and Belinda, paused at the doorway. She listened for a few moments, then continued down the hall to her room. The candles she had lit earlier still burned and she knelt at her prayer bench. For the next hour she prayed for her son's recovery, and the wisdom to guide her sons against the man she had believed her friend and now was defined as her enemy.

As she rose, she felt the weariness of having to make a decision to take revenge.

Revenge played upon Belinda's mind in that vague half awake, half asleep world where she envisioned herself a stronger woman, stopping those men before they hurt Conner.

A slight noise penetrated her consciousness and she blinked sleepy eyes as she turned toward the doorway. For a few moments she simply stared at the little boy. He was her brother come to life.

Belinda had not realized she mouthed Robert's name until the child shook his head and said, "No, I'm Marty."

"Yes. Yes, of course," she whispered. Belinda cast a fearful glance at Conner, afraid they had disturbed his much-needed sleep.

"Can I see him?" Marty crept closer to the bedside where Belinda still sat on the floor.

"We must not wake him."

"I know how to be quiet as a 'Pache. Hazer said so. He's been teachin' me and Kenny how to track."

Belinda scooted back to make room for the boy. She wanted to touch the straight corn silk blond head Marty had inherited from his father. Watching him as he looked at Conner, she noticed that he sucked noisily on his lower lip. Another of Robert's traits. She was overcome with sadness that Robert would never see his child grow to manhood.

"Kenny says Conner's gonna be all right."

Belinda heard the underlying faith in Kenny's belief and the defiance that dared her to dispute this. He shifted from one foot to the other, drawing her gaze down to the pebble-toed boots he wore. Despite the scuff marks, Belinda could see they were fairly new boots.

"You ain't saying the same?"

"Oh, yes, Marty, Conner will heal."

His gaze lowered to the floor. He noisily sucked his lower lip. Kenny said he had to stop, but when he was scared, it was hard for him.

"You like Conner very much?"

"Sure do. He was bringing me my badge. He promised to make me one of his deputies."

"Everyone must be proud of you." Belinda couldn't bring herself to ask if Jessie or Logan were especially proud. She did not want him to leave her.

"You're the... the l-lady that came to t-take me away?"

"I am your Aunt Belinda. Your father was my older brother."

"He's d-dead. So's my ma."

"It must have been a terrible time for you. I wish I had been there for you."

"I had Kenny."

Without the least bit of resentment, Belinda murmured, "I am glad that he was with you, Marty. You have become close to Kenny, and I can understand how depending on each other would make you feel—"

"You don't know how I feel. You don't know me. Kenny lied to Logan and Jessie so's no one could take me away. Kenny knows about the bad dreams an' he fixes them for me."

Belinda closed her eyes briefly. If he had said *go away, I don't want to come with you,* his declaration could not have been plainer. When she started out on her search to find him, she had not given much thought to what he would want. In the past few weeks she had undergone so many changes in her thinking that she could not answer Marty with a firm directive. Legally she was his guardian, it was her right to have him live with her. And morally...

"How come I don't remember you?" Marty asked.

The question fell artlessly from his lips, but it was one she had dreaded being asked. Conner shifted in his sleep and she seized the excuse to stand. Placing one finger over her lips, she motioned Marty toward the doorway.

Marty tugged on her skirt and, in a very hushed, stammering voice, asked, "Didn't you ever want to know me?"

Jessie reached the doorway just as they did.

"Marty. I told you not to bother her." For all that she reprimanded him, she welcomed Marty. He buried his face against her skirt and she wrapped her arms around his shoulders, holding him there. "Didn't I tell you that when your aunt is ready to talk to you, she would? And didn't I tell you not to ask questions?''

Marty's head bobbed up and down, but he didn't release his hold on Jessie.

"He has a right to ask questions, Jessie." Belinda looked into Jessie's eyes and found both resentment and sympathy for her. She wanted to dislike this woman who held her nephew within sheltering arms. Belinda could not. Jessie had been there for him, like Kenny and the rest of the Kincaid family when Belinda had not.

Seeing the way Marty clung to Jessie made Belinda feel woefully inadequate to deal with the young boy's needs. She had just told Jessie that Marty had a right to ask her questions, but Belinda knew she needed more time to form answers that were not composed of lies.

Belinda could not censure her deceased brother and his wife for keeping her away from their child. The boy had suffered enough without learning the cause of their being kept apart. But she did not want him to think that she had never wanted to know him. She had, from the moment he had been born.

"I came to see if you would join us for supper?"

"But Conner..." Belinda began.

"My husband's already eaten with your uncle. He'll sit with Conner." Jessie cradled Marty's cheek, gently lifting his head. "Go wash up. I'll be along in a few minutes."

Both women watched him until he darted out of sight into one of the rooms far down the hall. Jessie was the first to speak.

"We have lots to talk about, but it can all wait until tomorrow. No," she added when Belinda attempted to protest. "Those are Macaria's orders."

But it never came to pass, not the next day, for the night was torn with the shouts of stampede, and the ranch turned into an armed camp.

Chapter Nineteen

Belinda woke from a fitful sleep as booted feet pounded down the hall outside her room. She could hear shouting and it seemed the whole household was awake.

Grabbing her borrowed robe from the foot of the bed, she ran from her room. In various states of undress the family gathered in the front courtyard to listen as a winded rider told of the stampede.

"Swear we had no warnin', Logan. Tarabee went down before we could try and turn the herd. There's only three men holding those bastards off. Can't tell how many are up on the rim of the valley firin' down at 'em."

The furious clanging of several bells, one from the courtyard, and the others near various buildings scattered outside began ringing their alarming summons.

Belinda stood at the back, questions and orders flying too quickly for her to follow the speakers.

It appeared as if every man who worked for the Kincaids poured through the open gates, men still hitching up suspenders, buttoning shirts or buckling on gun belts. She had to stand on tiptoe to see. Logan and Ty were visible as torches lit the courtyard. They worked their way through the milling crowd.

Jessie and Macaria rushed back into the house just as Santo, with Sofia's help, hobbled into view from around the house where their small home was. They, too, were soon swallowed up in the crowd of men.

Belinda called out when she spotted her uncle, but he couldn't hear her above the raised voices. It took her moments to realize the bells were silent. The crowd seemed to shift to one side and she saw the reason why. Three men led saddled horses to the gates of the courtyard. Jessie dashed past, her arms filled with boots and weapons, while she yelled for Logan and Ty.

Belinda had steadily been stepping backward until the very wall of the house stopped her flight. She had never felt so useless.

"No quarter!" The words swelled to a roar as men mounted.

In minutes they were gone. The ground shook with the thundering hooves, then the night fell silent with the thudding as the massive gates were closed and barred.

Belinda focused on her uncle meeting Macaria in front of the gates. His arm slipped over Macaria's shoulders as they turned to walk back toward the house. Light and shadow wove over them, but there was enough light to see Phillip's head bent toward hers. If they spoke, it was in whispers to each other. They stopped near Jessie, and she, too, turned away from the gates, then beckoned to Santo and Sofia.

A blunted curse brought Belinda away from the wall to face the house. Conner, his chest tightly wrapped in linen strips from beneath his arms to the waistband of a pair of black pants, stood swaying on his feet, one hand gripping the doorframe. Kenny, who had his shoulder wedged beneath Conner's arm, was swearing at him.

"Help me get this ornery critter back to bed," he yelled, struggling to hang on to Conner.

"Let go. I'll tan your bottom—" Conner threatened.

"Too big for that."

"I'll show you—"

"Conner, stop it!" Belinda reached him first. "You are as pale as that linen holding you together. Kenny's right. You belong in bed. The boy has more sense than you do."

"They're my cattle. It's my problem. I'm still the law—"

"Yes, yes, you are." In a flash of understanding, Belinda knew how he felt. As useless as she had moments ago. But this was something she could do. "If you attempt to ride out now, you will only hurt yourself. What good will you be when your brothers bring those men in for justice if you cannot walk?"

She went closer, intending to replace Kenny's support with her own.

"Damn you, Belinda."

"Curse at me, lawman, and I will give you the same back." She knew his furious whisper was directed at himself, for his eyes closed and he stopped struggling with Kenny.

Before Belinda made her move, Marty's frightened voice came from within the house.

"Ma Jess! Ma Jess! She's yelling for you!"

Marty wiggled and squeezed his way passed Kenny and Conner. His nightshirt tucked halfway into his pants flapped like a tail as he ran for Jessie.

"What happened, Marty? What's wrong? Who's yelling?" Jessie demanded.

"Dixie." Marty gulped. "She's all wet and hollering the b-baby's coming."

"Oh, my Lord!"

"Calm, Jessie. We all must be very calm." Macaria left Phillip and came forward. "Belinda, you and Kenny will take my son back to his bed. Stay there with him so he does not add to his injuries. Conner, remember, you are to set an example for the young ones. Sofia, the kitchen, we have much to do with the baby coming early. Jessie, you will help me with Dixie."

"And me?" Marty wanted to know. "What's there for me to do?"

"Ah, my brave *niño,* for you there is work, too." Macaria knelt in front of Marty and placed her hands on his thin shoulders. "I give to you the most important work of all. You must keep watch for us."

"In the tower?"

"*Sí.* In the tower."

"You want me to be the lookout? I can use the field glass, too?"

"*Sí. Sí,* my child, you will do this." She released him and stood up with Phillip's assistance. For a moment they watched Marty jumping around before he ran to Kenny.

"Did ya hear? Oh, boy, Kenny, did ya hear?" He turned to Macaria. "Can I take PeeWee with me?"

"*Sí,*" she answered, hurrying into the house.

Belinda managed to get a reluctant Conner away from the doorway when Macaria suddenly stopped in the hall.

"Sofia, where is your daughter?"

"She is here, in the house. She wished to spend the night should you have need of her." Sofia looked over her robe-clad shoulder at her husband, who had stopped a few feet behind her. "Santo, you hear Rosanna say this?"

"*Sí*, I heard her. But my eyes did not see our daughter out there. Call her," he ordered with a hard edge to his voice. "Call Rosanna for *la patrona*."

Phillip stepped forward. "Go on, Sofia, help Macaria. I will look for your daughter."

Belinda, feeling Conner break out in a cold sweat, urged him back to his room. They all heard the moans coming from the last room down the hall. Dixie was not going to suffer in silence. Kenny, without being told, closed the door behind them as Belinda helped Conner into bed.

"I feel as helpless as a calf when a mountain cat comes hunting," Conner whispered in Belinda's ear as she tucked the sheet around him.

"Then we make a pair, lawman, I feel pretty useless myself."

"Don't." He worked his hand free of the sheet to grab hold of hers. "You're not useless. I need you right here with me."

"To hold your hand?" she asked with self-directed sarcasm.

"That's one thing."

"Fluff your pillows?"

"It'd be a mighty big help if you would."

"And I suppose you would like me to sit beside you and read you a story until you fall asleep?"

"How about a whiskey? And if Kenny weren't here, I'd tell you what else you could do to ease my awful discomfort."

"Heck, don't mind me none."

"Fetch me a drink, Kenny."

"You don't drink, Conner."

"Don't argue with me. I need one tonight."

Belinda glanced at Kenny. His face reflected his indecision. "I guess one drink won't hurt him, Kenny. He should not have gotten out of bed. Maybe the whiskey will help him to sleep."

"Gee, Conner, if you want to kiss her, go ahead. I ain't gonna look. I seen enough of that kissin' stuff with Jessie and Logan. He's always—"

"Kenny!" Belinda protested.

"Kincaids don't tell," Conner whispered in a voice that attempted to be stern but was filled with resignation.

"All right. I'm going. I'll even knock before I come in. Okay?"

"Do that," Conner answered.

Belinda heard pain and anger mixed in his voice. "Go quickly, Kenny," she added, thinking the whiskey might mellow the anger in Conner. She waited until the door closed. "Conner, your anger is misdirected. You cannot help being injured. Lord knows," she said, closing her eyes briefly. "You did nothing to provoke that attack. I didn't understand at first why you did not shoot those men."

"And now?"

"I've come to realize that you risked your life to prevent me from being shot. And they would have killed me."

"It was a thought."

"I wish I could wind the clock back to the minute you first told me to leave." She could not look at him now when guilt beat at her, and confession truly would bring her ease. "I could have summoned help."

"Belinda." Conner rejected the struggle it would take for him to get out of the bed, but not without frustration coloring his voice. "You couldn't have gotten back in time, even if you had known where to go."

"Then you did think about it."

"Stop. Don't do this to yourself or me. It's over. We're alive." *And they'll pay.*

And you are hurt. "I think you've done enough talking. I know you're brave, Conner. Braver than any man I've known. So you will obey me and rest."

"Yes, ma'am."

"Not that I have any right to give you orders—"

"Permission granted."

"Conner. Silence. Remember?"

"Yes, ma'am."

Belinda glared at him. She had to bite her lower lip to keep from laughing. Conner was making a buttoning motion over his mouth.

It was moments more before she could speak. "Much better, Mr. Kincaid," she stated in a prim tone. But the joking truly was at an end. Conner's eyes closed, and she saw the lines of pain etched on his face.

When she attempted to move away from the bed, his grip tightened on her hand. Before she could stop him,

Conner shifted on the soft mattress to make room for her to sit beside him.

Belinda hesitated. The events of the day had been harrowing, but sitting alone with Conner in his bedroom suddenly seemed the height of folly. Not for the act of sitting down beside him, but for the great temptation to curl up next to him.

She had done more than lose her virginity today. She had cast off twenty-six years of following what society deemed right and proper and allowed her desire for one man, this man, to cloud her thinking.

She was not sure if she should thank Conner Kincaid or hate him for setting her adrift from the rules that governed her life.

"Such a hard decision?"

She glanced down at their entwined hands. "I am not sure it's a wise thing to do."

"Don't be wise."

"I have not been sensible from the moment I met you."

"Such a bad thing? So troubled?"

"No, I—"

"Liar."

"You are not to talk, Conner."

He tugged on her hand. "Then you can."

Perhaps it was the soft glow of lamplight that added to the intimacy of being alone with him, but Belinda found it increased the temptation not only of Conner himself, but to tell him of her confusion. Confusion tangled with the guilt she harbored, her indecision over Marty, and her feelings for him.

Just as she made up her mind, Kenny knocked on the door, announcing, "It's jus' me."

When he opened the door, Dixie's scream entered the room with him. Belinda could not repress a shiver. She knew nothing about childbirth except that married friends spoke about their experiences in secretive whispers, and if she or another of their unmarried acquaintances dared approach them, the talk stopped. How was she supposed to know anything if no one would tell her? Conner had taught her more about her woman's body in a few hours than she had learned in twenty-six years.

She felt Conner's hand squeeze her own. A look revealed the compassion in his eyes. With a wry thought, Belinda had a feeling he knew exactly how the birthing process proceeded, and what's more, would not share it with her. But she took the comfort of his hand and tried for a smile to reassure him that she would not fall to pieces.

Kenny set the glass on the small table near the bed then backed away to the footboard. "The baby's coming real fast. Thought you'd want to know. Ty's gonna be madder than a calf on ice with its tail froze that he ain't here."

The look that Kenny shared with Conner served to nudge Belinda's anger. A sorry state. A boy half her age knew more than she did.

"Kenny, I know you must be eager to help out somewhere other than here. I'm worried about Marty being alone in the tower. It's high and he is a little boy. I know it is not my place, but I think he would welcome your company."

"You, too?" Kenny looked from Belinda to Conner and shook his head. "Jeez. What's with folks tonight? Santo chased me from the office. Jessie chased me out of the bedroom. Now you're getting rid of me.

Gettin' so a fella can't find a place to light 'round here anymore." Mumbling, Kenny left them alone.

Belinda would have called him back, but she caught the wink of his eye and his grin just before the door closed.

"Good idea," Conner murmured.

"I really am concerned about Marty being up there alone. Thank you for the warning about Kenny. He is wise beyond his years."

"You disappoint me. I thought you wanted—"

"To help you drink your whiskey so you can sleep," Belinda finished for him in a no-nonsense voice.

She lowered herself to the edge of the bed, then had to scoot forward to reach the glass. She ignored Conner's attempt to smile and slid one hand behind his neck to lift his head as she placed the glass against his lips.

His skin felt warm to her touch, but not heated, and she released a sigh of thanks that he had no fever. The damp ends of his hair clung to her fingers. The corded tension in his neck beckoned her to rub the knots away. Belinda could not stop the image that formed of how she had held him for more of the hungry kisses that had set her on fire.

With a rough shake of her head, she dispersed the image. Conner was injured. What was she thinking of? But as she focused on his features, she found that Conner was staring at her. For a few moments she thought he was aware of exactly what she had been thinking. She blinked several times, but the invitation was still there, brightening his eyes.

The sharp tang of the whiskey mixed with the faint scent of herbs and the light floral milled soap that she had bathed with. All of it warm. Spiced with memories of abandoned lovers. Intimate... blending and heating to cloud her senses.

Temptation. Utter folly... and Conner's gaze, darkening, drawing her closer, and closer to him.

At the touch of his hand caressing her thigh, heat bloomed beneath the layers of finely spun cotton, spreading to her hip as his splayed hand glided upward to urge her forward. Toward him, toward another taste of sweet, heated oblivion. His thumb, resting in the crease of her thigh, slowly rubbed back and forth, adding its own enticement of pleasures found and learned this day.

The glass tumbled from her hand, spilling the last bit of liquor. Potent fumes rose and seemed to fade as breaths mixed, warmed and grew rapid.

Conner's lips formed her name without sound.

Belinda's lips parted. She moved her hand to cradle his head. The golden length of her hair spilled to one side, draping across his bare shoulder, veiling the lamplight as she brought her mouth to his.

Insanity. Belinda knew it, but the rush of emotions Conner invoked beat rational thought in a race that engaged every pleasure point of her body. And more, his kiss brought her heart into the play.

To part from him was asking her to lose a piece of herself. But a fear she would lose all that she was gave her the strength to pull away.

"We should not—"

"Belinda, come ease all the pain."

She closed her eyes, trying to tell him no.

Conner used one finger in a featherlike caress that curved over her hip, dipped at the indentation of her waist and skimmed the hard tip of her breast.

"Your body doesn't say no to me..." he said softly. His finger rested against the pulse in her throat.

"I feel a yes right here," he added, and had the satisfaction of feeling her pulse increase.

In his vaster experience, Conner recognized the very unique, startling desire between them. He admired her courage, her willingness to be open-minded, but wished her scruples had been tossed out with the bath water.

"Belinda, *un beso*. One kiss, *cariño*."

Resolve melted beneath the soft caress of his voice. She opened dark eyes to look into his. There was no mistaking the tension. She felt it, a burning need between them, smoldering, ripe from exploding into flames. She did not want to withdraw. She did not want to be sensible.

"Such a dangerous fire." She breathed the words over his lips, lowering her head.

"Then burn for me."

A hushed entreaty that begged everything from her. "Belinda."

Without shyness, which suited her wild, fledgling feelings, she lowered her mouth to his. "Fire."

She felt him like a hard heat, brought to life because of his desire for her. He wanted her with the same scorching passion that flowed through her. Belinda circled his shoulders, then gently gripped them. Feeling the weight of her hands, he trembled and it gave her an immense pleasure to know that she had caused it with her touch. Wanting more of his warm mouth, her soft lips melted obligingly and temptingly into his.

"I want you," he whispered, his tongue tracing an enticing path over her bottom lip.

Belinda shifted slightly so she would not lean against his bruised chest. She lost herself in the fierce, intense kiss. *Fire* was the only word that echoed like a beguiling melody through her mind.

The echo grew louder.

Conner broke the kiss to whisper the word against her mouth. His fingertips traced lightly over and around the tautening peaks of her breasts. Her eyes, dark as velvet, fixed imploringly on the blatant sensuality of his mouth. Reading a hunger that mirrored his own, Conner brought her lips to his. A fleeting thought that he could still hear the faint echo of her whisper crossed his mind. Fire.

She drew away, staring at him. "Conner?"

They both heard the cry then. Not an echo, but an alarm.

"Fire! The long barn's on fire!"

Chapter Twenty

"For almighty sake! The horses! Belinda, help me with my boots. Damn! Those bastards. Get blankets. As many as you can find."

She hurried to get his boots, fear striking deep within her. "Conner, you cannot fight a fire."

"I can't! Who the hell is left to do it?" He hated the weakness of his body that forced him to lean heavily on her while he stomped into his boots. His pain was ruthlessly buried, and he almost snarled at her when she stopped him at the door.

"Put this shirt on." She shoved it at him.

To his amazement, Belinda stripped off her robe and struggled into another of his shirts.

"Get a pair of shoes or boots from Jessie. I'll meet you at the barn." Conner snatched the blanket from his bed. "Wet yourself down. The only fire I want touching you is one I start."

The front door was open to the night. Dixie's cries were weaker now, but they followed him outside. Phillip, with Kenny and Jessie's help, was throwing off the bar to the gates. Behind Conner came his mother at a run, her arms filled with blankets.

"I left Sofia with her. Santo is cursing. I wanted to lock him inside the office. Conner—"

"Belinda's coming. We'll have enough help to form a bucket brigade. The stream is full. There's plenty of water at the barn." As he started to run, pain knifed his chest. "Go on," he told her. "I'm all right."

As he reached the open gates, he could see the flames shooting up from the far side of the long barn where the horses, their precious blooded stock, were stabled. The fire had been started low to the ground, and was just now climbing the thick wooden walls. There was still time to get the animals out.

"Conner! Conner, wait for me," Marty called. "I had to put PeeWee back in the house."

"Get back, Marty. Stay with Sofia. She's alone. Better still, go back up in the tower. This may not be the only fire that's started. Go on!" he yelled when the boy hesitated. He couldn't wait. If he didn't keep moving, the pain would conquer him and Riverton would win.

Somewhere between the house and the long barn he realized that Belinda was beside him. Her grim expression more than matched his own. They could both hear the shrill frightened neighs of the trapped horses.

Fire was a rancher's enemy, but it was a horse's unholy terror.

Phillip worked the pump of the horse trough near the corral. Kenny filled the buckets, setting them aside in a row.

"Stay and help them," Conner ordered Belinda. He could see how his mother and Jessie struggled to open the barn doors. Conner tossed Belinda his blanket and ran to help his mother and sister-in-law.

The moment the doors opened, acrid-smelling smoke came from the tack room, filling the long barn. The smoke was drifting upward toward the open-beamed eaves. Both Jessie and Macaria held soaked blankets, ready to toss them over the horses' heads to lead the animals to safety.

"Take out the ones closest to the doors," Conner ordered the two of them. "I'll get the ones in the back." He ripped off his shirt as he ran, his ears filled with the terrified whinnies of the horses. Panic clutched his gut when a wet blanket slammed against him and he found Belinda once more beside him.

"Why didn't they stop you?" he shouted.

"There's no one else to help you, Conner. Tell me what to do."

He threw the dripping blanket over her. Her eyes were watering, and he knew her throat burned as his did. He hauled her after him, afraid to let her go, as he threw open the latches of the large box stalls. The horses, mares, colts, fillies and two stallions at opposite corners were kicking and rearing, trying to break free of the wooden slats that held them prisoner.

Conner threw up one arm to shield his eyes, and held tight to Belinda's hand as the smoke grew thicker, the smell of burning leather filling the air.

The yellow orange glow of flames licked through the wall of the tack room. He could barely hear Belinda's cough over his own as he forced himself down to the end stalls. The terrified screams of the horses rang in his ears.

Justin's Pride, the stallion his father had bought to begin his own breeding program, slammed against the stall door. His eyes were bulging, rolling with fear as Conner fought with the latch. Smoke billowed and he lost sight of Belinda. The stallion reared on his hind legs, pawing the air. Fear that the horse would shatter his legs when he came down sent Conner flying into the stall.

He flung the shirt over the horse's head, barely missed the treacherous fall of the stallion's hoof coming down near his arm. Conner wrapped the ends of the shirt into a tight fist beneath the animal's neck. Head tossing, whinnying with terror, the horse fought him and tried to rear again. Conner slipped, banging his elbow against the stall. Even without his injuries, he would be hard-pressed to hold the crazed animal.

Pain sliced through his body. Suddenly another pair of hands covered his own. Belinda! She had grabbed hold of the shirt from the other side. Conner regained his balance and tightened his grip on the shirt.

"Go!" he yelled. The horse, panicked now, half dragged, half carried them down the corridor. Conner's lungs were screaming for air, fresh and free of thick smoke.

Kenny ran forward with a short, looped length of cut rope when they cleared the doorway.

"No, Kenny!" Conner didn't dare give the horse over to the boy. "Open the corral gate," he ordered. Kenny ran ahead and, with Belinda's help, he managed to get the horse inside the fencing, where three other rescued animals milled in prancing agitation. "Where are the mares?"

"I brought them out to the pasture. Your mother took the filly to the breaking pen." Kenny swiped at his grime-coated face.

"Kenny, I'm going back. Help Phillip with the buckets before the fire spreads and brings the whole barn down." He started to run, then yelled back over his shoulder, "And keep her out here."

Kenny shot a look at Belinda, who was dragging her blanket in the horse trough. "Hell!" he shouted. "Ask me to spit up a storm, why don't you!"

"Spit one up, if you can, Kenny," Belinda called out as she ran after Conner. "The Lord knows we need one."

Jessie came at her, running and leading a half-grown horse. She yelled something, but Belinda could not hear her, and was not about to stop. Conner had gone into the barn alone. Her fear for him drove her back inside.

Plunging through the billowing smoke, she heard the hiss and crackle of the flames. Hot and wet, the blanket meant to protect her added to the smothering, frightening feeling of being in hell.

She could not see Conner. Her ears hurt as the pitch of frenzied screams from the horses rose to an unbearable level.

"Conner! Conner, where are you?" she cried, knowing he could not hear her but praying that somehow he would.

Coughing, Belinda wove her way to one side, feeling for the stalls. Heated wood met the searching touch of her hand. Tears streamed from her burning eyes. She could not see, no matter how many times she wiped them. By feel alone, she worked her way down the row of box stalls, finding that those closest to the doors were already opened.

Dear Lord, did I make a terrible mistake to come back inside?

Then she heard the shrill scream of an animal in pain. Belinda pulled herself hand over hand along the top slats. She could feel herself weakening, but somewhere up ahead was Conner and yet another horse.

As Conner plunged down the center with the young stallion, he caught sight of a dark form huddled against one of the stalls. There was one mare left to free, but he was afraid it might be too late to save her. But who had come back into the barn?

Instinct said it was Belinda. An instinct that wailed a warning to get her outside. He released his hold on the stallion, a terrible risk, but one he had to take. Belinda meant more. The horse needed no urging to run for the open doors, away from the terror. Conner ran for Belinda.

She lurched forward, having found the latch, and the imprisoned horse's terror torched her own. The metal was already hot. Protecting her hands with the blanket made her clumsy. She grabbed for the latch with her bare hands.

Conner locked his arms around her middle, lifted and swung her to one side, out of harm's way. He fumbled before he could open the latch and pull open the stall door. The mare bolted past him, bound for freedom. He prayed she didn't break her leg in her maddened flight.

Belinda sagged against the wood slats, overcome by smoke, blackness dancing in front of her eyes. She could not breathe.

Then Conner was there, snatching her up into his arms. He staggered beneath her weight and that of the soaked blanket before he regained his balance and ran for the doorway.

Gritting his teeth against the stabbing pain, he tightened his hold on his precious burden. Sweat streamed from his smoke-blackened body as he demanded every ounce of strength left in him to get them both outside.

Pain, like steel spurs raking his flesh, made it almost impossible to breathe. Pain, huge blackening waves of it, stole the cry welling in his throat when he felt Belinda's body suddenly limp in his arms.

Like a vicious enemy, smoke blinded him. Conner stumbled, then burst through the doorway into the night. He dragged in great lungfuls of air, but even out here the smoke taint was felt. He slipped in the mud as he made his way to the horse trough.

Ripping the blanket away from her head, he soaked one end in the water and used it to wipe Belinda's face. He repeated it over and over, using the shock of the cold water against her heated skin until she tossed her head back and forth, moaning in protest.

Hearing the flow of water, he looked around and found Santo there.

"Nothing is wrong with my arms. I can stand and pump the water the others need to fight the fire."

Conner swore beneath his breath. He couldn't tell the old man not to do it. There simply wasn't anyone else. Kenny ran up with four empty buckets banging against his legs. He plopped them down and bent over, holding his knees with his hands, heaving while Santo worked as quickly as he could to refill the buckets.

Kenny grabbed hold of two buckets and slipped in the mud before he staggered off behind the barn.

Conner plunged his head into the horse trough. When he lifted himself free and stood up, the searing shock of icy water falling on his flesh told him more about pain than he ever wanted to know. A convulsive shudder ripped through him, leaving him swaying on his feet.

But the shock served to revive him. He grabbed hold of the remaining buckets. "Watch out for her, Santo." A strangled cry strained his throat when he saw the flames leap high. Rage flooded Conner. Rage that gave him the added strength to plunge past Phillip and his mother and fling the water against the crackling fire licking at the protruding roof beams. He tore the buckets out of Kenny's hands as the boy returned with them. When the buckets were empty, Conner tossed them aside to be refilled and ripped the scorched, smoldering blanket from an exhausted Jessie to beat at the flames.

Steam hissed repeatedly as more and more water was thrown at the already charred wood. Cool droplets fell on Conner's skin. He felt nothing, saw no one. His absolute focus aimed at killing the fire and saving as much of the barn as he could before it spread to the other wooden buildings.

There was no sense of time for him. The world had been reduced to billowing, choking smoke, blistering heat and a reddened glow that refused to quit.

Someone had handed him an ax. And he hacked and tore the wood until a knifelike searing pain cut across his chest.

Conner doubled over, dropping the ax. He rocked to and fro, then went down to his knees in the mud. His stomach heaved and he bent forward, retching.

As if from far away, he heard a choked cry. The effort to lift his head seemed beyond his ability.

"Conner. Oh, God, Conner." Belinda reached out to touch his shoulder, pulling back at the last moment, afraid to touch him.

Her hoarse whisper penetrated through the blinding fog that filled his mind. He looked up to see Belinda standing beside him. Soot blackened her face and torn clothes, her hair hung wet and tangled, evidence of her own valiant fight. But he was on his knees before her, beaten and whipped, and the position was intolerable for him.

Conner managed to get one foot under him. His heart thundered in his chest as if it wanted to break free. He gathered himself for a last lunge to stand upright.

Belinda reached for him again only to have her hand jerked away by Macaria.

"Leave him. My son will not thank you for your help. He will stand on his own."

"No! He needs—"

"*Silencio!*"

"Come away from him, Belinda," Phillip urged, taking hold of his niece's arm just as Conner staggered to his feet.

Belinda shrugged off her uncle's hand but made no move toward Conner. He flung his head back, staring up.

"Go back to the house. All of you go back. There is nothing more to be done." His voice was devoid of emotion. He stood there, alone, as he had been alone for most of his life, even within the circle of his family.

Jessie hugged Kenny to her side. They were the first to turn away. Belinda resisted her uncle's gentle tug and stood her ground. He offered his arm to Macaria, and they too began walking back to the house.

"Didn't you hear me?" Conner asked, feeling Belinda's presence though she was silent.

"The fire's almost out, Conner. You won."

She listened to his ragged breathing, her own none too steady. And Belinda waited, hoping that he would not tell her to go again. She glanced at what was left of the long barn. Smoke drifted upward from the roof beams that had collapsed over the back half, but there were no new flames. She had worked with Kenny and Jessie to soak the wood before the fire reached the middle.

The horses still whinnied, but the sounds had lost the frenzied pitch they had held earlier. The night grew quiet, and still she waited for him.

"I helped my father build this barn."

There was no pride in his voice, just a statement of fact. "You saved the horses, Conner. That must count for something."

"Why did you stay?"

"I couldn't leave you to fight the fire alone." She hurt for him, more than she believed possible. But still, she would not reach out to him. He appeared so remote, a bruised and battered warrior who took no pride in the supreme, almost inhuman effort he had put forth.

And she had an insight into the man that Conner was, one who did not take pride in any accomplishment, regardless of its cost, but a man who simply did what had to be done.

"Conner?"

"You said those words to me before."

"Yes. At the creek when those men came."

"And now," he said softly, turning to look at her.

"And now," she repeated.

"You don't follow orders worth a damn."

"So I've been told. Very headstrong, that from my first tutor. My grandmother, may the Lord rest her soul, claimed I was a spirited child. Inherited, of course, from her side of the family."

"And your uncle? What does he say?"

"Uncle Phillip said that I would always learn a lesson best by making mistakes. But they would be my mistakes, and I would never forget the lesson."

"A very wise man. My father offered similar advice. Break the rules and laws that govern man only if you're willing to pay the price."

She attempted to smile, but understood how tightly he controlled himself. The touch of his fingertip wiping a smudge of soot from her cheek made her hold her breath. He was a weary shadow warrior, and her heart went out to him, for she did not know what to do to ease his pain.

"You're a hell of a woman, Belinda Jarvis. I'd be proud to escort you to my home."

She did not know where Conner's strength came from, or her own as she took his hand and walked back to the house with him. Men had paid her lavish compliments before, but none had she treasured as much as she did his simple words.

Chapter Twenty-One

Hours later, dawn not yet a hint in the sky, they were all gathered in the large front parlor. The remains of a hurried repast covered the table against the wall. Bathed and dressed, burns and blisters soothed with salve, Belinda offered another heated pot of coffee. Conner was the only one to ask for more.

Marty curled in one corner of the large leather couch, snuggled beneath a gaily woven blanket, PeeWee nestled in his arms. Kenny sprawled on the opposite end. Both were asleep. Macaria, chased from the bedroom by Sofia more than two hours ago, sat beside Phillip on the smaller settee. Conner had claimed a high-backed chair before the fireplace and Belinda returned to its mate across from him. Jessie kept vigil by the window. Santo had left them sometime before and had not returned.

Dixie no longer cried out, at least Belinda had not heard her for a while. She looked up and saw Sofia pause in the doorway. Signs of exhaustion were evident as each one turned to look at Sofia. She gazed only at Macaria as she made a stately walk across the rugs scattered over the wide-planked floor. Despite the lateness of the hour, and her own tiredness, her head was high, her manner formal.

Macaria rose and stood in place, hiding the need to run and ask, no, demand news. Sofia would not come to her unless the child had been delivered. But she waited, for Sofia, despite their ages, and their long friendship, would insist on making a formal announcement. *Hurry, hurry, old friend, we need joy in this house on this of all nights.*

"*La patrona,* the child is born. A *princesa, patrona.*"

"A girl?"

"*Sí, patrona,* a little *corderito.*"

"Lambkin," Macaria whispered, hugging her close. "Ah, Sofia, friend of my heart, it is great this joy you bring to me." Tears gathered in Macaria's eyes as she stepped back. "Dixie? She is well?"

"She is resting. Soon she will sleep."

"And the child? Come, come, my friend, I must see them. Ah, Sofia, a little girl."

Phillip, having risen when Macaria did, remained unnoticed as they rushed from the room. He smiled at Conner. "If ever an occasion called for a drink, I believe we have one now. Whiskey?"

"Make it a large one."

"Ladies? Sherry?" Phillip asked.

"Save mine," Jessie answered. "I want to see Dixie and the baby."

"I would like a glass, Uncle," Belinda replied.

"Then the three of us shall make the first toast to a new generation of the Kincaids."

Phillip moved off to the liquor cabinet where Macaria had earlier served them brandy with their coffee. He kept up a light stream of meaningless chatter, casting looks over his shoulder at Conner. As he had mentioned to his niece, the man was remarkable. He couldn't believe he was still awake, a remote, controlled expression guarding what brooding thoughts darkened his eyes.

Conner roused himself to take the glass, joining in several toasts. He drank the liquor without tasting it, for the bitter pill of betrayal had numbed his senses.

He was waiting for Santo to come back. The old man had insisted he be the one to go. No argument that Conner could muster had moved him from his decision. In the end, Conner had to respect the man's desire to right a terrible wrong. He tilted his head back against the chair and closed his eyes. He had thought he knew the limits he could push his body and his mind, but tonight had shown him new truths about the punishments a man could deliver to himself and still survive.

Belinda. Just thinking her name disrupted his somber thoughts. But he couldn't allow her to interfere with what he had yet to face. He had no need to look at her to know he had her total attention. She was truly magnificent, striking in her beauty despite the terrors of the day. To keep himself awake, Conner thought of Hazer and what he would say about Belinda. A woman with sand in her bottom and her head on straight. Stubborn, opinionated...and if he called her, she would come to him without a question.

But he couldn't call her. Couldn't touch her. He might falter and never go through with it if her softness tempted him to let down his guard.

Belinda watched him as the silence lengthened. She worried as he steadily sipped from the glass. She felt his tension like a living thing that grew with every weighted passing minute.

Conner obviously waited for someone or something to happen. But what? What more could Conner or any one of them endure this endless night?

Conner's eyes were the color of slate when he lifted heavy lids and focused on her. Belinda quickly judged he did not really see her sitting across from him. Conner never noticed her uncle coming to his side, silently taking the empty glass forgotten in his hand. Belinda had a strange feeling that Conner listened to some noise that was beyond her hearing.

Moments later he rose from the chair, glanced toward the doorway, then looked, really looked at Belinda. "You must excuse me."

Belinda heard it then, the rhythmic thump that came from the hallway. She thought it was Santo finally returning. Conner was halfway across the room when Santo appeared in the doorway.

"*Patróne,* it is time," Santo solemnly announced.

Conner inwardly winced hearing Santo name him master, but took no issue over the term. "Where is she?"

"Who, Conner?" Macaria asked, standing behind Santo.

"Rosanna."

For long seconds, Macaria stared at her eldest son. Never had she heard this cold, deadly voice from him. He sounded like his father, Justin, stern and unyielding, facing what had to be done.

And like his father before him, Conner would not be deterred. "I will come with you," Macaria said. "I wish to speak with Rosanna about her neglect tonight."

"*Madre,* you will not come with me. This is for me and Santo to attend."

"Santo, what is this? Am I an old woman to be cast aside within my home? What does Conner wish with Rosanna?"

"*Patróne,*" Santo pleaded.

At his sides, Conner's hands curled into fists. He had no wish to hurt his mother, less to deliver a verbal blow to Santo. Hearing the demand in his mother's voice, along with the tiredness besieging them all, he had to answer her.

"Rosanna must answer for the fire she set."

"Conner! No!" Macaria cried. Her bewildered gaze lit on Santo's stoic expression, then on the hard set of her son's features.

"Santo, where is your reason? Tell him," she demanded. "Tell my son this is not possible. Your daughter was raised from birth in my home. Never will I believe she would do this thing to us. Tell him!"

Santo stood with his head bowed, still and silent. Macaria pressed one hand to her chest, then anger rose, hot and potent.

"Deny this, Santo. Look at me and tell me my son lies."

"Where is she, Santo?" Conner's sharp voice cut across his mother's pleas.

"The office, *patróne*. It is the place for a matter of honor." Shame and defeat colored the old man's voice. One of his blood had betrayed his honor and loyalty to the family he had vowed to serve with his life. His tall, spare frame seemed to shrink where he stood.

Conner stood in front of him. The tanned, webbed face had aged with deeper creases, startling against the white mane of hair. Conner rested one hand on Santo's shoulder, feeling its bony strength that seemed to bend beneath his touch. "This is not your shame," he whispered to the man he loved like a father.

Santo did not answer him. He turned, awkward with the crutches until Macaria stepped away from him in the hall.

Conner looked back at Belinda. "I know you are exhausted, but I must request that you wait here awhile longer." In the hall, he stopped before his mother.

"*Madre*, if I could shield you all from this pain, I would. Believe that I do not make this accusation without knowing the grave consequence. But, *Madre*, stay out of this."

She reached out a hand to him and he shook his head, his gaze filled with regret.

"I have no choice."

"You will kill Sofia when she learns—"

"Then go to her, *Madre*."

"What will you do to her?"

His answer was silence as he walked down the hall to the office door where Santo waited with his daughter.

Macaria entered the parlor. "Phillip, forgive—"

"Nothing," he said, a few long strides bringing him to stand in front of her. Phillip brought her hand to his lips. "Is there anything, anything at all I can do to help?"

"Can you pray?" She lifted weary eyes to look into his. "Pray for an end to this night, Phillip." She attempted to pull away, but he held her hand fast in his.

"I'll come with you. I would like to see your first grandchild." He glanced back at where Belinda still sat in the chair. "Join us?"

"No, Uncle. I will wait for Conner."

"Do you know why he accused Rosanna?" Macaria asked Belinda.

She gazed into Macaria's dark eyes. "No, I have no idea why he asked me to wait for him, or what I could tell him about her. I do not know the young woman." *But I have suspicions, Macaria.* Afraid she would give herself away, Belinda closed her eyes and rested her head against the chair. As they left the room, Belinda hoped that neither one had noticed how tightly her hands gripped the arms of the chair.

Macaria glanced at the closed door of the office as she walked by with Phillip. Her pace quickened when she heard the key turn in the lock.

Conner removed the key from the lock and handed it to Santo, who stood close to the door. Then he faced the doe-eyed dark beauty whose pose and gaze spat defiance at him.

Rosanna, little sister to the Kincaids, was no longer a child to be indulged. Her lush hips rested against the edge of his desk, her arms behind her, supporting her. Rosanna's black hair, a cloud of rippling curls, was pinned away from her face with the combs he had bought for her fourteenth birthday. Dirt stains smudged the hem of her dark blue skirt. Conner saw the damp spots indicating she had knelt recently. His gaze traveled upward to the wide, mobile mouth that often wore a smile. There was none on her lips now.

"Whatever my father told you is a lie."

"Rosanna, you will listen to what I say, you will not speak unless I ask a question. Is that understood?"

"Why did my father bring me here? I have done nothing."

"Defiant to the last." Conner raked both hands through his hair. " Santo," he said, "sit until we are done." But he did not look at him. Rosanna held his complete attention.

"I will not waste time asking foolish questions. I know you started the fire, Rosanna. Silence!" he commanded when she opened her mouth to interrupt. He felt the cold rage tearing at him, and he feared not being able to control it. "I want to know how much Riverton paid you to betray us and why. That is all I wish to hear from your lips."

"What will you do with me?"

"Answer me," he replied in a very soft, very hard edged voice. "Or I will not be responsible for my actions."

"He hates you. He will do anything to destroy you and your family. He paid me *mucho dinero, el patróne,*" she spat in a mocking manner, sliding one hand to her hip. "All in gold."

Conner rubbed the bridge of his nose with his thumb and forefinger. The pounding in his head had increased tenfold in the past few minutes.

"You sold us out to Riverton. You gave him the information about the mine payrolls and shipments," he stated, unable to look at her. Pieces slipped into place, one by one, then faster and faster. Sickened, he had to look at her. "You almost cost Logan his life."

Santo, fearing that Conner would falter, made his own demands. "You will tell me why you dared dishonor—"

"Dishonor? It is you who dishonor me, *padre*. Always they come first, for you and *madre. La patrona* wants, so run and fetch, Rosanna. *La patrona* needs ... hurry, hurry. She is sad, Rosanna, sing for her. She desires, Rosanna—''

''Cease! You will not speak so disrespectfully of *la patrona*. She gave you the very milk from her breast when your mother could not. She clothed you. Always she made a place for you. She has given—''

''What?'' she screamed. ''The crumbs from her table? *Sí,* always she comes first with you. Then the sons. Never do you think, what do I do for my children? What do I give to Raphael and Rosanna? Even the land you claimed was deeded back to them. To your sacred Kincaids.''

Conner's slap came as a shock to her. She had never once seen him raise his hand to her or any woman.

''Apologize to your father,'' he whispered from between clenched teeth, fighting against losing his temper.

''Never. What I have said is not a lie. That is what you find bitter. I tell the truth. He would give his life for you before he thought of me.''

Santo gasped. Every word she spoke brought the venom of a viper's strike to pierce him. One crutch fell as he clutched his chest.

''Damn you!'' Conner rushed to Santo, kicking the crutch out of his way. Taking the old man's weight, he led him to the large chair in front of the desk. ''Get brandy for him.''

Stricken by her father's ashen face, Rosanna ran to the liquor cabinet. She couldn't stop shaking, and brandy sloshed over the edge of the glass as she poured it into a glass. She brought it to her father, but Conner took the glass from her and blocked her attempt to get near him.

"Easy, old friend. Here, sip this slowly." Conner remained bent over Santo, holding the glass for him as he sipped and color returned to his face. He remained a few more minutes, until Santo's breathing was easier.

"Let me take you to lie down. I will finish this."

Ageless eyes met Conner's compassionate gaze. "I will stay." He motioned the glass away.

Very carefully, Conner set it down on the desk. He wanted to throw it, he needed to vent the anger churning inside him. When he thought it safe, he faced Rosanna.

"Greed was your reason. What of Enrique? What made him help you?"

"That weakling?" Rosanna's full-throated laugh mocked Conner and her father.

"You were promised to marry that weakling, daughter."

"Did I marry him? Do you believe me such a fool. I used him. Many times he told me things that I sold. He is like Raphael, a fool in my clever hands. They truly believed you would reward them."

"And you knew better?"

Rosanna tossed her head, ignoring Conner's question.

"Answer me. Answer *el patróne.*

Santo's deliberate use of the title was a goading reminder to his daughter of the high respect with which he held Conner.

But it also served, for Conner, as an unwanted reminder of the place he had held and never wanted. He glanced at Santo. He sat with pride and dignity in every proud line of his body. Conner knew Rosanna's answers pained her father, as they did him. But you couldn't tell from the old man's bearing how devastating it was for him to hear Conner verbalize his suspicions about Raphael.

"Answer him!" Santo demanded.

"*Sí*. I know better. I know there is nothing for me but to work here until I am old and beaten down. A slave like my mother to the Kincaids."

Conner moved to her with astonishing speed. She tried to run, but he already had his hands around her throat.

"A slave would wear a collar or, at the very least, a mark of ownership."

Rosanna trembled. He dragged her nearer. Their faces were so close she could feel the heat from his skin. Stark fear crumbled her defiance.

Santo watched in silence.

A cold sweat broke out over Conner's body. He dropped his hands and backed away from her. All he could think of was what he had almost done.

He moved swiftly around the desk, jerking open the large bottom drawer where he kept the strongbox. He lifted it to the desk top, flipping open the lid, and took out a canvas sack.

"Judas only received thirty pieces of silver. Your betrayal is worth more, Rosanna, much, much more." He threw the sack across the desk. It landed against her hip, but she made no move to touch it.

"Go on. You're greedy for gold. There are fifty-dollar gold pieces inside. Five thousand dollars' worth. It was to have been your wedding present," he stated in a cold, relentless voice. "Of course, we were going to pay for the wedding and the trip to San Francisco you wanted so badly. And my mother, the woman who made a slave of you, ordered the satin for your wedding gown from France, and the lace and the silks, no expense to be spared for our Rosanna.

"And this," he added, lifting the gilt-edged deed from the box. "This was the balance of your gift. One thousand acres in the south quarter made out to you and Enrique. Despite what I believed about him, despite my suspicions, my mother insisted this be done. She wanted everything for your happiness, Rosanna.

"But she is not a wise woman, this softhearted mother of mine. She nursed a viper who put us through hell."

Conner was breathing heavily. He didn't think he could continue with his cold delivery, but when he looked at Santo, at the hard, implacable features, he knew he had no choice.

"Take your Judas gold, Rosanna. But not the deed to our land." He ripped the paper into shreds then let them fall while her eyes watched him like a wary animal watched a predator.

"I do not want your gold."

"Think of the money as payment for the service you have tendered this household. There will be no debts between us. I want you off Kincaid land by morning. And if you think I am weak because I don't kill you now, I won't be in the morning. You will keep your life because of the love I bear for your father and mother."

He quickly went to Santo and helped him stand. "Lean on me, old friend, it is finished now."

"No." Santo stared at his daughter. "I grieve the loss of my child. I have no daughter. My wife has no daughter," he said in a strong, ringing voice. "My son will claim no sister. You are wiped from our memory as if you had never been given life. You will go as you are, as *el patróne* has ordered. You will never return."

"*Padre.*"

"You have none." He leaned heavily against Conner. "Take me from this room. I will not breathe the air with this foul betrayer."

"You think you have won, *el patróne*," she cried out in a shrill voice.

Conner kept walking. Santo handed him the key as they stood by the door, but as Conner slipped the key into the lock, his blood turned cold when Rosanna spoke.

"Go look in the silken purse of the *fine lady* you brought into your *fine house, señor*. Go and see who is the true betrayer beneath this roof."

"What lies—"

"Leave her, Santo. I didn't hear anything." But he had heard her. Rosanna was many things, but would she make a claim so easily disproved against Belinda when the girl had barely escaped with her life? Yet to even consider there was any truth...no! He refused to play her game.

"Do you not ask yourself how Charles knew where to strike this night? How could Charles know where there are no guards?"

Conner unlocked the door and urged Santo out into the hall.

Before Conner fathomed her intent, Rosanna shoved past her father, knocking him into Conner. She flew down the hall to the guest room given to Belinda.

"Go. Go after her," Santo ordered as Conner steadied him against the wall.

Conner ran. He wanted her to have no chance of planting some false evidence against Belinda. Coming through the doorway, he almost slammed into Rosanna.

"There, go look." She pointed at Belinda's reticule sitting on the low dresser. "Are you afraid?" she mocked.

"You were ordered to leave this house."

"Is that all you can tell me? Look at it. Look," she dared in a rising pitch. Rosanna grabbed the silk pouch from the dresser and tore open the drawstring. "Here," she declared, throwing a small, folded paper at him. It fell to the floor at his feet. Enraged, she rushed to sweep it up and pushed it into Conner's hand.

Her gaze shifted from Conner to the door. Belinda stood there, one hand covering her mouth. Behind her stood Macaria and Phillip.

"I am guilty. I will leave this place gladly. But see first the viper you nestled in your arms, Conner."

"Conner, wait. I can explain."

He gave no indication that he heard Belinda's softly spoken protest. He opened each fold slowly, dreading what he would find. He noted the fine trembling of his hand but couldn't stop it. His gaze locked on the map he held. He studied each dark dot, each place marked to show where they had posted guards around the land that bordered Riverton's.

"A most damning piece of evidence," he murmured in a very controlled voice. Then he dropped the map to the floor. His boot heel ground the paper into the carpet.

He leveled a cold look at Rosanna. "Is there more?"

Head held high, defiant to the end, Rosanna walked out of the room. No one spoke to her, their attention was on Conner and what he would do.

Belinda could not wait, she stepped forward, stopping behind him.

"Conner, I copied that map from one that Charles had. I overheard him buying the map. I was going to use it to bargain with you if you continued to refuse to let me see Marty. But I brought it with me with the intention of giving it to you so you would know that Charles had this information."

"Your confession is unnecessary, Belinda."

"What did you say?" She grabbed his arm, but he caught hold of her hand and drew her to stand in front of him.

"Since this is your first visit to my home, Belinda, you couldn't have copied the map here. When did you have time to search? You didn't even know anything about it." He lifted his hands and very gently threaded his fingers through her hair to cup the back of her neck.

Belinda searched his features, studying his weary eyes. No accusation gleamed in their darkness. "Thank you," she whispered, "for your belief and your trust."

"You're very welcome." He ignored the tremor of his hands as his thumbs caressed the sensitive skin beneath her chin, then tilted her head up. Her dark eyes held a potent magic as they gazed into his. Conner couldn't resist his need. He lowered his mouth to hers.

Due to their audience, the kiss was, of necessity, chaste and far too brief, but filled with promise.

"Your bed," he mouthed with barely a sound against her lips, "is very tempting."

"Your mother. My uncle." She brushed the words over his mouth in a regretful reminder.

"Forgive me." His forehead touched hers. "I'm not thinking. It wasn't meant as an improper suggestion. I'm afraid I've reached the end of my endurance."

Belinda took a moment before she jerked her head back. Conner's hands slipped from her neck. His eyes shuttered closed and he pitched forward. Only her uncle's fast reflex saved them from both toppling to the floor.

Belinda spent what remained of the night in Conner's bed. Alone.

The most incredible display of color heralded the dawn by the time she finally closed her eyes.

She had discovered a most frightening feeling.

She was in danger of falling in love with Conner Kincaid.

Chapter Twenty-Two

Logan and Ty led a weary, somber group of men past the burned barn late the next afternoon. Kenny, who had ridden out to meet them at Marty's first warning shout from the tower, had told them what transpired while they were stopping the stampede and rounding up the scattered, frightened cattle.

There were whispers from a few of the men, but one rode without remorse when he viewed the destruction the fire had left. Charles Riverton sat as erect as his bound arms would allow, and smiled as they rode past the barn.

Kenny scowled at the man, wishing he was older, bigger, he'd show him what it meant to mess with the Kincaids.

Just as the men pulled ahead, veering off to the corral near the bunkhouse, Jessie stepped out of the bunkhouse kitchen. For a few moments she stood there, wiping her hands on her apron, hiding their trembling as she studied each man walking his horse past her. Shoulders slumped, dust laden and tired, each one nodded, or attempted a smile for her.

"Smell that hot coffee," Hazer said.

"There're hot biscuits and bacon waiting inside," she called out in a choked voice when she finally saw Logan. He drew rein to wait for her and, with a glad cry, she ran to him.

Jessie stood looking up at her husband, blinking back the sudden spurt of tears. Dark stubble covered his face, his clothes were dusted with reddish brown dirt, but he had never looked more handsome to her. She spared a quick smile for Ty, knowing by his presence that Kenny had not told him about the baby. But then Jessie knew firsthand how well Kenny kept secrets.

Logan held out a leather-clad hand for Jessie. "Casey," he ordered, "take Riverton down to the woodshed and lock him up till Conner decides what to do with him." He leaned over, kicking his boot free of the stirrup, so Jessie could mount in front of him. Holding her close, without a word exchanged, Logan absorbed the incredible feeling of coming home that stole over him. With his chin he nudged aside her single braid to kiss her bare neck.

"I swear, sweetheart, you're sweet as water to a thirsty man."

When he lifted the reins, Riverton's shouts stopped him.

"What the hell does Conner decide?" Charles demanded. He twisted around as far as his bound arms allowed, to keep Logan in sight. "I'll have a fair trial. I have powerful friends, Kincaid. And you've got no proof that I had anything to do—"

"Your men stampeded our cattle. Folks around here don't need more proof of guilt than that. Conner's the law. In case you forgot, Riverton."

Ty continued, his voice rising to cut across Riverton's tirade. "Conner says you get a trial, you'll have one. Should he want to see you hung on the old cottonwood outside town, that's the way it'll be. If he figures you should get lost in the canyons yonder, that can happen, too."

Ty ignored the rest of Riverton's threats and looked at his brother. "I've got a hurting pair of empty arms, I'm for home."

"I'm right behind you, Ty."

Jessie leaned back against Logan's warm body. "It's a terrible burden to place on Conner," she murmured.

"And you know Conner wouldn't have it any other way, love." He cradled her closer, urging his horse at a walk toward the open gates. "Can you wait," he asked her softly, "till we're all together so I tell only once what happened?"

"You're home and unhurt. I know all that I need," she replied. Her hands covered his as she offered another prayer of thanksgiving.

"You would have been so proud of our boys, Logan. And Belinda fought alongside us. She didn't quit till Conner did. I have a feeling . . ."

"Keep your feelings for me. Ah, Jess, I love you. I never want to live through the hell of last night again." *And I never want to see your lovely eyes bruised with sorrow and fatigue again.* Logan briefly thought of the sketchy details Kenny had provided about Rosanna. He added that grief to what he carried for the loss of three good men.

"They're here! They're here!" Marty shouted from the tower. He waved at the small party riding through the gates then scrambled down the ladder.

Macaria stood with Phillip near the front door. Her lips moved in prayer when she saw that her sons were weary but not wounded. Logan set Jessie down, then dismounted. Ty, however, sat on his horse, a bewildered look in his eyes as he glanced around for Dixie.

"She is well, my son," Macaria hastened to explain. "Go to her, Ty. She waits in your room for you."

His initial fear subsided. His mother would not wear a joyful smile if anything had happened to Dixie. Ty gave himself a mental kick. After the ordeal of fighting the fire, his whole family had to be exhausted, and expectant mother or not, if he knew his wife, she had been right there in the thick of the battle. He wished for the hundredth time that Logan hadn't stopped him from beating Riverton to a bloody pulp. He swung his leg over the horse and stood for a few moments before he tossed the reins to Marty.

"Give the horses grain and plenty of it, son."

"I'll take care of 'em. Don't worry." His eyes held a merry expression as he shot looks over his shoulder at Ty while he walked the horses back toward the gate.

Ty shook his head, tilted his hat back and pecked his mother's cheek. "Riverton's tied up in the woodshed," he whispered. "Me, I'm for my wife and bed." He was already stripping off his gloves and the sweat-dampened bandanna from his neck as he walked into the house.

"Logan, there is hot water for you, my son," she told him as he approached with his arm around Jessie's waist. "There will be no talking until you and Ty have rested and eaten."

He wasn't about to argue with her. He didn't know if he could stand long enough to wash. "Just tell me one thing. Where is Conner? We brought him a present."

"He must have seen you return. He went up the hillside to your father's grave. He wanted to ride out after you, but we managed to convince him to wait." She frowned when the expected shout of joy was not forthcoming from the house. Looking at Logan, she said softly, "If you will promise you will pretend surprise, I will tell you of the blessing we received."

"Promise," he said. "Blessing, huh? Like in Dixie and a baby?"

"*Sí*, the baby. A sweet little girl, Logan. Both are well," she reassured him. "Do not spoil the news for your brother when he comes to tell you."

Logan glanced at the open doorway. "He must know by now and not a peep out of him. Maybe I'd better go see if he's passed out. It'd be just like him."

"No, you don't." Jessie locked both arms around his waist. "This is their time, alone." She smiled up at him.

"Well, if it was me, I'd be shouting down the house." He hugged Jessie and whispered in her ear. "I'd like some time alone, too, Mrs. Kincaid."

"But Conner will want to—"

"Go," Macaria ordered. "I will tell Conner."

"Come along, Jessie. Did I ever tell you what a good, dutiful son I am? *Madre* only has to order, and I obey."

Her soft laughter helped to chase his weariness.

"Have I ever told you, outlaw, that you have a most lecherous smile?"

"The better to please you with, wife."

Their banter stopped before they reached Ty's room. Without a word spoken, they crept past the closed door. But the silence had them share a look of concern.

Logan and Jessie needn't have worried. Ty had not passed out. Nor did he shout his joy. The darkened room scared him at first, just as seeing Dixie in bed, under the covers had. But the moment he stepped closer and saw what his dozing wife held tucked against her side, Ty could barely think, much less speak, as he gazed down in awe.

He and Dixie, with love, had created this tiny angel. He blinked back the wetness stinging his eyes as he fell to his knees beside the bed. His heart pumped furiously, and he felt small as the tide of emotions rose.

"Ty." Her whisper brought his head up. She lifted a hand to touch his beard-stubbled cheek.

"I'm here, love. I—"

She smiled. "I know. I keep looking at her and—"

"A girl? We have a little girl? Now I have two angels to love."

Dixie shifted the baby and herself to make room for Ty.

"Let me wash my hands." When Ty joined her on the bed he kissed his wife.

Dixie took his hand. "Touch her, Ty. I promise she won't break."

His finger trembled as he traced his daughter's tiny features. "She's beautiful." He stared as his finger touched the corner of her small mouth that opened in reflex, seeking what Ty couldn't give her.

Dixie freed the soft cashmere shawl wrapped around the baby. She lifted up one tiny hand, marveling, as she had while waiting for Ty, at how perfectly formed she was.

"Have you told them what name we chose?"

"No. I want you to do that."

"The first Kincaid princess. I want to promise her the world. Dixie, was it hard for you?"

As countless women had done before her, Dixie looked at her husband and lied. "The moment I held her in my arms I forgot the pain."

"Thank you for the sweet lie. And for our baby. Reina Justine Kincaid, welcome to the world."

Conner had watched his brothers return with Riverton from the hillside where their father was buried. Two ironwood trees shaded the plot. He wished he could feel relief that their enemy had been caught, some sense that it was over. But he knew what he still faced as he made his way back to the house.

At the last minute he veered away from the front gates and went around to the back ones that led to the garden.

Belinda had been there when he left the house earlier.

He couldn't begin to explain to himself why he sought out her company at a time when he needed to be clearheaded. If there was one thing Belinda did well, it was cloud his thinking.

Unfortunately, just as he discovered her whereabouts in the far corner of the garden, he heard his mother's and Phillip's voices as they walked on the rose-bordered flagstone path.

Belinda sat on a wooden bench built to encircle an aged juniper tree. The berries Sofia used for cooking hadn't ripened yet, but he recalled the scoldings she had delivered when he and his brothers used the berries in peashooters. She appeared lost in thought, oblivious to his approach.

"I had hoped to find you alone, Belinda. We need to talk. But it seems we are about to have my mother's company."

Surprise rippled through her that Conner had sought her out after avoiding her most of the day. Kenny had come to tell her that Logan and Ty returned with Charles. Although she had come to this quiet corner to make a few important decisions, she also wondered what Conner intended to do with Charles.

She gathered the skirt of the gray twilled silk gown that Macaria had lent her, to make room for Conner to sit. But he had glanced down the path and missed her silent invitation. When he looked back at her, Belinda stared straight ahead, hands folded primly in her lap.

"Such a somber mood for a lovely lady? I wish you hadn't pinned your hair up. I like it better down."

"Conner, about what happened—"

"We'll talk. Later."

He stepped away and she looked beyond Conner to see that her uncle accompanied Macaria.

Conner appeared to withdraw as they joined them.

"I sent your brothers to rest and spoke with Hazer," Macaria said. "He informed me that Charles was there with his men. That is how they were able to capture him."

"From what I heard," Phillip began, taking his niece's hand in his own, "Albert may have been with him. The men are riding back with pack mules to bring the bodies into town. I'm going to go with them. If Albert is dead, I want to know."

Belinda wished she could feel some remorse, but the thought of her cousin scheming to kill her wiped away any feeling of grief. She nodded her acceptance of his decision.

"Charles is locked in the woodshed," Macaria informed Conner. "What will you do with him?"

"Who do you ask, *Madre*, your son or the sheriff?"

"To me they are one and the same." She held her son's steady gaze with her own for long seconds before she looked at Phillip. She was thankful to have had him with her through this ordeal. His strength and quiet acceptance had shored her flagging spirits.

"Whatever decision you make regarding this man, my son, we will all stand beside you."

"Belinda must decide for herself where she stands on this matter, but I, too, offer my complete support to you, Conner," Phillip assured him. "Charles was my friend. I feel as betrayed by the way he used me and my niece as you do for what has been done to your family. I've been told by your mother that hanging is the usual payment for a cattle rustler. And that it is commonly carried out without any delay."

Phillip's voice churned with anger as he added, "But that bastard tried to kill my niece. And if you don't see that he's punished, I will."

Belinda jumped to her feet. "Stop it, Uncle. What you are demanding of Conner is murder. You do not have that right. No one does."

"Is that your choice?" Conner asked her.

For long moments she stared into his eyes, shocked that he allowed her a glimpse into the war he fought within himself. Abruptly he turned back to his mother.

"Civil it is. He'll stand trial. To make sure there are no accusations leveled against me or my family and friends," he said with a nod toward Phillip, "I'll send word to town for Rob and Tom Sweet to come and get him. They'll be charged with keeping him alive."

Conner offered his arm to Belinda. "If you'll both excuse us?"

He didn't wait for an answer but swept her along the path and out the back gates. With a quick turn he pressed her up against the high wooden fence.

"I have one question to ask, Belinda. Will you stay?"

Chapter Twenty-Three

Belinda stayed. Conner temporarily removed himself from office, appointing Rob Long as deputy. Word was sent for the circuit court judge to make his stop at Sweetwater months early and Conner impressed upon him the need for a speedy trial.

The ever-faithful Mrs. Dobbs visited the jail every day. Rob, on Conner's instructions, never allowed her a moment alone with Charles. Everything, food and clothing was searched before being given to the prisoner.

Mark found himself courted by the other territorial papers for information and *The Gazette* had to increase its weekly copies. But one thing he never reported was the ranting heard when letters to former political associates were returned unopened to Charles.

Albert's body was never found. Belinda did not know if her cousin lived. She learned through the almost daily telegrams to and from her man of business, that no one had seen Albert in the city and when he inquired at Albert's rooms, his landlady was in the process of packing his belongings for storage in the basement. His rent was due and she had no intention of holding the rooms for him.

The coming trial hovered in the background as Belinda experienced the wonder of falling in love with Conner.

The days melted one into the other, a time to be treasured. She had always longed for freedom, and Conner gave her that gift, encouraging her to say what she pleased, listening to her express her thoughts, laughing and teasing and kissing her senseless. But he never again made love to her.

It was a cloud on her happiness, but she understood why a few weeks later when he had bluntly asked if she had had her monthly courses. Blushing furiously, too shocked to answer him, she managed a nod before fleeing to the house.

Much later, alone in her room, she had calmly reasoned out why he had asked and fully faced the risk she would take by making love to him again. There was no question in her mind that Conner cared a great deal for her, but he had never said that he loved her. The future was simply not discussed.

Conner was a man she could spend the rest of her life with. And seeing Dixie and Ty with their baby, sharing their happiness, brought an ache to her that grew and grew. She wanted to explore more of the passionate nature Conner revealed. And she wanted the perfect lover—one Conner Kincaid.

In the end, she decided she could not force a declaration from him.

They rode together most days, sometimes with Jessie and Logan alone, or with the boys. The weeks were sweet with berry picking, picnics and swimming on moonlit nights in the pond.

She never withheld herself from him. The perfume of crushed, sweet-smelling grass often scented the place where she lay with her head pillowed on Conner's shoulder while they talked of everything from childhood to the growing problems in the territory as settlers and miners poured into lands claimed by the Indians. She told him of her problems in filling a growing demand for beef, and they learned that despite all else Riverton had done, some good had come from him. The railroad would build a line passing through the town.

When the talking died to whispers, he would take her in his arms, kissing her until a fever spread, some nights leaving her abruptly until passion cooled.

It was a lengthy exercise in frustration.

And then there was Marty. Belinda had reconciled herself to allowing Jessie and Logan to retain the role of parents. Marty loved the gifts she had shared between him and Kenny. But it was her understanding, from the mornings she spent with him, that she would destroy his happiness if she took him away.

Legal rights aside, Belinda had come to love her nephew and she had finally decided that this was where he belonged. She knew that Jessie was anxious about her decision.

One morning, finding Jessie alone in the kitchen, Belinda knew she could not put off talking to her any longer.

"I hope we can work it out so that you will let him visit me, Jessie. I want to remain a part of his life. I cannot simply walk away from Marty. There is his inheritance to consider, too. Someday he may want it. I just needed to tell you that I won't be taking him back with me."

"I had no idea you were still planning to go, Belinda. I . . . we all assumed that you and Conner—"

"He hasn't asked me to stay. Not forever," she added, unable to meet the compassion in Jessie's eyes.

"Do you love him?"

It was a measure of how much Belinda had changed that she did not immediately tell her it was not her business to ask such a personal question, but instead toyed with the coffee cup in front of her.

"Belinda, don't you know?"

"He did ask me to stay. I think he only meant until after the trial. As for loving him," she whispered, "I—"

"Belinda, look at me." Jessie put her own hands over the cup. "Look at me. If you can imagine yourself with someone else, then you're not in love with him. If you believe that without him in your life, there is no life, then you love him. I know you have your wealthy friends back East and your businesses. But if they really mattered, would you have stayed this long? Marty is part of the reason, but I think Conner is the other part.

"Maybe the major part. Even your uncle believes you're in love with Conner. And why are you still wondering how he feels? Why haven't you asked him?"

"Asked me what?" Conner said, coming in the back door. "I've just had word Judge Beltane has arrived."

"Has he set a date?" Belinda asked.

"Two days. He wants that much time to review the evidence I put together and talk with the lawyers that Riverton's hired."

"You'll be staying in town then?" Jessie asked.

"I leave tomorrow morning." He cast a longing look at Belinda's back.

Belinda gracefully slid from the bench and, without looking at either of them, announced that she would find her uncle to tell him the news.

"He just rode out with my mother. They both know."

Two days. Two days left. Belinda repeated this over and over. She had to do something. But flinging herself into Conner's arms and demanding a declaration of love and a promise of marriage required courage, boldness and some sense of that love being returned. She had the first two in abundance, but lacked the third, and to her, the most necessary ingredient.

Conner left for town in the morning. Belinda rode in each day with her uncle and Macaria in the carriage, Logan and Ty riding alongside. The trial didn't last very long. Not one of Charles's business associates or political friends came to speak on his behalf. And judged by a jury of his peers, he was sentenced to twenty-five years in Yuma prison.

Conner didn't believe that Riverton would survive. Justice had been served, not quite the way he thought it would be, but then he'd learned that following the law meant following a hard mistress.

The next morning Jessie found Belinda alone and resumed her campaign the moment Conner joined them.

"I bet Belinda would love to go for a ride," Jessie suggested, eyeing her brother-in-law with a glare that spoke volumes. When Conner didn't appear to take her hint, she added, "That's what we were talking about when you came in, Conner. Belinda was wondering if she should ask you to take her for a ride." Then, in a sharp tone, with a pointed look at the lady in question, Jessie prompted, "It is true, isn't it? You do want to go riding with him?"

Yes! she all but screamed. Belinda wanted to go, but she thought of how it would end—Conner kissing her until her knees were weak, leaving her restless and heated, yearning again for the fulfillment she had known in his arms. There was only so much punishment a body could take. Belinda had had her share.

"I did mention it, but I have changed my mind."

The moment Belinda left the kitchen, Jessie lit into Conner. "You are the most thickheaded Kincaid. How could you let her go? Any fool could see she wanted to be with you. Any fool can see that you're halfway in love with her. Any fool—"

"Jessie, I'm not a fool."

Conner found Belinda in the garden sitting on her favorite bench. Marty was giving her another lesson about his pet ferret PeeWee, extolling the animal's hunting exploits in great detail. Seeing Conner, he stopped talking.

"There're some orphan calves that need feeding. I know Kenny and Santo could use some help with them, Marty."

"Oh, but Aunt Belinda loves hearing how PeeWee can hunt. Don't you?"

"Marty," Conner said in a voice that brooked no more argument, "I want to talk with your aunt alone."

"Oh." He looked from one to the other. "Gonna do more of that kissin' stuff?"

"If I am, I sure don't want you around for an audience."

"Conner!" Belinda protested. But Marty was laughing.

"I'm going. Would you like me to leave PeeWee with you?" He offered his dearest pet to Belinda.

Conner stepped in again. "No, she doesn't want him." With a firm hand on Marty's shoulder, he turned him in the direction of the house. "Off with you."

Watching the boy depart, Belinda sighed. "I have a great deal to learn about little boys." Her tone was wishful. "They ask a great many questions. Some that are impossible to answer."

Conner had a few of his own she would likely classify the same way.

"At least you don't get cornered by Ty very often. He must be the proudest papa this family's ever had. He can't stop talking about his daughter's every inch, every sound and every move, for anyone who'll stand still long enough to listen."

"I am sure his love coats each word. Have you ever thought about having children, Conner?"

"I've thought about it. Most men do. I've just never found a woman who wanted to settle down with a small-town sheriff and part-time rancher."

"I see." Belinda found the tips of her slippers required her attention. Her uncle had gone to Riverton's home and packed all her belongings. Today she wore a two-piece cream printed calico polonaise dress trimmed with a dark green piping and slippers to match.

"I don't think you do, Belinda."

The sudden serious note begged her to look up at him. She found the strength of will to resist.

Conner tried a different tack. "I don't think your uncle will be returning with you." She turned a startled glance on him. "He mentioned wanting to look at some land north of Sweetwater."

"He never mentioned that to me."

Conner looked at her nettled expression. "He didn't think you'd be interested. He knows what your plans are. You're leaving at the end of the week."

She could no longer hold his gaze, and looked away.

"You are planning on leaving, aren't you?"

"It was always my intent."

"You don't sound very sure of that, Belinda."

"I have my home, friends, businesses. I told Jessie I won't be taking Marty with me. Not this time. But I want him to visit with me." She was intently aware of him, despite the few feet of distance he maintained. Would she ever lose that awareness? *When there were a few thousand miles between them.* She did not want to think about that.

"I had hoped..."

"What?" Dark and luminous, her gaze fixed on him. She took in the lean power of his body and his unsmiling face. There was a restlessness about him he couldn't hide and she wondered what caused it. A despair wrapped around her. How could she say...no, if Conner wanted her, he would have to be the one to speak first.

"You've enjoyed the past few weeks, haven't you?"

"Very much."

"You're making this difficult."

"Difficult?" she repeated. "Since I have no idea what it is that you're attempting—"

"I want you to stay, Belinda."

"You asked me that weeks ago. I stayed."

"You're not making it difficult. You're making this impossible. Up," he ordered, snatching her to her feet when she didn't move fast enough for him. "Do you want me to go down on bended knee?"

"Whatever for, Conner?" But she knew! Her heart beat furiously and a curious warmth unfurled inside her, setting off a series of tiny tremors.

"I've never proposed to a woman."

"I cannot tell you how very happy that makes me." Her smile was radiant. Conner's grin was sheer wickedness.

"I want you to marry me. I can't sleep. I can't eat. I can't carry on a sane conversation with anyone because all I hear is your voice, and all I want to do is be with you."

Belinda found herself in his arms, but she covered his lips with the tips of her fingers. "There is something more you need to say, Conner Kincaid."

"That I love you," he whispered. "I do, you know. More than I thought I could ever love—"

"Conner, I cannot sew."

"Then I'll take extra care not to tear my clothes. Definitely a poor bargain for me. But we'll make plenty of work for a seamstress."

"I have no cooking skills."

He kissed each temple. "Ah, but I disagree. You heat me to the right temperature with a look from those wide, dark brown eyes. And love, we can afford to hire a cook."

"I will not be a docile wife, Conner."

He removed her hand and placed it against his heart. "Belinda, if you don't want to marry me, a simple no will do. I thought—"

"Conner! Of course I want to marry you. I just don't want you to think I'll be like Jessie or Dixie—"

"You won't have babies...my babies? You won't love me and fight me and love me some more?"

She caught hold of his ears and drew his lips down to hers. "Be serious, you impossible, thickheaded Kincaid."

And he saw then the underlying fear she had. He didn't realize he could love her more, but he did at that moment, when he understood that she measured herself against his brothers' wives and found herself too different from them. And he knew that before he could put her fears to rest, he had to let her say them.

"Tell me, Belinda, what sort of a wife will I have?"

"My social skills are considered to be excellent."

"We host dinners for everyone in the territory." He pecked a kiss on her nose. One on each cheek, then skimmed his lips across hers. "Next."

"I really am very good at making money."

"Got a little printing press of your own?"

"Conner, be serious! These are important—"

"Yes, very important and I am serious. If you make money and we make love, what's there to worry about? You tend to forget, Miss Belinda Jarvis soon-to-be-Kincaid, you've got the law on your side." He couldn't wait a moment more and took her mouth in a cherishing kiss.

Minutes later he lifted his head. "As I was saying, you've got the law at your beck and call, dedicated to serve—"

"Conner, why won't you make love to me?"

"Because I wanted the next time to be as my wife. I did everything wrong before. You deserved to be courted with flowers and candy, serenaded by moon-light—"

"And who," she asked with an impudent smile, "would be singing love songs to me?"

"I'm told I have a moderately fair voice. Belinda, *querida,* how could you think I didn't want you?"

He drew her hand down between them, holding her gaze with his. "Feel what you do to me, love. I ache with the need I have for you, and only you. But I wanted you to know me and not be caught by new-found passion. I had to give you time, time I stole that day—"

"You gave me the most incredible pleasure I have ever known, Conner Kincaid. Pleasure I found only in your arms." The last was a bare whisper of sound, for she gave in to the hunger for his kiss.

Conner indulged her. Soundly. Hotly. With all the love that flowed from his heart to hers. And when desire threatened any rational thought, he broke the kiss.

"How long will it take you to plan a wedding?" he asked, nibbling her ear.

"Properly, at least eight months."

"Too long. Try three."

"Six."

"Two. Accommodate me, love."

"Compromise, Conner. Three."

"One and that's my final offer. Expectant brides can't dance all night."

"But I," she replied, with a merry twinkle glowing in her eyes, "am not an expectant bride."

Conner scooped her up into his arms. "Are you open to bribery?"

"Conner Kincaid, I am shocked. You are the sheriff, remember? You cannot take bribes. You certainly cannot offer any."

"Wanna bet?"

Her eyes gleamed with assurance. Her smile curved on the wicked side. "What are you offering?"

"Temptation. A man. Just a man who loves you."

"Definitely tempted." She kissed him, long and slowly, playing a game of tease and conquer with her tongue. When she opened her eyes to see the sensual heat from his gaze, she nestled her head on his shoulder. "Definitely a man. Definitely loved. Honorable and wise. The perfect man to wear a lawman's badge. The perfect choice for a husband. Lawman, we have a wedding to plan."

"I like a woman who knows her own mind."

"And it is filled with nothing but thoughts of loving you, Conner Kincaid."

* * * * *

If you enjoyed this book by

THERESA MICHAELS

Here's your chance to order more stories
by one of Harlequin's favorite authors:

Harlequin Historical®

#28843	FIRE AND SWORD	$3.99 U.S. ☐	
		$4.50 CAN. ☐	
#28876	ONCE A MAVERICK	$4.50 U.S. ☐	
		$4.99 CAN. ☐	

(limited quantities available on certain titles)

TOTAL AMOUNT	$
POSTAGE & HANDLING	$
($1.00 for one book, 50¢ for each additional)	
APPLICABLE TAXES*	$_____
TOTAL PAYABLE	$_____
(check or money order—please do not send cash)	

To order, complete this form and send it, along with a check or money order
for the total above, payable to Harlequin Books, to: **In the U.S.:** 3010 Walden
Avenue, P.O. Box 9047, Buffalo, NY 14269-9047; **In Canada:** P.O. Box 613,
Fort Erie, Ontario, L2A 5X3.

Name: _____

Address: _____ City: _____

State/Prov.: _____ Zip/Postal Code: _____

*New York residents remit applicable sales taxes.
 Canadian residents remit applicable GST and provincial taxes. HTMBACK1

HARLEQUIN®

BRIDE'S BAY RESORT

UNLOCK THE DOOR TO GREAT ROMANCE AT BRIDE'S BAY RESORT

Join Harlequin's new across-the-lines series, set in an exclusive hotel on an island off the coast of South Carolina.

Seven of your favorite authors will bring you exciting stories about fascinating heroes and heroines discovering love at Bride's Bay Resort.

Look for these fabulous stories coming to a store near you beginning in January 1996.

Harlequin American Romance #613 in January
Matchmaking Baby by Cathy Gillen Thacker

Harlequin Presents #1794 in February
Indiscretions by Robyn Donald

Harlequin Intrigue #362 in March
Love and Lies by Dawn Stewardson

Harlequin Romance #3404 in April
Make Believe Engagement by Day Leclaire

Harlequin Temptation #588 in May
Stranger in the Night by Roseanne Williams

Harlequin Superromance #695 in June
Married to a Stranger by Connie Bennett

Harlequin Historicals #324 in July
Dulcie's Gift by Ruth Langan

Visit Bride's Bay Resort each month wherever Harlequin books are sold.

 HARLEQUIN ®

BBAYG

Harlequin® Historical

Don't miss your opportunity to read a very
special historical romance from three-time
RITA Award winner

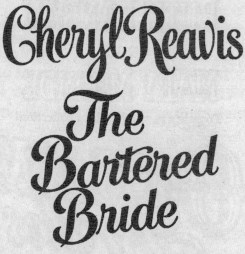

Cheryl Reavis

The Bartered Bride

Keep an eye out for this unforgettable story.
Coming this June from Harlequin Historicals!

Bestselling authors

ELAINE COFFMAN
RUTH LANGAN

and

MARY McBRIDE

Together in one fabulous collection!

OUTLAW
Brides

Available in June wherever Harlequin
books are sold.

HARLEQUIN ®

HARLEQUIN®

Don't miss these Harlequin favorites by some of our most distinguished authors!
And now, you can receive a discount by ordering two or more titles!

HT #25645	THREE GROOMS AND A WIFE	
	by JoAnn Ross	$3.25 U.S./$3.75 CAN. ☐
HT #25648	JESSIE'S LAWMAN	
	by Kristine Rolofson	$3.25 U.S.//$3.75 CAN. ☐
HP #11725	THE WRONG KIND OF WIFE	
	by Roberta Leigh	$3.25 U.S./$3.75 CAN. ☐
HP #11755	TIGER EYES by Robyn Donald	$3.25 U.S./$3.75 CAN. ☐
HR #03362	THE BABY BUSINESS by Rebecca Winters	$2.99 U.S./$3.50 CAN. ☐
HR #03375	THE BABY CAPER by Emma Goldrick	$2.99 U.S./$3.50 CAN. ☐
HS #70638	THE SECRET YEARS by Margot Dalton	$3.75 U.S./$4.25 CAN. ☐
HS #70655	PEACEKEEPER by Marisa Carroll	$3.75 U.S./$4.25 CAN. ☐
HI #22280	MIDNIGHT RIDER by Laura Pender	$2.99 U.S./$3.50 CAN. ☐
HI #22235	BEAUTY VS THE BEAST by M.J. Rogers	$3.50 U.S./$3.99 CAN. ☐
HAR #16531	TEDDY BEAR HEIR by Elda Minger	$3.50 U.S./$3.99 CAN. ☐
HAR #16596	COUNTERFEIT HUSBAND	
	by Linda Randall Wisdom	$3.50 U.S./$3.99 CAN. ☐
HH #28795	PIECES OF SKY by Marianne Willman	$3.99 U.S./$4.50 CAN. ☐
HH #28855	SWEET SURRENDER by Julie Tetel	$4.50 U.S./$4.99 CAN. ☐

(limited quantities available on certain titles)

	AMOUNT	$
DEDUCT:	**10% DISCOUNT FOR 2+ BOOKS**	$
ADD:	**POSTAGE & HANDLING**	$
	($1.00 for one book, 50¢ for each additional)	
	APPLICABLE TAXES**	$_____
	TOTAL PAYABLE	$_____
	(check or money order—please do not send cash)	

To order, complete this form and send it, along with a check or money order for the total above, payable to Harlequin Books, to: **In the U.S.:** 3010 Walden Avenue, P.O. Box 9047, Buffalo, NY 14269-9047; **In Canada:** P.O. Box 613, Fort Erie, Ontario, L2A 5X3.

Name: _____

Address: _____ City: _____

State/Prov.: _____ Zip/Postal Code: _____

**New York residents remit applicable sales taxes.
Canadian residents remit applicable GST and provincial taxes.

HBACK-AJ3

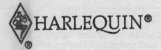